PRAISE FO

"This is a dark fantasy romance from Katee Robert, and honestly, this is exactly what I hoped she'd always write."

—Culturess

"Katee Robert knows how to capture romance readers' hearts."

—*Entertainment Weekly*

"Full of unique world-building and compelling characters."

—Paste

"Thanks to its wildly fun romance and adventure, *Hunt on Dark Waters* will soon be a staple for any romantasy lover's bookshelf."

—BookTrib

"This promises more good things to come in future installments."

—*Publishers Weekly*

"Robert continues to shine with their inclusive characters and flawlessly executed romance tropes. . . . A clever-witch-meets-stern-pirate, open-door, one-bed delight."

—*Library Journal*

"Robert fans will enjoy this fresh, new setting on the high seas, as well as the enticing spice."

—*Booklist*

"Katee Robert's *Hunt on Dark Waters* is a fast-paced and delightful fever dream of fantasy creatures, mysterious magic, and sizzling sexual innuendo."

—*BookPage* (starred review)

BERKLEY TITLES BY KATEE ROBERT

Hunt on Dark Waters

Blood on the Tide

KATEE ROBERT

BERKLEY ROMANCE
New York

BERKLEY ROMANCE
Published by Berkley
An imprint of Penguin Random House LLC
penguinrandomhouse.com

Library of Congress Cataloging-in-Publication Data

Names: Robert, Katee, author.
Title: Blood on the tide / Katee Robert.
Description: First edition. | New York: Berkley Romance, 2024. |
Series: Crimson Sails; 2
Identifiers: LCCN 2023050035 (print) | LCCN 2023050036 (ebook) |
ISBN 9780593639108 (trade paperback) | ISBN 9780593639115 (ebook)
Subjects: LCGFT: Fantasy fiction. | Romance fiction. | Erotic fiction. | Novels.
Classification: LCC PS3618.O31537 B56 2024 (print) |
LCC PS3618.O31537 (ebook) | DDC 813/.6—dc23/eng/20231024
LC record available at https://lccn.loc.gov/2023050035
LC ebook record available at https://lccn.loc.gov/2023050036

First Edition: May 2024

Printed in the United States of America
1st Printing

Book design by Daniel Brount

For fans of Pirates of the Caribbean *who wished that there were more lady characters and that those lady characters kissed a bunch*

Blood
on
the
Tide

CHAPTER 1

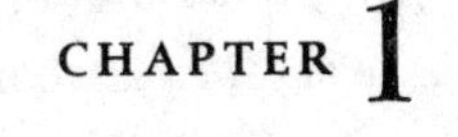

Lizzie

IN NEARLY TWO HUNDRED YEARS, I'VE NEVER ONCE WONdered how long it takes a vampire to drown.

Now it's all I can think about.

We might be damn near immortal, but we're not unkillable. It would take me longer to succumb to the lack of air than my human counterparts, but I couldn't hold out indefinitely. Eventually the cold sea would rush in and drag me to the depths for good.

Dark thoughts. Morbid thoughts. Impossible to escape while sailing on what amounts to a thimble in an Olympic pool. Everywhere I look, I see water stretching out to the horizon in all directions. Even in my cabin, protected by some kind of pocket dimension magic, I swear I can feel the dip and sway of each wave we crest.

Fixating on drowning, on the feeling I'm experiencing that certainly isn't *fear*, is still preferable to contemplating the sequence of events that led me to Threshold—more specifically to end up sailing on the *Audacity* with my ex and the new love of her life.

Only a few months ago, Evelyn was in *my* bed and making eyes at *me*. Now it seems like all she can see is that giant of a man who glowers at everyone who comes close. I can't even find fault with his battle prowess; Bowen is a powerful telekinetic and doesn't shy away from using his magic to defend Evelyn and the crew. Taking a hit from him felt like being rammed by a semitruck. I don't crave a repeat experience.

But every time I turn around, I find myself staring at them, analyzing all the ways they're so obviously in love. Comparing it to the way Evelyn and I were . . . and finding the past lacking. She never looked at me like that. I didn't even know I wanted her to, and then the possibility was gone before I realized what I'd lost.

It doesn't matter. It can't matter. I'm destined to marry another bloodline vampire within our extended family, all the better to create progeny to build power and ensure we don't fall behind the other bloodlines. There's little risk of that at this point, but my mother didn't become one of the most powerful vampires in our realm by resting on her laurels. She'd never be content for me to settle with a woman, let alone a human woman. If she knew I was dabbling with Evelyn, she would have killed her on the spot.

"Sickening, isn't it?"

I don't glance over at Nox where they lounge against the helm. They always seem to be lounging, draping their lean body over the nearest available surface. They're captain of the *Audacity*, and a royal pain in my ass. They see too much and delight in poking and prodding at sore spots. They jerk their chin, and I follow the motion to find Evelyn leaning against Bowen's chest and staring up into his eyes.

The tightness in my chest that never quite goes away squeezes harder. "Fuck off, Nox."

"Lizzie, my darling, at some point you're going to have to make your peace with the fact that you're second best. You could always fall tragically into my bed. The best way to get over an ex is to get under a new one."

Nox is beautiful in a near alien kind of way. Gray eyes, pale skin, white-blond hair cut short on the sides and slightly longer on top, the kind of bone structure to make the angels weep, if they ever existed. They're also one giant complication, and I've had enough of *those* to last me several lifetimes. "Pass."

"Lizzie, you wound me." They don't sound like they mean it, though. It's just as well. If they were to push in the slightest, I wouldn't hesitate to separate their head from their body, captain or no, elemental magic user or no.

Trust Evelyn to come to a different realm and end up in a plot to overthrow the current power structure. I'm still not quite sure why I haven't left this ship and crew to go my own way, but at least with Nox acting the part of a double agent and working for the rebellion in Threshold, things are never boring. In the three months since I reluctantly joined with the crew, we've fought monsters, ferried refugees to portals that will take them home, and drank our weight in wine in nearly every port we've put in at.

Our current task falls on the rebellion side of things. A week ago, Nox got word on the wind—the literal wind—that one of their assets had been taken by a Cŵn Annwn crew. Technically, *we* are a Cŵn Annwn crew as well, one of the peace-keeping monster-hunting crews that sail the seas of Threshold.

In reality, Nox and their people would like nothing more than to bring down the Cŵn Annwn and the Council that rules them, as the Cŵn Annwn are like any other policing force across history—inclined to abuse their power over the very people they supposedly protect.

I won't still be around when the rebellion finally takes the fight to the Council. I wish Evelyn wouldn't be, either, but she's up to her nose in this rebellion, and I don't see that changing no matter how many times we argue about it. At least tonight there will be some action to keep boredom at bay. I might even get to murder people soon. That should cheer me right up. "How close are we to the ship that took this asset of yours?"

Nox narrows their eyes, shifting from flirty rake to ruthless captain in the space of a heartbeat. "Close. The *Drunken Dragon* completes the same circuit from Viedna to Khollu to the Three Sisters and back again. Brady isn't smart enough to know what he has, so he'll still be heading north on the same path he always does. We should be able to catch sight of them on the horizon soon."

All this cloak-and-dagger shit is a pain in the ass. I prefer a more simplified—and hands-on—approach to dealing with my enemies. Sneaking around, pretending to be part of the very group they want to bring down . . . It's all so *tedious*. Better a bloody fight that lets everyone know who the victor is. If it's bloody enough, you won't have to fight again. Not while the memory is fresh.

If this asset of Nox's was important enough to divert us from our previous course, they should be good enough to take care of themself. "What's so important about this one person that you're willing to risk someone finding out that you're not a perfect little Cŵn Annwn soldier?"

"Maeve is a vital part of our network, and I need her back where she belongs." Nox speaks coldly, but I think I detect a softness under the words. They like this little victim.

"If you say so." I don't really give a fuck about the cause everyone on this crew seems to believe in so strongly. There have been corrupt governments since the beginning of time, and if the rebellion somehow manages to depose the Cŵn Annwn's Council, something even worse will step into the power vacuum left behind.

This rescue mission is wasting my time. I don't care about this asset who's been taken by the *Drunken Dragon* or whatever noble purpose Nox and Bowen have dragged Evelyn into. The only reason I'm still here is because Threshold is a big watery world, and without a ship and crew of my own, it will take me years to track down the *Crimson Hag* and my stolen family heirlooms.

I can't go home without them. If I'm even able to go home at all when the portal back to my realm has been destroyed. I push the thought away. There's no point in worrying about how I'll get home until I have the stolen jewels, and I won't have *those* until I find the *Crimson Hag.* And before I can do that, we have a damned rescue mission to pull off.

I pinch the bridge of my nose. "This Maeve could be dead."

"Has anyone ever told you that you're a terrible pessimist?"

Nox's grip tightens on the helm. "It's possible that she's dead. But we're going to act like she's not until I have proof otherwise." They curse under their breath. "Maeve's a good girl. People talk to her, share secrets that they never would with a stranger. Even if she wasn't good at her job, she deserves better than to suffer at the hands of Brady and his crew. They're the worst that the Cŵn Annwn have to offer. They should have been put down years ago, but they're too damn good at their job, and the Council ignores any complaints that are filed against them." Nox shakes their head and gives me a mocking smile. "I realize that you don't care about any of this, so I'll stop now."

"Much appreciated," I say dryly. I'm no white knight. If anything, I'm the villain. The people in my life would certainly say so. Without Nox at the helm, I never would have put aside my personal aims to go play savior.

Against my better judgment, my gaze cuts back to Evelyn. She's stopped playing grab-ass with Bowen, and she's currently carving a circle into the deck of the ship. It's supposed to create a shield when triggered, which frees up Bowen to use his telekinetic powers for attack instead of defense. Evelyn is a damned good witch, so I have no doubt it will work.

Her pale skin has tanned a bit in the sun, and her blond hair is nearly to her shoulders now, constantly wavy from the wind and salty air. She laughs more, too. I never noticed how little she laughed when she was with me. She's also taken to pirate fashion wholeheartedly, though she's skipped wearing the traditional Cŵn Annwn crimson in favor of black pants that fit her full thighs and big ass to perfection, and a billowing white top that would be at home on those romance novels she loves so well.

Happiness looks good on her.

I hate it.

"Captain! The *Dragon*!" The call floats down from the crow's nest.

"Fucking *finally*," Nox says under their breath before raising their voice to nearly a roar. "Look alive, chaps!"

I give them a sharp look. "Surely you don't mean to attack another Cŵn Annwn ship out in the open?" We might have a crew full of powerhouses, but so do most Cŵn Annwn ships. I don't relish the idea of a sea battle against another ship. The monsters we've come up against in the three months I've been aboard are enough to give me nightmares—not that I'd ever admit it aloud. Give me a fight on solid ground any day of the week. Not this watery bullshit where one wrong move means your enemy might not even have to kill you—the sea will.

"Of course not." They snap their fingers at their navigator, Eyal. He's a tall, lean man with dark brown skin and gorgeous bright blue locs. "Keep us on this course. I don't want it to look like we're in pursuit."

Eyal nods, but I have questions about the order. "We *are* in pursuit." We're moving fast, too, thanks to the air elemental users on the crew filling the sails with their magic. I can clearly see the *Drunken Dragon* now. It has to be a ship nearly the same size as ours, and yet it looks no bigger than a quarter. I shudder. I fucking *hate* the open water.

"You're lucky that you're pretty, darling." Nox leans close. "I can only take one person with me, but I need someone who can do crowd control without risking my asset. We have two options for who that person is. It's you or Bowen. Choose."

I stare. An attack on an entire ship with only two is a

massive risk, though both Bowen and I are more than capable of taking out a group of humans within seconds. Except we aren't talking about mundane humans. Most of the Cŵn Annan crews are filled with magic users and paranormal beings, some of whom are easily as powerful as I am. At least in theory.

I should tell Nox to take Bowen. If he dies, then Evelyn can fall weeping into my arms, and . . . I glance at my ex again. She's finished the circle and is sitting on her heels, chatting easily with two crew members.

Happy. She's so fucking happy.

Damn it. "I'll do it."

Nox leans closer. "Don't worry. I won't tell anyone about your noble streak."

I'm not noble. I wouldn't know what noble looked like if it bit me in the ass. "They might have information on the *Crimson Hag* aboard that ship. I want to get to it before any of your ham-handed crew fucks up my evidence." The sooner I find that ship, the sooner I can get back to the familiar: death and darkness and familial obligation.

"Sure, darling. Whatever you say." Nox once again raises their voice, roaring orders. I follow them to the stern, watching closely as they shrug out of their dramatic crimson coat and hand it off to their quartermaster, Poet. "Keep this safe for me, love." They keep stripping, taking off their crimson vest and crimson shirt, then peeling off their crimson pants. Nox really commits to the bit when it comes to being one of the damned Cŵn Annwn. "These, too."

"You know, your cabin is right there. You don't have to strip out in the open."

"Lizzie, has anyone ever told you that you're a stick-in-the-mud?" I didn't realize Poet brought replacement clothing until Nox pulls on a formfitting black catsuit and grins at me.

"They'll be in your cabin when you get back." Poet—a large woman who looks like she kicks down walls for fun—has broad shoulders and a thick waistline. Her light brown skin is covered with sailing tattoos and her long brown hair is tied back from her strong face. She turns severe dark eyes on me. "Don't get our captain killed."

I smile, baring my teeth. I like Poet for the most part, but she's disgustingly loyal to Nox. "It's your captain's plan. If they die, it's on them."

"Lizzie, you're a constant delight." Nox throws an arm around my shoulders, laughing when I snap my teeth at them. "Truly, I mean it. A constant source of amusement."

They don't give me a chance to formulate a response. They throw their weight backward, toppling us both over the side of the ship. The drop sends my stomach into my throat. The ship is taller than it looks, and it's a long fucking way down.

Holy shit, holy shit, holy shit.

We hit the water hard enough to steal my breath. My curses are a string of bubbles leaving my lips. Oh fuck, I didn't realize Nox meant we were *swimming* to the damned ship. It's cold and wet and so dark that I can't see a single thing. There could be anything in the depths below us, and I wouldn't know it until it appeared right before me—and maybe not even then. The pressure of the water makes it impossible to move, to breathe, to think, to . . . but I can't breathe because I'm *underwater.*

If this is how Nox plans to kill me, they chose well. It's

everything I can do not to panic . . . except I *am* panicking. I can't move my limbs. My body isn't responding to the increasingly shrill commands my brain shouts. I have to swim to the surface. I have to reach the boat and get out of the water as soon as possible. I can't be here. I can't . . .

A pocket of oxygen forms around my mouth and nose, courtesy of Nox's elemental powers. I hate the harsh breath I drag in, hate the relief that fills me, hate that I'm reliant on them to keep me alive during this little excavation. Being able to breathe doesn't decrease the horrible feeling in my chest, though. It just gives me enough space to think about exactly what kinds of monsters might be lurking just out of sight, waiting to make a meal of us. Would that be worse than drowning? Better? I have no idea, but I don't want to die.

Nox pulls me tight against them, close enough to be lovers. The air pocket expands and then their voice is in my ear. "Breathe, Lizzie. I've got you." And then we're shooting through the water, propelled along by their magic. They are one of those rare beings with access to all four elements. It makes them damned hard to kill, but I'm distantly able to admit that they're useful for situations like this as well.

The movement helps calm my thoughts. Nox isn't going to kill me or leave me to the depths. I can't believe the thought even crossed my mind. Everything is perfectly fine. Except for the fact that I'm still in the damn water.

Within a few minutes, we slow and then ascend to the surface in the shadow of the *Drunken Dragon*. The pocket around my mouth melts away as I drag in salty sea air. "I hate you."

"Liar. You're quite fond of me." They swim to the ship and haul themself out of the water.

I follow as quickly as possible, wanting to put the dark depths out of reach. Something could still rise to slap me off the side of the ship, but at least I'd have a chance to see it coming once I'm in the open air. I can't stop myself from breathing a shaky sigh of relief when my feet leave the water.

Dragging myself up and following Nox's path gives me an excellent view of their athletic body. Hard not to notice that the perfection of their face seems to extend to every part of them. If they weren't such a pain in the ass, maybe I *would* take them to bed.

"What's this asset of yours look like?"

Nox glances over their shoulder down at me. "Red hair. Freckles. Short and plump. Her name is Maeve. Don't murder my girl, Lizzie. I'll have to do something unfortunate if you do."

I don't bother to answer. Accidentally murdering the asset would be sloppy, and that's a word that will *never* be attributed to me. "Worry about yourself. Don't get stabbed or blown up while I'm doing all the heavy lifting of killing everyone."

For once, Nox doesn't have a smart answer ready. They just keep climbing, tension in their lean body. I follow. The thrum of excitement in my blood is a welcome emotion. A familiar one.

This is what I do. What I was made for.

I'm not a person intended for peace, and while there have been a few fights in the last three months of sailing on the *Audacity*, there hasn't been anything challenging enough to work off the tension constantly coiling inside me.

I send out a pulse of my power, the bodies of the crew lighting up in my mind. Too many heartbeats to stop at once, especially since half of them are warded. I poke at the closest to me, testing the ward as I try to move the blood in that person's body to my will. It responds sluggishly, but it *does* respond. I grin, letting the chains of civility fall away, taking away the last of my lingering fear with them.

This is going to be fun.

CHAPTER 2

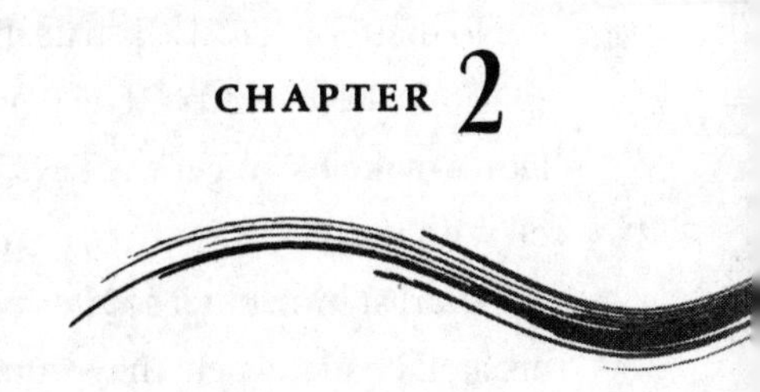

Maeve

I'VE BEEN IN SOME TIGHT SPOTS IN MY TIME, BUT THIS IS the worst to date. I crouch in the stinky cell in the brig, warily eyeing the five men leering at me from the other side of the locked door. I've been on the *Drunken Dragon* since they caught me out in the open three days ago. I should have known my skiff couldn't make it from Viedna to Khollu without something bad happening. But it wasn't the storms that hit this time of year that got me into trouble.

It was the damned Cŵn Annwn.

The ones who supposedly protect Threshold from monsters but are more monstrous than any of the creatures they murder. I press myself against the grimy wall as one man reaches through the gap in the door to attempt to paw at me. Perhaps I should be grateful it took them this long to decide to come down here to menace me, but it's hard to be grateful for anything right now. I'm exhausted, dirty, and in serious danger.

Worse than all that combined is the fact that I'm missing a vital part of myself.

No matter what else is true, I'll go down fighting.

"Come here, pretty." The pawing man makes another grab. "Don't make us go get the keys. Unless you do want us in the cell with you . . ."

I snarl at him, but it sounds pathetically weak in my human throat. If I had my pelt, they wouldn't dare try to touch me with those awful filthy hands. They'd be too worried about me ripping out their throats. If I was whole . . . But I'm not. If I can't get out of this catastrophe, I never will be again.

I'm still trying to figure out my next move when the jingle of a key stops my heart in its tracks. I'm out of time. If I get trapped in the cell with them, it's over. My only hope is to run, to place my bets on the captain not being a total monster willing to allow his crew to assault his prisoner. If they're here with the captain's blessing, or at least his nonexplicit consent, then I'll have to throw myself over the railing and hope for mercy from the sea.

But the voice that speaks next isn't gruff and ragged from a life of sailing. It's soft and light and damn near melodious. "Am I interrupting something?"

My would-be attackers don't get a chance to respond. I don't see what happens. One moment they're starting to turn toward the new intruder, and the next, their limp bodies hit the ground, blood blooming at their mouths and eyes and ears. Revealing my . . . savior?

At first, I think they might be one of my distant cousins from the north, their dark wet hair clinging to their face and shoulders, but then I notice their clothes. This person, this savior, comes from one of the realms, not from Threshold. They have to, because I've never seen pants that mold to lean legs quite so effectively, or a top that doesn't appear to have seams. Maybe the captain scooped them out of the sea when they went through the wrong portal and ended up here?

They step lightly over the bodies—because they *are* bodies; not a single one of them has drawn breath since they hit the floor—and insert the key into the lock. "You must be Maeve."

Now that the light from the window behind me is shining on their face, I can't quite find my words. They're beautiful. It's a kind of beauty that would make my hackles rise if I had them, the sort designed to lure in the unwary. This is a predator right down to their bones.

The door swings open on rusty hinges. I make no move to step forward. "You have me at a disadvantage. You seem to know who I am, but I have no idea who you are."

Instead of waiting for me to make my decision, they step into the cell. Suddenly, there's not enough room. Not enough air. Not enough anything. Their eyes flash crimson, and an unmistakable pulse of magic flares in my blood. It doesn't hurt, but it's incredibly unsettling.

I jerk back a step. "What are you doing?"

"Checking you for injuries." They're still watching me closely, and there's something in their expression that makes me think of a wolf eyeing a particularly juicy deer. "You seem well enough, if a little dehydrated."

I have to put some space between us, but I can't do that with them between me and the door. "Is this a rescue mission, or are you planning to pick up where those bastards left off?" I flick my fingers at the fallen pirates.

"This is a rescue mission, which I suppose makes me one of the good guys. For once." Their nose, which I am horrified to discover is rather cute, wrinkles in distaste. "How novel."

I don't know what I would say to that, because I don't get a chance. Hurried footsteps approach, revealing someone I actually *do* recognize. My chest goes tight, and something resembling a sob lurches into my throat. "Nox."

"We're getting you out of here." They stop in the doorway, their expression going pinched. "Is there a reason you're blocking the exit, Lizzie?" Without waiting for an answer, they shoulder past her. "Ignore her. She's just mad she didn't get to kill more people."

Lizzie. What an unassuming name for such a terrifying woman.

Lizzie nimbly shifts to the side. "Just getting a feel for our little captive."

I can't quite read Nox's expression, but they seem worried. "We need to get moving. The *Audacity* is almost here to collect us, and it's important that we don't linger. It will make people ask questions about what happened to the *Drunken Dragon* and its crew."

"So, what you're saying is that it would be better if there was no ship for people to ask questions about." Lizzie steps out of the cell and walks to a lantern hanging across the way.

I haven't had cause to be on many Cŵn Annwn ships, but I've been on board the *Audacity* a few times, and it's nothing like this cesspool. The *Drunken Dragon* is only a ship, with no convenient pocket dimension to house the crew. They all sleep in one massive room, swaying on hammocks. And if the smell is anything to go by, there's no indoor plumbing, either. The ship will go up rather quickly if Lizzie sets something on fire.

"I realize that I brought you here for a specific purpose, but it's incredibly disconcerting how much you enjoy violence," says Nox.

Lizzie shrugs, her expression curiously blank. "Dead men tell no tales."

Nox narrows their eyes. "Is that supposed to be a joke?" They shake their head sharply. "Never mind. Don't answer that. I should've brought Bowen with me." They hold out a hand to me. "Let's get you out of here."

I don't know what to make of their interaction, but I *do* know I want to get out of here. Nox is a known entity. That's good enough for me. I slip my hand into theirs and allow them to lead me past the curiously still Lizzie. Even in this body, my senses are enhanced. I shouldn't be spending time focused on the stranger, but her breathing is significantly slower than a human's, and her heartbeat is as well. What is she?

Nox leads me past a massacre. There's no other way to describe it. But the strangest thing is that there's no blood spattering the worn wooden planks. It seems like most of the crew just dropped where they stood. The only evidence of violence is the same as that for the men in the brig—blood from their mouth, nose, and eyes.

I know Nox is capable of killing with their elemental magic—they can trap the air in your lungs until you suffocate. Or summon actual water and drown you on dry land, which is obviously something that happened here, judging by the puddles near some of the people's heads. "So many."

"This crew has been a problem for a long time. You know that as well as anyone."

I do. There are ships among the Cŵn Annwn for which the locals know to avoid getting caught alone with members of the crew. To keep the pretty ones tucked away so that they don't catch the eye of the captains. Technically, the Cŵn Annwn aren't supposed to conscript locals into their ranks, but some of their captains care less about the rules than about the power they wield. The Council doesn't care as long as they continue to kill monsters. There's no one to stop them . . . Or at least there never was before.

This rescue is still a bold move, even for Nox. "It was a risk to come for me. You shouldn't have done it."

They shoot me a charming grin. "Come now, Maeve. You know I wasn't going to leave such a lovely lass to these bastards. Let's get you out of here and safe."

Safe. It's a nice thought. I don't know if it's ever been true, though. Maybe my childhood, when the only thing I had to worry about was keeping within the rocky shores of the bay near my home on Viedna. Or waiting for the seasons to change and my favorite kind of fish to come back for hunting. Or living up to the expectations set forth by my mother and grandmother.

I haven't been that kind of safe in a long time. Certainly not since I joined the rebellion, but even more so now that I've lost my pelt. It's like what I imagine losing a limb might feel like. I keep instinctively reaching for it only to remember its loss all over again, as if for the first time. "I have to go to Khollu."

"We'll talk about what happens next after we get you back

to the *Audacity.*" They hustle me across the deck to another crimson-sailed ship.

Reality catches up with me and I dig in my heels. "Wait. I can't be on Hedd's ship. It's just as bad as this one." Maybe Nox can shield me a little, but ultimately they have to keep their cover. They can't let the Cŵn Annwn know that they're a double agent for the rebellion.

Which means they can't protect me.

I look at all the death around me, and all the evidence of rebellion. "What have you done?"

Nox, instead of seeming as worried as they should be, slings an arm around my shoulders and guides me to the railing. "A lot of things have changed since I saw you last. I'm captain now."

I twist to look at them. "What?" There's no way Hedd would have given up the position, even if he was voted out. Which means he must be dead, but . . . *how*?

"I'll explain when we get over there. This isn't the place for that chat." They motion to someone on their crew, and it feels like a giant hand wraps around my waist and lifts me gently into the air. I freeze, too aware of how easy it is for a telekinetic to do more harm than good when they carry someone. My heart is in my throat. I'm not afraid of heights, but there's something deeply disconcerting about staring at a long drop between my helpless body and the surface of the sea. From this height, it would feel like crashing into a solid surface if I fell. My concern is apparently for nothing. A few seconds later, I'm deposited safely on the deck of the *Audacity.*

A person with shoulder-length blond hair and suntanned skin hurries up with a blanket. "You must be freezing. I'm

Evelyn, she/her. Did they hurt you?" She drapes the blanket around my shoulders with a warm smile. "It looks like Lizzie killed them all, so I guess that's . . . Well, that's something."

This woman is pretty in a way that makes me blush, but her bubbly energy immediately sets me at ease. She's about my size, full body poured into a pair of skintight pants and a shirt that shows off a significant portion of her chest, most of which is covered in vaguely familiar magic glyphs. A witch, though I've never seen one who tattoos their spells onto their skin.

I'm saved from having to say anything by Nox and then Lizzie landing lightly on the deck. Behind Lizzie, the *Dragon* is already alight in flame.

Nox waves two members of the crew over. "Make sure the fire takes the ship to the bottom of the sea. Quickly." They're already turning away, barking orders at the rest of the crew.

If I don't catch them now, they're going to take me right back to Viedna.

I rush after them and grab their arm. "Nox, I need you to listen to me. I *have* to go to Khollu." Bronagh lives there. Even if he's not there right now, he'll return there eventually. I just have to hope he still has my pelt when he does. It's a long shot. My pelt could be anywhere by now, sold for a tidy profit. I might chase rumors for the rest of my life and never find it. The thought makes me shake. "Nox, please."

Nox shakes their head. "Things are moving faster than we expected. I need you in your home village and keeping an eye on the southern route."

My skin heats, and it has nothing to do with potentially flirting with the pretty blonde. No, it's shame making me wish the deck would open up and swallow me whole so I don't have to admit the truth. "I won't be much use to you as a spy. Not in my current condition."

Finally, they slow down enough to turn and face me. "What are you talking about?"

"My pelt." I can't make myself meet their gray eyes. "It was stolen. I have to get it back. I can't go home until I have it."

CHAPTER 3

Lizzie

A SELKIE WHO'S LOST THEIR SKIN. WHAT A CLICHÉ. I hang back and wait to see what Nox will say. Even taking this detour to save the selkie was a risk. We're supposed to be hunting some . . . I forget. It's not mermaids again, and Evelyn has argued long and hard against "murdering" dragons, but there's some monster of the deep that we're supposed to be dispatching right now. It's all wasting my time. Hunting monsters might get my blood going with the thrill of facing down an opponent who actually has a chance of taking me out, but I can't fully enjoy myself with the damn sword of my family hanging over my neck.

At the beginning of all that, my mother paid a surprise visit, which led to a series of increasingly frustrating events. In order to ensure my lovely mother didn't skin my paramour alive, I told Evelyn to run. Evelyn, being Evelyn, ran right through a portal—and took my family's priceless jewels with her.

And then promptly lost them.

Or, rather, got herself kicked off the ship currently in possession of said jewels. It's an unmitigated disaster, and it's compounded by the fact that Nox refuses to chase down the *Crimson Hag*. If they won't do that for me, when I'm actually valuable in a fight, they certainly aren't going to change course for an asset they obviously want back on her home island, coaxing secrets from the Cŵn Annwn ships that pass through.

Sure enough, Nox is already shaking their head. "I'm so sorry, Maeve. I'm on a hunt right now, and we've already diverted too much time. If we take any more, someone's going to start asking questions." They hesitate. "And your position is too vital to remain vacant for long. It's not your skin that made you valuable to the rebellion. It's your human form."

It's harsh, but one doesn't win rebellions with a bleeding heart. If they have a chance in hell of succeeding—and I'm not certain they do—then they can't prioritize one person's loss over the benefit to the collection. It's something I understand intimately. My mother considers the Bianchi family to be a single unit rather than a gathering of multiple people with their own thoughts and feelings and ambitions. If you're born into *our* bloodline family, then you are expected to obey first, second, and last.

Maeve doesn't burst into tears like I expect. "Nox, you don't understand."

"I do. Better than I'd like to." They actually sound remorseful, which makes this whole conversation more uncomfortable. "I'm sorry, Maeve."

Maeve. A sweet name for a sweet little thing. Short and curvy in a way that makes you want to grab for her hips and pull her against you. Her curly red hair is a tangled mess, but it intrigues me all the same. And the damn freckles. I haven't had a lover with freckles in a very long time.

Not that I'm thinking about taking this quivering creature to bed. I prefer my partners to have a little more spice, a little sharper teeth. I don't know what selkies are like in Threshold, but in my realm, all the stories surrounding them are tragic and bittersweet. Victims in waiting—that's all they are.

I force myself to turn away only to be faced with Evelyn and Bowen. He's a big brawny brute with shoulder-length dark hair and a perpetual frown on his face. Except when he looks at Evelyn. He pulls her in for a quick kiss and then he's off, doing whatever it is that he's supposed to be doing to get us the fuck away from the burning ship.

Evelyn practically has stars in her eyes as she watches him go. It makes my stomach curdle. The feeling only gets worse when she turns to me, gentle understanding in her expression. I hate when she looks at me like that. There's an intimacy there that I used to crave, but now it feels like sandpaper against my skin.

She's not mine any longer. And while I'm not too proud to murder to get what I want, I know a losing battle when I see one. I lost Evelyn the moment I told her to run. Continuing to chase her will only make me look like a fool, and she'll still end up in that asshole's arms.

She scoops a bag off the floor that I hadn't noticed previously. "I brought you some dry clothes. I thought you could use them."

"I'll change in my cabin. There was no reason for you to go to the effort." I pluck the bag from her hands and move past her, ensuring my long stride carries me away from her as quickly as possible.

I head down the stairs, and there's a small part of me that continues to be surprised at the fact that the inside of the ship is larger than the outside. I've experienced pocket realms before, but this one is so sophisticated it feels absolutely seamless. There's no staggering moment where you're not sure which way is up or down, not even a dip in the floor from the ship to the pocket realm. It's more impressive than anything we have back home. Add in the fact that there's running water and indoor plumbing—and apparently a hot water heater in some capacity—and there are worse places to live.

But none of that changes the fact that I shouldn't be here.

We already know that time moves differently from realm to realm. It took me the better part of a year to find the portal that would bring me to Threshold. And yet, for Evelyn, it was a couple of weeks at most. I don't expect the conversion to be static, either, so there's no denying the fact that a significant amount of time is passing while I've been here, failing to retrieve the family jewels.

I can't go home without them. Heir or not, my mother will rip out my throat for failing so spectacularly. We can't have someone *weak* leading the family when she's gone. If she's ever gone. At this point, I have no doubt that she intends to live forever.

If I was anyone else, I wouldn't go home at all. My mother isn't known for her patience, and if she didn't need me to create little vampire babies, she wouldn't have deigned to give me a second chance after my failure to protect the family heirlooms.

She simply would have killed me then and there, and moved on with her life.

I fight down a shudder. Best not to think too deeply about how she's taking my absence. Successful or no, there will be a price to pay when I return home. I'll endure it just like I've endured all my mother's lessons and then come out stronger on the other side.

A quick shower does wonders for my morose mood. I dress in dry clothes and pull my hair back into my preferred high ponytail. I'm in the process of debating if I'm up to dealing with people when the door opens and the selkie steps inside. She stops short. "Oh. Sorry. I didn't realize someone was already in here. This is the cabin that Nox sent me to."

I'm going to rip out the captain's spine and feed it to them. There are other cabins. When Evelyn, Bowen, and I helped Nox to stage a mutiny and dispatch the last captain of the *Audacity*, half of the crew went with him to the watery depths. We've been refilling those ranks slowly since, allowing other sailors to join up, but we're nowhere near fully crewed. Nox could've sent this woman to one of those empty cabins. Instead, they sent her to me. Since they do nothing without purpose, it's enough to make me wonder . . .

"Nox won't help you with the pelt problem?"

The selkie blinks those big dark eyes at me. "With all due respect, I don't know you. You're obviously a conscript, which means I can't trust you. I don't know why you're asking something you already know the answer to, but I'm not interested in playing whatever game this is."

I step aside as she darts past me into the bathroom. It was the tiniest show of backbone, but I can't help the reluctant approval that flares inside me in response. Weakness is for prey, and I would have categorized this woman as such, but maybe there's more to her than a damsel in distress.

Or perhaps I'm looking for an excuse to explain away my attraction to her. I like pretty things, but I learned a long time ago that I tend to break them. While some of those pretty things were meant to be broken, there are those that leave me with the taste of regret on my tongue. Over my long life, I learned to indulge only with partners who have their own claws and teeth and thorns.

They tend to survive longer.

Evelyn must have fucked up my head more than I realized if I'm considering taking someone to bed who looks like they'll fold if I speak a harsh word. I shake my head and leave the cabin, once again searching out our wayward captain. Nox might play the frivolous fool, but there's a canny mind behind those pretty eyes. I suspect they have a secondary reason for assigning Maeve to my room.

I walk through the door of Nox's cabin without knocking, only to stop short at the sight of a naked Nox. They truly are well formed. I've never found tan lines intriguing before, but I can't deny that it only adds to the allure of them. They raise their blond brows. "Unless you've decided to take me up on more than flirting, normally people knock when they come through my door."

I kick the door shut behind me and cross my arms over my chest. "If I wanted to take you to bed, you'd know it."

They laugh, completely unfazed. "The fact that you haven't tried to rip out my throat means you aren't totally opposed to it. But since you're clearly determined to keep breaking my heart . . . What do you really want?" They grab a shirt from their bed and drag it over their head.

"You're really not going to help the selkie retrieve her pelt? After you went through so much to save her?"

"The selkie has a name." Nox pulls on their pants, somehow making it smooth instead of awkward. "But, no, as much as I would like to, I can't chase down the pirate who stole Maeve's pelt. It was risky enough saving her, and I can't afford for the Cŵn Annwn to look too closely at our actions. If we keep diverting from our normal sailing routes, someone on the Council is going to start asking questions." Nox hesitates and there's something almost like guilt on their face. "And I meant what I said earlier. I'm sorry for Maeve's loss, but her ability to shift into a seal is the least of her value to the rebellion. The needs of many outweigh the needs of a single person."

It's just as I suspected. The same reason that Nox won't actively help me. For the first time since coming to this godsforsaken realm, I feel something aside from pure frustration. "This selkie. She's a local? Not someone who wandered through the wrong portal like the rest of us?"

Nox sits on the edge of the bed to pull on their boots. "Again, she has a name."

I'm aware of that. I'm not entirely certain why I'm so resistant to saying that name, but it's clear that Nox won't continue this conversation unless I indulge them. I roll my eyes. "Fine, is Maeve a local?"

"You already know she is. Where are you going with this?"

I give them the look that the question deserves. "Exactly where you led me when you assigned her to my room. I don't know why you're bothering to act so surprised."

They burst out laughing. "I'm beginning to think you don't trust me." It's slightly startling to watch them transition from the defensive, protective captain to the flirty rake. Obviously I knew it was a mask all along, but witnessing them put it on real time feels like watching someone strip out of their lingerie.

"It's a wonder how you find the time and energy to play games when you're so concerned about this adorable little rebellion," I finally say. "When are you actually going to get around to *rebelling* instead of playing the obedient hunter?"

The flinty look appears back in their gray eyes. "Watch yourself, Lizzie. I like you, so I let you get away with the disrespect, but there are limits."

I merely raise my brow and allow the question to stand.

Nox pushes to their feet and rolls their shoulders. "You already know that I can't help you. At least not in a timely manner. Maeve can. If *you* help *her* first. But do it quickly. I meant what I said about her value to the rebellion. She's the only asset we have in Viedna, and we need her back home and doing her work."

I stare. "You don't give a shit about helping me. But your heart is practically bleeding for the poor selkie without her skin. What a cliché."

"You're a vampire with mommy issues. One could say the same thing about you."

I almost strike them down right there. Only years of control keep my rage under wraps. Nox really does see too much. It's inconvenient in the extreme. "If she's such an asset in Viedna, that means she's hardly well traveled. I don't see how that serves me in the least. I might as well steal a map and go it alone. A suspicious woman would accuse you of trying to pass off two responsibilities instead of dealing with it yourself."

"Don't sell yourself short. You're convenient to have on this crew, even if your attitude is sour enough to curdle milk. If I thought for a second that you'd stay, I'd try to convert you to the cause." They stride to me, and I'm startled into taking a step back, allowing them past me to the door. Nox grins. "Though I'll admit, even I get tired of watching you glare at Evelyn and Bowen. New lovers make everyone a little sick to their stomach, but it's not as simple as that for you, is it?"

I narrow my eyes. "Be very careful what you say next."

"Do you think you can rip all the blood from my body before I have a chance to burn you to ash?" There's a feral look in Nox's gray eyes. As if they're not quite sure they're bluffing, either.

There's a significant part of me that wants to pick up the gauntlet they just threw at my feet and beat them to death with it. But even though they're irritating in the same way that my little brother is, Nox shows every evidence of being a good captain. No doubt whoever took their place would be less effective at their job—and more annoying to deal with.

Besides, if I kill them, Evelyn will get that horrible disappointed look on her face again. As if I'm proving her right, as if I am validating her decision to think the worst of me. It shouldn't be enough to hold my strike, but somehow it is.

I step back, allowing the captain more room to pass by. "We won't find out today."

"Pity." They actually sound like they mean it, disappointment lacing their merry tone. "Another time, then."

I follow them out of their cabin, their threat once again reminding me of my brother Wolf. Once upon a time *I* was the one who set *him* on fire, all at the altar of my mother's approval.

I don't think he's ever forgiven me for that. Not that I seek his forgiveness. That's not the kind of family we are.

A flash of red catches my eye, and I turn to see the selkie speaking with Evelyn. Throwing my lot in with a stranger, even a stranger who is desperate to reclaim something stolen from them the same way I am, is a risk. The question is whether the risk is worth the reward.

That, I have to think about.

CHAPTER 4

Maeve

THE VAMPIRE IS WATCHING ME AGAIN.

In the week since I've been aboard the *Audacity,* it seems like every time I turn around, there's a weight of a contemplative gaze on the back of my neck. It's *always* her. Every time. The only small mercy is the fact that she's taken to avoiding our shared room. I don't know if I would've gotten a single hour of sleep otherwise. I'd like to say it's her being considerate, but all evidence points to the contrary.

I'm not used to people taking one look at me and deciding they dislike me. Usually, my face is enough to have strangers spilling secrets and placing their trust in me within a few minutes of meeting. I look younger than I am—and innocent. It allows people to underestimate me, which is something that's served me well. Served the rebellion well.

But Lizzie doesn't trust me. She doesn't seem to like me much, either. Which is fine. Better than fine, even. I have my hands full arguing with Nox about the need for me to reclaim my skin. They refuse to divert their course to Viedna, my home island. Tucking me back safely where the rebellion needs me most.

It's not enough.

My connection to my skin was severed the moment it was stolen from me, but there's a part of me that's certain I can feel the distance between us growing greater with every day that passes. I can't help but fear that if too much time and distance pass, I'll never be whole again.

I wish I could hold Nox's refusal against them, but I'm participating in the same rebellion they are. No one individual is more important than the cause. I may contribute a significant amount of information and assist with guiding people back to their portals, but ultimately I'm only a single person in a vast network that spans the length and breadth of Threshold.

"It's frustrating when they won't do what you want."

I yelp and startle several feet backward. I hadn't realized Lizzie was so close until she spoke right at my shoulder. Embarrassment heats my skin. I tuck my hair behind my ears and move closer, even though my instincts demand more space between us so that I can maneuver in the event of an attack.

Lizzie shows no indication that she considers my response an overreaction. She just watches me with fathomless dark brown eyes. I've always been told that my eyes are true black rather than a deep brown, but hers have less to do with color than with power. There are old legends about avoiding looking a vampire in the eyes to prevent them from mesmerizing you, but Evelyn quietly confided to me that while there *are* bloodline families with the power to glamour—they do it using their voice—that's not the bloodline Lizzie hails from.

I still get a thrill when I meet her gaze.

"What do you want? You've been watching me for days. Unless you plan on eating me, I need you to back off."

"Eating you?" The way she says it gives the words an insinuation that I absolutely did not intend. Probably.

If anything, my face flames brighter. "That's not what I meant."

"I suppose I should reassure you that I have no intention of . . . eating you." Lizzie hasn't looked away from my face. I'm not even certain she's blinked. It's eerie in the extreme. "We've both lost something vital to us. Nox isn't in the market for playing finder. I'm not certain if you have a timeline on reacquiring your skin before the magic breaks, but it seems better to accomplish that task sooner rather than later."

She's not saying anything I haven't already considered myself, but it still feels like she reached out and struck me. "I suppose you have a point in all of this verbal circling."

Lizzie blinks as if I surprised her. Her lips shift in something that's almost a smile. "I'll help you reacquire your skin. In return, you will act as a guide and help me find the *Crimson Hag*."

The *Crimson Hag*. It's the Cŵn Annwn ship Bowen used to be the captain of. As best I can tell from the gossip on board, his crew voted him off after he sided with Evelyn in a fight against a dragon. It's a story that seems to defy belief. In the few encounters I've had with Bowen previously when he's come through the port on my island, he seemed to be the very essence of the Cŵn Annwn: Cold. Unquestioning. Absolutely ruthless when it comes to hunting down the so-called monsters of this world.

Funny how the Cŵn Annwn are the ones to decide who's a monster and who isn't.

The man now part of the crew on the *Audacity* seems a changed person entirely. I don't know what happened between losing his ship and coming on board, but there's a new fervor in his eyes that matches Nox's. They're true believers in the cause.

Which means they're no help to me in my current predicament.

"What did the *Crimson Hag* steal from you?" I finally ask. I can't pretend having Lizzie at my side wouldn't be an asset. She and Nox took out an entire ship full of the Cŵn Annwn. It's the kind of protection that would cost a small fortune if I were paying for it.

And all she wants in return is a guide.

"A set of priceless family heirlooms. I need to reclaim them before I can return home."

I can't trust this woman. She's obviously dangerous in the extreme and ruthless enough to murder her way to her goals. But if she needs a guide, then she has a vested interest in keeping me alive. And if we're retrieving my pelt first, I can always escape her if I need to. She might be fearsome, but in my other form, I can swim faster and hold my breath significantly longer. She'll never catch me.

Still . . .

I clear my throat. "I'll think about it. We have a couple days before we reach Viedna. I'll give you my answer then."

"So be it." She lets me walk a few steps before she speaks again. "Maeve."

I don't want to stop, don't want to turn back and look at her gorgeous face again. I do both. "What?"

"Find something else to do for a while before you come back to the room tonight."

I blink, understanding making me blush against my will. "Are you fucking someone in our room?" The question comes out sharper than I intend, but it's not for any jealous reason. I don't *know* Lizzie. She's as gorgeous as some fey creature designed solely to lure the unwary through a mushroom circle—and just as dangerous. I'm not certain I want to be trapped in close proximity with her, even if it's looking increasingly like she's my only chance to get my pelt back. Having anything other than a working relationship is a fool's bargain.

"No." She doesn't blink. "I need to feed. I don't mind an audience, but it makes people like you uncomfortable to witness."

People like me.

What does *that* mean?

She walks away before I can decide if I want to respond—or what I'd even say. It's just as well. We have vampires in Threshold . . . I think. I've heard rumor of them a time or two, but I've never encountered them personally. They're said to be ravening beasts that hunt in the darkness and hide from the light. The sun doesn't seem to bother Lizzie in the least.

I've got to stop thinking about the vampire. I'll do that. Right now . . .

To distract myself, I try once more to convince Nox to change their plans. I know it's a lost cause, but since it's becoming clear that the alternative is to ask Lizzie for help, I'm getting desperate. "*Please,* Nox. If I have to take the vow—"

"No." They cut me off sharply. "In fact, *fuck no.* I am not putting that chain around anyone's neck, let alone someone I actually care about. I'm sorry I can't help, Maeve. Truly, I am. But things are in motion, and not even I can stop them."

"What things?"

They take a deep breath, obviously striving for patience. Their legendary flirtation is nowhere in evidence. "You are an informant and a very vital part of our network in this region of Threshold."

The cold finger of fear slides down my spine. "Why are you saying it like that?"

"I'm acknowledging that you have been instrumental in getting numerous people home and saving lives, because what I say next is less kind." They meet my eyes steadily. "You are not Cŵn Annwn. This is your fight because you're a citizen of Threshold, but it's not your fight in the same way that it's mine and everyone else's on this ship. You could go back to your life, stop working with the rebellion, and live to a ripe old age, unbothered by the shit we're fighting for."

My throat burns and my skin heats. I've considered Nox a friend, but I want to scream in their face at how dismissive their words are. "That's not fair."

"That's reality, love." Their smile is bittersweet. "You don't have to hunt down your pelt. That bastard will bring it around again, wanting to use it against you. Just be patient."

I stop short. "I thought we were friends."

"I'm not speaking of this." They take my shoulder and turn me toward the door of their cabin. "And I'm not having this conversation again, Maeve. I'm sorry about your pelt, but I have my orders, and those take precedence."

I hate the burning in my eyes. Hate how my body betrays my anger with tears. Hate how anyone witnessing it will assume that I'm weeping to gain sympathy. "Then, why save me at all?"

"Even monsters have attacks of conscience, love." Nox nudges me out the door and closes it firmly behind me.

If they understood what a pelt is to a selkie, they wouldn't be so quick to dismiss the loss. If Nox was a shifter, they might have more sympathy, but perhaps not. It would get in the way of the rebellion's grand plan, after all.

I shake my head. I'm tired and heartsore, and want nothing more than to strike out at anyone in my vicinity. If I wasn't missing a vital part of myself, I would be more sympathetic to Nox's situation. Gods, I *am* part of the rebellion. I believe in the cause.

The Cŵn Annwn are more monstrous than the creatures they hunt. The Council sits down in Lyari, gorging themselves on the resources they claim to deserve for the duty of keeping Threshold safe. They don't care that the majority of their captains run their respective ships however they like, abusing their power wherever they go. Many of them aren't overly worried if their victims are monsters or strangers or people born and raised in the realm they're supposed to be protecting.

They need to be brought down. For everyone's sake. Even without the rebellion, there's fear and resentment simmering just below the surface. If we're not careful, violence will erupt unplanned, and there's every chance the Cŵn Annwn will take it as an opportunity to make an example of the first community to flare up. To ensure it never happens again.

With the rebellion, with the proper organization, there's a chance to avoid that fate, to make a change in Threshold for the better. *That's* the cause Nox is fighting for. It's so much bigger than me and my personal loss.

I take a deep breath and exhale slowly through my nose. Nox is a dead end. That leaves very few options. I very much don't want to have to travel with the vampire for . . . gods know how long. Threshold is a big place, and even if you're only counting the permanent islands, it could be months before we find what we're looking for.

The thought makes my chest hurt.

Belowdecks, I'm nearly to my room when the door opens in front of me. I stop short, suddenly remembering what Lizzie said. She's *feeding.* On Poet, apparently, because that's who stumbles into the hallway.

I can't help searching her neck for evidence of a bite. There's nothing. But there *is* a heavy look in Poet's eyes of someone well pleased. Her hair is mussed a little and her cheeks are flushed. She catches me looking at her and grins. "I don't like the vampire much, but I do like her bite. Damn."

What does her bite do to put that look on your face?

I chomp down on my tongue until copper floods my mouth. Under no circumstances will I ask that question. The less I know about this feeding process, the better. Or maybe Lizzie and Poet are fucking, and Lizzie lied about feeding. Either way, it's none of my business.

If you're sailing together for weeks, the vampire will have to feed . . . on you.

I forcibly shut that thought down as I slide past Poet and keep walking, heading for the kitchens. I'm almost able to outrun the strange anticipation I feel . . .

Almost.

CHAPTER 5

Lizzie

I'LL DIE BEFORE I ADMIT HOW PATHETICALLY GRATEFUL I am to hear the call go up of land sighted. Thank the gods. I crave solid ground beneath my feet instead of the constant rolling of the deck. To see absolutely anything other than the endless blue of sea and sky. I was not made to be a pirate.

On the ship, there's no escaping all that *water.* It surrounds us, just waiting for a vicious storm or a particularly determined monster to sink us. There would be no help, no way to escape. Just the depths opening up to pull us down, down, down . . .

I force myself to stand at the railing, though I'm careful to keep out of the way of the crew rushing about to prepare to go ashore. The weather is nice today, cool with a faint breeze that prickles my skin. I wish I could enjoy it. Instead, my gaze is pulled to the choppy waves, the swells making the ship dip and sway. When I finally return home, I'm going to stay landlocked for a few decades, until my unease of being on open water fades.

The little blot of dark gray become larger as we approach.

Viedna. The island the selkie calls home. It's low and sprawling, the shoreline rocky and bare until it meets the deep green of the low trees. There must be some kind of reef, or whatever it is that causes waves, because they seem to increase the closer we get, crashing violently upon the rocky shore. It's strangely peaceful.

Nox guides the ship around to the east, skirting the coastline as the surf becomes smoother and less tumultuous. The ship eases between rocky outcroppings, and I pause at the sight of two small pale gray bodies sunning themselves. Seals. One of them lifts its head and lets out a little squeaky sound and, for all appearances, seems to go to sleep.

I don't have to turn my head to see Maeve standing at the bow, her long red hair streaming behind her in the wind. That damned hair means I never miss where she is on the deck. It draws my eye despite my best efforts.

She still hasn't agreed to my offer.

I can be a patient hunter when the situation calls for it, but there's something about this woman in particular that makes me want to push her until I get a proper answer. Until I get the *right* answer. Because there is only one right answer. *Yes.*

"Lizzie."

I don't look over as Evelyn comes to stand beside me. Ever since she turned down my offer to find a way to bring her home, she's been treating me like I'm spun glass. It makes me want to set something on fire. Since I've promised to be on my best behavior, and Nox would *not* appreciate fires on their ship, I've managed to refrain.

For now.

Evelyn leans on the railing, the wind bringing her scent to

me. I can't quite stop myself from inhaling deeply. Damn it. She turns her head and gives me a faint smile, her green eyes filled with the same bittersweet feeling sprouting thorns in my chest. "You're going to con the selkie into going after your jewels."

Of course she would correctly guess my plan. I bite down on the urge to point out that I'm not conning anyone. I prefer a straightforward deal; *Evelyn* is the one always looking for her next mark. "She hasn't said yes."

"She will." Evelyn waits until I look at her properly to continue. "There are some good people aboard the *Crimson Hag.* They might have made a shitty decision to vote Bowen out as captain, but that doesn't mean they deserve to die."

Ah. So this is why she's come to me. To beg for mercy for near strangers. I've heard what she's said to Bowen when they talk about the *Hag*—and what she hasn't said. Just like I've listened to the crew's whispers about that crew. Those aboard the *Audacity* don't like me much, but one of the skills I've learned over the years is to fade into the shadows. Not literally. I'm simply very good at dimming my energy until those around me don't necessarily register that I'm near. Historically, it's been good for hunting when the prospects are slim.

Those *good people* aboard the *Crimson Hag* wouldn't have stopped the new captain, Miles, from cutting Evelyn to pieces and using her remains to bait the monsters they hunt. She broke their silly little vows, and now not one of them would say a single word in her defense.

And yet here she is, asking me to spare them. "Everyone dies eventually, Evelyn."

"Not everyone needs to die because you sent them to an early grave." She tucks a strand of her blond hair behind her ear, and it immediately whips free. "Look, I'm not going to pretend I'll cry if Miles gets eaten by a mermaid, but Kit? Aadi? Some of the others? They were good to me."

Damn her for attempting to appeal to my better nature. She should know by now that I don't have one. "Do you really think these *good* crew members haven't been murdering their way through Threshold in the meantime? The last time you saw them, they were chasing down that mother dragon and her kit. They probably killed them both."

Her mouth tightens. "Don't do that."

"I have no idea what you're talking about." But I do. I'm being intentionally cruel. Evelyn is a realist most of the time, but every once in a while she gets these rose-tinted glasses that drive me out of my mind with frustration. People—whether they be vampire, witch, or boring old human—are inherently selfish, cruel creatures. They will always put themselves first, and they will always villainize the things they don't understand.

Better to strike first and not give them the chance to stab you in the back the moment you turn around.

"Please, Lizzie. For me."

She's manipulating me. She's not even trying hard to cover it up. Irritation flares, and I step away before she can reach out and put a hand on my arm. "Stay out of trouble after I'm gone, Evelyn. If I have to hunt you down and save you again, it's going to put me in a mood."

"Gods forbid." She still has that look on her face, and it makes me want to snarl. She hasn't gotten *soft*, exactly, but she's lost an edge that I didn't realize I craved until it was missing. Not that this woman is mine to crave any longer.

A flash of red in the corner of my eye draws my attention despite myself. The selkie watches us, her expression carefully blank. The urge to reach out and touch her with my magic is nearly overwhelming. I've very carefully not thought about what her vibrance would taste like, have kept myself well fed to avoid any . . . temptations.

I force myself to refocus on the port taking shape in front of us. Some of the islands in Threshold are so wildly different as to be on another planet. Viedna isn't one of those. The closer we get, the more the rocks and trees and mood remind me of western Ireland. Though the houses up on the little hill just inland from the bay are different. They are domed, with bright geometric patterns on the outside that give me an instant headache. I'm not sure how I missed them before. They're an eyesore to be certain.

Next to me, Evelyn shivers and pulls her coat tighter around her. "I definitely prefer the northern islands. This cold cuts right down to my bones."

The cold doesn't bother me the way it does her. I glance around to find most of the crew burrowing into heavy coats and cloaks. There are exceptions—Nox, for one, seems completely unbothered. And . . . the selkie. She's in a sleeveless white dress that should make her look like a virgin sacrifice; that much white just begs for the red spill of someone's lifeblood. She doesn't so much as shiver in the face of the wind whipping about. Interesting.

"What do you know about Viedna?" I find myself asking.

Evelyn gives me a sharp glance but doesn't comment on the fact that I've never expressed interest in any of our stops before. She worries her bottom lip. "They're pretty neutral when it comes to the Cŵn Annwn. The town leader is a big fan because of the steady trade they bring, and he does a lot of pandering to the Council. It means their ships pass through pretty regularly. Maeve's family has owned a tavern there for a few generations, long enough to be a town staple. Anyone who comes through Viedna stops by for a drink, which makes her an invaluable asset. I'm sure Nox has mentioned that last bit a time or three."

I've sailed with two crews since arriving in Threshold, and both treat ports as a vacation just for them. When my family has cause for celebration, things get . . . messy. But I've never witnessed revelry like sailors drinking to fate and fortune and a thousand other toasts to greater powers, some familiar to me and many more not. After my first experience witnessing Eyal weeping his eyes out, so deep in his cups I could barely make out his words as he confessed something to me with the utmost seriousness only the drunk and dying seem to manage, I chose not to accompany the crew on their tavern escapades.

"I see," I finally say. Despite my best intentions, my gaze slides to Maeve again. She hasn't been gone from home for long, but there's still that strange blankness on her expression. She stares down the approaching village as if it's a death sentence with her name on it.

"Lizzie." Evelyn is painfully serious. "Leave her alone. Find another way to get to the *Hag*. She's been through enough."

"I'm surprised that, bleeding heart that you've become, you don't want me to help her reclaim her pelt."

Something like guilt blossoms in Evelyn's green eyes. "The rebellion needs her here."

She has truly bought into all the rebellion shit. I've been aware of it, of course, but every time she says something like this, it spins me for another loop. I sneer. "Worry about yourself, Evelyn. I'm not the one planning to face down the entirety of the military force that patrols this world. That's *you*." And I'm *not* worried about her. I certainly haven't considered restricting her blood flow until she passes out and then hauling her to the nearest portal that seems relatively harmless to save her from what feels like an inevitable death.

I'm a member of the Bianchi family. I know what a losing fight looks like. One of the first things my mother ever taught me was not to step onto a battlefield unless I knew I could win. With my superior speed and strength, not to mention my magic, there are few fights I stand to lose.

But the one Evelyn and Nox and the others seem determined to have?

It's impossible. No one but the Council even knows how many Cŵn Annwn crews are active. Evelyn, Nox, and this *rebellion* are playing a game of whack-a-mole against an enemy who's more powerful, more numerous, and not afraid to raze entire cities to the ground.

Not that I have empirical proof on the last point. I've simply seen how they conduct business, and it's a logical jump to make. The only reason the rebellion has functioned for so long is because the Cŵn Annwn don't know they exist. The moment that changes, it's all over.

I have to get out of here before then. I'd prefer to take Evelyn with me, but she's made her choice known. She's staying to be part of this impossible battle. She's a vicious fighter and more than capable of protecting herself, but there are limits to her magic resources. In a battle of attrition, she's dead in the water.

It's not my business. Not anymore. Maybe not ever. She was never really mine. There was a moment when she might have been, when I could see a future spinning out between us, but things ended before that nebulous fantasy could be realized. There's no going back now.

Gods, I'm becoming as morose as my brother. Wolf pretends to be chaotic so that no one looks too closely at how deeply he feels every cut. It's not a problem I shared with him until recently. I look forward to digging this new weakness out with my bare hands at the first available opportunity.

Putting some distance between me and Evelyn is the first step.

The hardest step, perhaps.

I barely wait for the first boat to be lowered into the water before I vault over the railing and descend to it. Nox is already aboard, and they raise their eyebrows at me. "Careful there, love. Someone might accuse you of running from something."

"Shut up and row." I belatedly register that the selkie is also aboard. Of course she is. Nox is determined to make her someone else's problem, which means they won't want her to linger on the ship. The selkie and I have that in common.

"And tear up these pretty hands?" They flutter their fingers. "I think not. Sit down."

I almost keep standing just to avoid obeying their command, but a wave chooses that moment to rock the boat and remind me that I'm now *inches* from the water instead of yards. I sit too quickly to be perfectly nonchalant and dig my fingers into the wood of the bench seat I'm perched on.

The selkie is very pointedly not looking at me. Eyal and

Bowen accompany us, which means I can relax a little. There's few places safer in Threshold for Evelyn than the *Audacity*. I'm glad she's staying behind. At least for this trip.

"Poet, you're in charge, mate," Nox calls. They raise their hands and a wave rises behind the boat, sending us skipping over the surface toward the beach.

My stomach sours and the bench creaks precariously beneath my grip. There's no dock to speak of here, which gives me something to focus on beyond the possibility of drowning. The larger vessels that the Cŵn Annwn favor require deeper water, so they all approach the way we are now—by dropping anchor farther out and then using rowboats to reach shore. But I would have thought there would be local fishing boats at least. Most of the islands we've visited to date have done so.

Theoretically, those fishing boats could be used to hop to nearby islands, but one thing I've learned about Threshold is that most people won't risk being caught on the open water by the Cŵn Annwn. There are too many stories about *mistakes* that result in locals being forced to take the vow and join a crew. The only exception is the trade ships that sail specific routs under the Council's colors. But they're just as bad as the fucking pirates. There was one at the last island we stopped at, and their "deals" were just short of highway robbery. Most of the people in that village couldn't even afford the cheapest item.

Not that I care.

I don't.

I'm not like Evelyn. I don't have a heart just waiting to bleed out at the misfortune of others. She used to pretend that she didn't feel that way, but being with Bowen has pushed that part of her to the forefront. It would be cute if it wasn't so irritating.

"Don't cause trouble, vampire."

I swallow down a snarl and turn a carefully blank look on Bowen. "I'm not the one who has the potential to lose control of my power and murder an entire village. Worry about yourself."

His jaw goes tight, but Nox makes a low sound in their throat. "Children. Behave in front of our guest."

For her part, Maeve watches the interaction with interest . . . at least until she catches me looking. Then she turns away, refocusing on the beach.

We reach it shortly, Nox's elemental powers guiding us up onto the rocks. They're smaller on this beach than the one I first saw, more like pebbles than boulders. I look around slowly. I'm sure Evelyn would call it peaceful, enjoying the crash of the waves and the distant call of some kind of seabird, but it makes my skin crawl. I don't trust the quiet. Too often, it precedes an ambush.

I follow the others off the beach to the dirt road that curves up the tiny hill that the village occupies. The sun hasn't quite set, but lights are just starting to appear in windows of the buildings closest to us. I can't tell if the lack of foot traffic is because they saw us coming or because it's got to be close to the dinner hour.

Nox passes the first handful of houses, their attention on a larger building positioned in a slight expansion of the road that must make this the village square. The patterns painted onto our destination's walls are a true eyesore, bright yellow and purple and green zigzagging and spiraling and . . . I blink against the dizziness threatening. "What the fuck?"

"It's a spell."

I didn't realize Maeve had fallen into step beside me until her voice snaps me out of my daze. I pointedly look down at the ground. That, at least, is normal and expected and doesn't make me worry that I might vomit. Finally, I ask, "What kind of spell? Warding? Or just repelling?"

"Repelling. It's meant to ward off bad spirits and those with ill intent." There's something in her tone, something almost like mirth. "It doesn't usually affect humans."

I'm not human, for all that I look it. I'm no spirit, either, but one could argue I have ill intent. "Charming," I grit out.

"Maeve." Nox speaks without turning back. "Stop tormenting my vampire. We're just here to drop you safely with your mother and grandmother. Everyone else, we'll get a drink, pick up any news, and then head out again. No trouble. You especially, Eyal."

Eyal raises his hands in defense. "Hey now. That was one time."

"You drinking yourself under the table is at least a monthly occurrence." Nox says it with no heat and a boatload of charm. "It's not personal. We just don't have time for it tonight."

"Fine, fine, I'll behave." Eyal moves with an easy rolling gait that speaks to his shifter nature. I'm not quite sure *what* he shifts into. It's not a wolf—I'd smell the mange on him a mile away. It's something . . . I still can't quite put my finger on it, and it drives me to the brink of frustration. Oh well. I suppose it won't matter much in a few hours.

I'm not returning to the *Audacity* tonight . . . or ever again.

CHAPTER 6

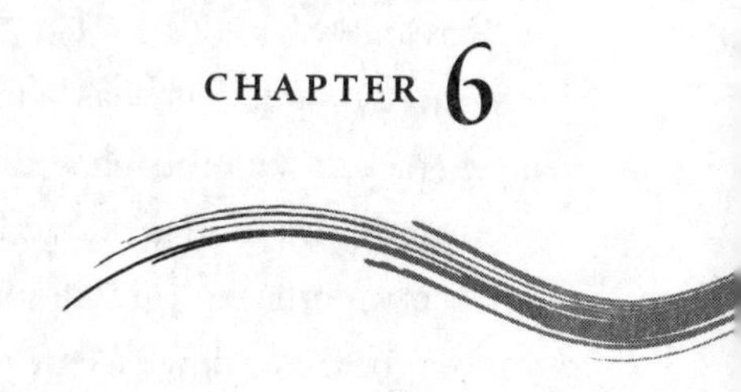

Maeve

For days, I've been trying to figure out how to tell Nox that my mother and grandmother don't know about my missing skin. For days, I've failed to find the right words. I know what Nox would say—my family loves me and won't think less of me for falling into such a simple trap.

Maybe they're even right. Maybe my mother wouldn't get that stony look on her face and blame my foolishness of getting involved in the rebellion. Maybe my grandmother wouldn't shed enough tears to drown me, lamenting on how worried she always is and how I'm going to put her into an early grave. My family *does* love me, and desperately, but all that means is they worry.

Even worse is the fact that losing my skin had nothing to do with the rebellion. I have nothing to blame but my own terrible judgment and the loneliness that sometimes becomes too much to bear. Without those two working in tandem, I'd like to believe I never would have been seduced by Bronagh.

Shame becomes a physical thing that plagues my steps as the distance shrinks between me and the tavern where my family lives and works. It's too late to run. I already did that. I even convinced myself that I was being brave and resourceful in trying to track down Bronagh without help.

Maybe if I'd admitted the truth as soon as I realized what happened, my mother and grandmother could have helped. Maybe I wouldn't be facing down a journey with no definitive end.

That bastard took my skin. He played me with sweet words, seduced me with his touch and gifts, and the moment I dropped my guard, he stole part of me and sailed away. With each day that passes, the distance grows greater. There's no guarantee he'll hang on to it, either. A selkie skin can go for a high price on the black market. It's a bragging right that the worst of Threshold loves to hold close.

I need to *move*. To get out of here. To find a ship, find a crew . . .

The enormity of the task before me makes my knees threaten to buckle. Nox is right in their own way; I've never been anywhere but Viedna. I can measure the distance of my world in a finite number of steps I've traversed more times than I can begin to count. I know every rock and tree and the quirks of the currents beneath the waves. But only here. Only on this island.

Out in the greater world? I thought I'd have a chance, but evidence points to the contrary. I don't have the skills or experience to do any of this. The last time I tried, I ended up as a captive and put the entire rebellion at risk because Nox had to come save me. What makes me think I can do this?

Without intending to, I allow myself to fall farther and

farther back, the distance between me and the door to the tavern growing. If Nox notices, they make no sign of it. The others follow their lead.

Except for Lizzie.

I'm not quite sure how she manages it, but she slows until her pace matches mine, eventually coming to a stop just outside the merry lights decorating the exterior of the tavern. I love those lights. I hung them with my grandmother when I was fifteen, a project that took days and a few misadventures. They're a sign of happier times, of when I was a different person. More innocent. They used to represent home and safety and everything a person could want. But looking at them right now, all I can think of is the many ways I've failed.

I miss my grandmother like an ache in my bones. I miss my mother even more.

It doesn't matter. I can't face them. I don't know why I thought I could. I make an abrupt turn toward the dark pathway that leads between buildings deeper into the village. Lizzie matches my steps effortlessly. It takes me a few minutes to gather my wits about me enough to question her presence.

"You don't have to play guard. I'm as safe in this village as I am anywhere else." The words are bitter on my tongue. I *was* safe in this village. Until I brought misfortune upon myself. The flavor of self-pity doesn't sit well with me, but combating it feels as impossible as reclaiming my pelt.

I expect Lizzie to be derisive or maybe insult me. That seems to be her preferred method of communication. Instead, her voice is carefully neutral when she says, "Your family doesn't know your skin is lost."

"What an amazing deduction you just made." I know better than to show anything other than calm in the presence of a predator. I might as well throw blood in the water—and then myself for good measure.

But instead of looking angry or striking back, she merely slides her hands into her pockets and continues walking by my side. "Have you thought about my offer?"

I've thought of nothing else. No matter which way I look at it, I really don't have a choice about accepting it. Lizzie isn't a local, but she is fearsome in her powers. She's not a bad ally to have at my side. "I noticed in your offer there's nothing about feeding you."

"Maeve . . ." She says my name slowly, as if tasting it. As if tasting *me*.

My eyesight is better than most in the darkness, which is why I see her lick her lips. As if she can already taste me there. I should be scared out of my mind. I like my blood exactly where it is, contained within skin and muscle and bone. I'm a predator, for all that I don't look it right now. I don't feed other predators with my body.

So why is there a little tingle down my spine? Something that isn't quite fear.

"What?" I finally manage.

"You seem to have an extreme interest in how I feed. If you want me to bite you, just ask. Really, you're trying too hard."

I have to stop myself from snapping my teeth at her. She's so incredibly aggravating. My irritation is the only excuse I have for being perfectly honest. "Even if I was going to say yes to your help, it wouldn't work. I'm already too far behind, and if the trail goes cold, my chances of finding him—of finding my skin—are practically nonexistent. He'll sell my pelt before I have a chance to stop him."

Lizzie shrugs. "So we start tonight. Let's steal a ship and get out of here."

I stare, but she doesn't appear to be joking. Or to have a sense of humor at all. "This is my village. You can't honestly expect for me to steal from my own people."

She tilts her head back and looks at the sky above. The stars twinkle merrily, much more distant from our current problems. I envy them. Lizzie laughs softly. "Look at it this way, selkie. It's not stealing. We have to get back here somehow, and we'll bring the ship back with us when we do."

As if that would make it any better. Unfortunately, her plan has a few key issues. "Even if I was willing to follow that logic, there are no ships in Viedna."

She doesn't stop short, but there's a slight hitch in her step. "Impossible."

"Hardly." I turn around the corner of the last building and head toward the rocky shore. My feet know this path from many years of traveling it. Every stone and crack as familiar as the freckles on my skin. "Everyone who lives here is a selkie. We don't need boats to fish and feed ourselves. The rest of the population either have no desire to leave, or they catch a ride on one of the trade ships that pass through regularly."

"Inconvenient," she mutters, "but unsurprising. Nothing about the situation has been easy from the beginning. There's no reason it should start now."

I ignore her and keep walking. Usually by the time I hit this point in the trail, peace and joy fill my chest, twisting in anticipation of diving below the surface and losing myself in the depths. The crash of the surf soothes me, promising a joy I only experience when swimming.

No longer.

I stop on the rocky beach and look out to where the waves are frothy and white and perfect. Deadly. Not for my other form, but they would break this human body against the rocks. I can hold my breath longer than a mundane human; I don't feel the cold as intensely as they do, but without my tail, my serpentine body that so easily cuts and swirls and twirls through the water . . .

I sit on the edge of the nearest boulder and fight against the bitterness threatening to swallow me whole. If I'm not able to find Bronagh, this is the life that waits for me. One where I'm always cast to the side, where I'm forced to watch my family and friends enjoy the very things no longer accessible to me.

Maybe there will come a day when that won't feel like a sharp burning on my tongue that makes me want to cry. I don't know if falling into that acceptance is a good thing or a terrible tragedy. I don't know anything anymore.

I'm so lost in my thoughts that it takes me several long moments to register the feel of Lizzie's eyes on me. I glance over to find her watching me closely. Even now, there's a part of me that wants her despite myself. She's beautiful and dangerous, and there's certainly no risk that I would get attached with how distant she holds herself. Maybe if I lost myself in a few hours of pleasure, the world would feel a little less dim in the morning.

"Do you think your family will blame you for the loss of your pelt? Is that why you're avoiding going home?"

The question washes away my lustful thoughts. I twist around to stare at the waves once more. "Of course not. They love me just as much as I love them. They would mourn the loss as if it were their own." And then it will finally be real. Lizzie doesn't respond, so I find myself elaborating. "It's happened before, you know. There was a time when stealing a selkie skin was an honored tradition among sailors. They would take some of their victims as spouses, trapped in one form and perpetually mourning, but just as often they would sail away with no intention of returning. Once that happens enough, bruises enough generations, you learn to cope."

"Cope." The word sounds like an insult from her lips.

"What else would you have us do? In the water, we're nearly unmatched. Even with magic, most humans don't stand a chance. We're faster. More agile. We've had to be." I swallow thickly. "But like this?" I wave a hand at my body. "We're just as human as anyone else. Just as easily cut down."

She moves so fast not even my superior eyesight can track her. One moment she's standing several feet away, appearing relaxed—or as relaxed as the vampire ever gets—and the next she's crouched in front of me, my chin in a painful grip between her fingers. "That's about enough of that."

I try to jerk back, but I might as well be encased in stone. I knew she was strong. Apparently I had no idea. "Let me go."

"Only if you're done with this pity party."

Shame is a fire in my blood. She's right, and I hate that. "Let. Me. Go." A growl inches into my voice and surprises me so much that I go slack. Where did that come from?

"Better." Her grip softens slightly, but she doesn't release me.

The faint pain centers me, allows me to keep speaking. "Even if nothing else was in play, my family has never been happy about my involvement in the rebellion. They'll blame

Nox and their people for my loss, and will stop informing on the Cŵn Annwn. The rebellion can't afford that loss."

"The rebellion." Her lips twist. "All I ever hear about is that fucking rebellion. The way I see it, you have two options. You can turn around and walk back to the tavern and be embraced in the tearful arms of your family. You can settle into a life where you're only half of who you were meant to be."

I can't quite catch my breath. "Or?"

"Or we can figure out how to steal a ship and go get your skin back." She finally drops her hand and rises gracefully to her feet. With the stars in the night sky behind her, she's a sliver of shadow before me. "It's your choice."

It's no choice at all. It never has been. If I have to learn to live without my skin, then I'll do it. But not until I'm certain I've done everything in my power to attempt to retrieve it. I lick my lips, tasting the salty sea air. My need to be beneath the waves is a craving in my blood that I don't know how to combat. I've never had to before. I want to get back to a point where I never have to again. "I might have an idea."

"I thought so." She steps back, gracefully avoiding turning her ankle on the rocks beneath her feet, and motions for me to stand. "Let's go."

Just like that.

I turn toward my village and allow myself a moment to memorize the sights and sounds and smells. The bright lights twinkling in the windows. The faint scent of people cooking dinner as they wind down for the day, eager to get some rest before they start again in the morning. The quiet. Most of all, the quiet. I wish I could say goodbye during the day, when people are bustling around and laughter and conversation fill my ears. This will have to be enough. I tuck the memory away, promising myself that I won't let it dim with time . . . that I won't let enough time pass for it *to* dim. I won't forget them. I'll be back.

"This way." I lead her to a path that's nearly invisible in the night and head north along the coastline. Once again, Lizzie falls into step behind me with a grace that I might envy under other circumstances. Considering she's haunting my steps, I'll save that envy for another day. The hair on the back of my neck stands on end to have a predator so close behind me. I don't trust her, and yet I have to trust her at the same time.

"Where are we going?" The question is absent of even a hint of curiosity. That's an interesting trick.

I pick my way along a particularly tricky section of the path before I answer. "I wasn't entirely honest when I said there were no ships here. We don't have *ships* but we do have *boats*—that's how I got off the island in the first place. They're just not meant to sail over long distances. There's the added problem that if the Cŵn Annwn see us, we're liable to end up in the brig, just like where you found me."

Lizzie laughs softly, the sound trailing down my spine and seeming to sink its fingers beneath my skin. "If the Cŵn Annwn find us, we won't be the ones to meet misfortune. They will."

"What are you going to do—kill them all?" The very idea is absurd.

"Yes."

I start to laugh but stop short when I realize she's not joking. She means it. If the Cŵn Annwn try to stop us, she'll kill them all. Or at least she'll try. "Shouldn't we attempt literally anything else before we try to murder a ship full of Cŵn Annwn and potentially bring the whole fleet down on our heads?"

She laughs again, low and throaty. "Maeve, you really need to dream a little bigger."

Oh gods, what have I gotten myself into?

CHAPTER 7

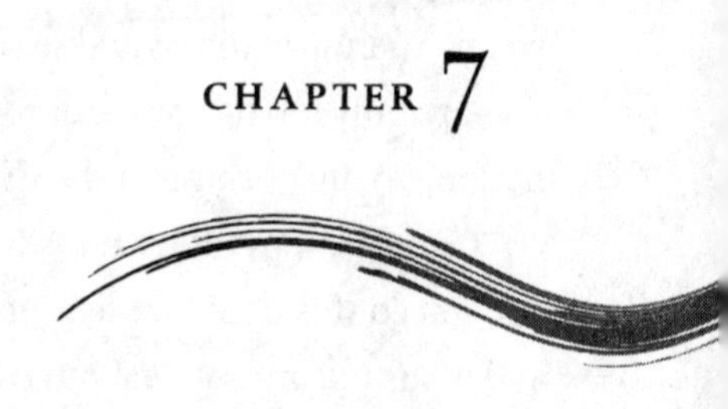

Lizzie

When you said there were boats on the island, I didn't expect you'd lead me to a death trap that will sink the moment we put it in the water."

Maeve looks at me with such exasperation it almost makes me smile. Or I would if I wasn't fighting down a tight feeling in my chest that makes it hard to breathe. Because what she's crouched next to is not a vessel meant for the open sea. It looks more like something children put together during a game of pretending to be pirates. Yes, there's a sail, and yes, it's *technically* boat shaped, but the first high wave will sink us. To say nothing of a storm.

"It's not a death trap. It's our only way off the island." She shakes out the sail and sneezes as a cloud of dust erupts. It's a cute sneeze. Maeve wrinkles her nose. "Besides, Khollu is only three days away, and it's not the storm season. We'll be fine."

"That reasoning sounds like bullshit from where I'm standing." The boat is so shallow, I'll be able to reach out and touch the water if I want to. The very idea has my skin prickling. This thing doesn't look like it will last an hour once we put it in the water. There are storms and sea beasts, and all manner of things that are only too happy to murder us before we reach our destination. To say nothing of the Cŵn Annwn.

The prickling under my skin gets worse. I need this selkie and I need this boat, but fear has wrapped its arms around me and holds me immobile. I can't do this. "When I asked you to be my guide, I thought you were smart enough to know a suicidal plan when it was staring you in the face. Getting in that thing and sailing for another island is the very definition of suicide. We'll never make it." We'll drown, and that will be the end of both of us. Foolish to the point of suicidal. And who will mourn us? Well, me. Maeve has people who love her. My mother will simply be furious to have lost one of her heirs, and my brother will breathe a sigh of relief that I'll never darken his doorstep again.

Maeve steps into the boat and starts attaching the sail. I'm pretty sure it has moth holes in it. There's no way she's being serious right now. "Like I said, it's only a few days to get to Khollu. It won't be a comfortable trip, but between the two of us, we should be able to row even if we're becalmed."

Becalmed. With so many air elementals in the crew of the *Audacity*, it never occurred to me to worry about that. *Another* thing that could befall us. Damn it, I hate admitting that I've made a mistake, but clearly the selkie is not the asset I anticipated. "There's no way I'm getting on that thing."

"Okay," she says easily. She yanks back the tarp covering the back half of it and bends down to grab a crate tucked up against the side. The motion brings my attention to her wide ass, and I almost forget my reservations as my mouth waters. She is so damned *bitable*.

"What do you mean 'okay'?"

"I mean, okay, I'm not going to force you to sail with me." Maeve straightens and dusts off her hands. "If you follow the path back to the village, Nox will likely still be in the tavern. You can join up with them again and wait for however long it takes to run across the *Crimson Hag*."

I glare. I had thought to keep all the leverage in this little partnership, but the selkie is proving to be smarter than is comfortable. She knows I can't afford to walk away from this opportunity. If I could, I never would have offered this bargain in the first place. "Let's get this pathetic little death trap in the water." I have been tortured for longer than the trip to Khollu will take. I can survive this. And the first thing we're doing when we reach that island is taking over a *real* ship.

The shore here is made of the same small smooth rocks as the bay to the south. They shift under my feet, making me grit my teeth. Viedna isn't a very large island—we made the hike from south to north in a few hours. I caught sight of a few houses along the way, bright patterns little more than a flash deeper in the trees, but there's no buildings near us. I send my power pulsing out cautiously, pleased that there isn't anyone lurking nearby. We're in the clear. The sun is barely a hint on the horizon, pale fingers of light doing little to combat the darkness.

The perfect time to steal a boat.

Maeve holds up her hand. "Give me just a second."

I watch with interest as she darts up a little incline, scrambling over the rocks like she's part goat. She's obviously done this a number of times before. I can't pretend to know this woman, but anyone willing to jump on a *boat* and sail off after her stolen skin is someone I can't imagine being content living on this tiny little island.

The island is beautiful. Even in the short time I've been here, I can acknowledge that. Low pale gray cliffs, rocks that cause the waves to crash and roar in a way that's very pleasing when you have two feet planted firmly on the ground. Enough greenery to keep things interesting and probably provide for the people who live here. I didn't get a good look at the people themselves, but every building I saw was well cared for, even if they're all painted with those damned bright patterns that give me a headache. I can understand, at least in theory, that it's a nice place to live.

But it's so . . . constrained. It has to irk Maeve to be trapped here, relegated to hearing tales of sailors and Cŵn Annwn and traders rather than experiencing them herself.

I shake my head. What am I thinking? I don't need to have sympathy for this woman. I have none to speak of. I just need her assistance for the time being.

Even so . . . I know what it's like to be trapped. Both by family obligation and by an inability to travel freely. It doesn't matter where I go, the responsibility of being a member of the Bianchi family follows, crowding closer than my shadow. There's no escaping it. But at least I had a change in location to keep things interesting. My family maintains residences in several key locations across Europe and Asia, and in the last couple of centuries, we've expanded into North America. It's important to make your presence known; otherwise, other people will begin to forget you. Or, rather, they'll forget to fear you.

My mother's worst nightmare.

Most leaders rule through either love or fear. I've never met a vampire who's chosen the former. Well, I suppose that isn't quite true any longer. My brother's paramour is certainly doing her best to rule her people with an even hand instead of terror, but Mina is only half vampire, so she hardly counts.

My mother certainly is never going to rule through love. The emotion is completely foreign to her, and if she had the capability for it, she's long since purged it. Fear is all that's left. Fear is all that I've ever been taught. I'm quite good at it.

Granted, this selkie doesn't seem to fear me all that much.

It's just as well. I find traveling with cowering, weeping messes to be increasingly irritating. If that were the type of person she is, I'd be far more likely to eat her and be done with it.

As Maeve reappears, a bag of what is obviously food dangling from her fingertips, my mind decides to offer up all the different ways I could . . . eat . . . Maeve. I am a vampire, after all. Eating people is baked into my very DNA. More than that, she's a beautiful woman. It's enough to make me wonder what she'll taste like. Salty or sweet or some combination thereof?

I look at the bag with interest as Maeve gets closer. It's larger than I first thought, filled to the brim in a way that makes the fabric stretch to contain the items inside. "What do you have there?" I ask, mostly to delay the moment when we have to enter the water and leave the safety of dry land behind once again.

"If we're very, very lucky, then it will only take three days to get to Khollu. Maybe you can go that long without eating or feeding or whatever you want to call it, but I can't. If I had my skin, it would be easy enough to hunt, but since I'm stuck in this form, the only option is bringing food with us."

Three days. She said that before, but the reality of that timeline hadn't quite registered.

I turn and look at the boat that Maeve wants us to spend three days on. It's not *quite* as small as I first thought. In addition to the small sail and oars, there's a little space to sleep and take shelter in from the weather at the back of it.

Still . . . *three days*. In a best-case scenario.

I don't want to admit that I've gotten soft while traveling on the *Audacity*. The pocket realm sometimes made me forget that I was even on a ship. There will be no forgetting on this boat. More than that, even on the *Audacity*, I never quite forgot my fear of the sea.

How many storms have we weathered? At least a dozen, and I've white-knuckled my way through every single one while hiding in my cabin, certain I could hear the crash of the waves even through the barrier of the pocket dimension. There will be no hiding if we're caught in one while sailing *this* contraption. The waves won't even have to sink us—if it rains hard enough, it will fill the hull and we'll sink. That's the problem with the sea. There's too many fucking ways to die and nowhere near enough methods to stay alive.

"We're going to die," I say flatly.

"There's no need to be dramatic. It's only until we reach the next island." Maeve tosses the bag she obviously had stashed somewhere close onto the boat with an ease that nearly distracts me from the feeling twisting my guts into knots. "When we get there, we'll jump on a trade ship and head wherever Bronagh has gone to. He'll have stopped in Khollu first, regardless, because that's where he lives. We'll find more information when we get there, because if there's one thing Bronagh loves, it's to brag to anyone who'll stand still long enough to let him."

If we're forced into close proximity for days on end, maybe I'll get the story of how she lost her skin in the first place. I know how the old tales say it's done. A sailor waits and watches for a selkie to come ashore and shed their skin so they can sun themself in their human form. Then he steals the skin and forces that selkie to be his wife.

But Maeve lives on this island. Not in the sea. She's hardly leaving her valued other self lying around to be picked up by an enterprising sailor. Something else must have happened. Perhaps he was a lover. The thought rankles, and I easily shove it aside. What do I care about this woman's past lovers? I might be interested in her, but it's a passing thing. At the end of this, when I find my family jewels and a portal that will take me closer to home, I'll be gone.

And I'm never coming back to this godsdamned place.

Something twinges in my chest at the thought. I absently rub the back of my hand over my sternum. "There's one further complication."

"You'll need to eat." Maeve grabs the edge of the boat and starts pushing it into the water. "I suppose you'll have to feed on me, unless you're keen on taking a swim and attempting to hunt some deepwater predator."

The thought makes me shudder. On land, there's a solid chance that I am the biggest, baddest predator around. And if I'm not, I'm more than capable of surviving most violent encounters. In the water? It's a different story altogether. I'm fighting not only the thing that wants to tear me to shreds but also my lungs' capacity to hold air. The poor odds of surviving keep me up at night.

Besides, I *do* like the thought of feeding on this selkie. My bite is orgasmic. Within seconds, she'll be coming apart in my arms, shuddering sweetly and whimpering through her release. The image washes away some of the coldness that has invaded my bones at the thought of getting in that damn boat.

Yes, seducing her will pass the time nicely.

"Lizzie." Maeve's voice is carefully neutral. "Your eyes are glowing red. It's really creepy."

Fuck. I didn't mean to draw my power around me. It's been too long since I've taken a lover, and being in close proximity to Evelyn has me tightly wound. I might have fed on several of the willing crew members and enjoyed their pleasure that way, but despite several offers, I haven't taken any of them to bed. Maybe I should have. Maybe if I had, I wouldn't be panting after this complicated, strange woman.

Or maybe you're just terrified of the sea and losing control.

I smother the nasty little voice. I am not *afraid*. I am logically and understandably wary. It's a completely different emotion. "My eyes going crimson is a side effect. Don't be alarmed." I take a breath and make an effort to shield myself. I can't quite tuck my powers away neatly; they're thrashing inside me, wanting to wrap around this pretty woman and show her exactly what I'm capable of. I've never had this kind of control problem before, but I've never climbed aboard a death trap and hoped for the best. "Let's go." Before I give up on this reckless plan and hurry back to Nox and resign myself to spending *years* not chasing the *Crimson Hag*.

"That's what I'm trying to do."

I help to push the boat deeper. Water pours into my boots and makes my pants cling to my legs. The sky is lightening steadily, but it's as if the rising sun doesn't penetrate. I'm now waist-deep in the water, and I can't see more than an inch past the surface.

"That's far enough." Maeve hauls herself easily over the edge.

I almost turn around and flee back to shore. I actually shift back on my heels to do it. I desperately don't want to get on this boat and sail off to drown in pursuit of a selkie skin and jewels I'm not even sure I care about any longer. Not enough to *die* for them.

But going back means facing Evelyn again, means seeing how damned happy she is, how much she's bought into this new life with her new love and her new purpose. To see the barely veiled pity in her eyes when she looks at me.

No way to go but forward.

I grit my teeth and drag my body over the edge of the boat, making it sway violently. My stomach surges into my throat, but Maeve doesn't seem concerned in the least. She's in the process of getting the sail exactly where she seems to want it. It's much easier to focus on her than on the fear harshly demanding I return to shore.

Yes, I'll just . . . focus on Maeve. It's surprisingly easy. The strength in her soft body intrigues me. Most shifters I've encountered are significantly stronger than they look, but shifting is part of them, something that can't be stolen as easily as one steals a pelt. Obviously Maeve maintains some benefits of her magic, even if she's lost her ability to shift.

"Sit there out of the way and I'll get us going."

I almost obey but catch myself before I move an inch. "I know how to sail." At least in theory.

The look she gives me is disbelieving enough to spark my pride. Maeve shakes her head. "I was on the *Audacity*. I know exactly how much sailing you're capable of. This will go faster if you stay out of my way."

Despite the irritation that arises in the wake of her words, once again I can't help but admire the steel in her spine. It flickers before me, peeking out between the self-pity and the softness. I don't understand the self-pity. Yes, she lost something incredibly valuable, but it's a waste of time and energy to sit around crying. This person who stole from her is hardly going to bring it back just because she feels bad. With every day she spends weeping, her pelt moves farther and farther from her.

Personally, I'm a fan of wholesale slaughter when something's taken from me.

Then why didn't you kill Evelyn and Bowen?

Again, I ignore the voice inside me. Murdering Evelyn might be something my mother would have done, but my feelings for Evelyn are far too complicated to end in her death. The world would be colder without her in it, running around and causing chaos.

Besides, if she honestly tried to kill me, things might have played out differently, but she was only ever defending herself. I'm horribly, unforgivably sentimental when it comes to that woman. It's the only explanation I have for leaving Bowen alive, too. It would have made her sad to see him dead.

What the fuck is wrong with me? I've never worried about things like this before. There may have been people I cared about on a superficial level, but not enough to change the way that I acted. Even before Evelyn stole from me, there was only the slightest softening in her direction. I'd barely allowed myself to think about what a future with her might hold, let alone do anything to act on it. But . . . I cared enough to give her a chance to run, to avoid the bloodshed that would result in my mother finding a human witch in my bed.

Maybe it's Threshold itself causing this uncomfortable change in me. Maybe the very air and water and blood of its occupants are magical in a merciful kind of way. I examine that concept from every angle as we sail away from Viedna. I very carefully don't allow myself to look at the shrinking island being swallowed by the endless blue sky and sea as morning takes a proper hold of the world. No matter that I'd like to blame my actions on environmental magic shifting a centuries-long habit, it's an impossible concept to even entertain. There's no way there's any truth to that theory. If there was, then the Cŵn Annwn would be out of jobs.

Maybe you're different because you're away from your mother's influence.

Unease filters through me. I can't afford to be soft. I may not be under my mother's thumb currently, but I *am* going back home. Once there, I will have to become the heir she formed me into. If she senses so much as a hint of softness, she won't hesitate to carve it out of me, bit by bloody bit.

To distract myself from the memories threatening to take hold, I focus on the selkie. She moves around the boat, adjusting the sail with an ease of someone who's done this many times before. Considering she told me that selkies don't use boats or ships, it's enough to make me wonder how she learned it.

"You're staring." Maeve speaks without looking at me.

"You're the most interesting thing I have to look at." I'm sure as fuck not going to look at the sea. I'd prefer to pretend it doesn't exist at all, that we're floating along on air currents instead of ones made of water. I drag in a ragged breath. *Maeve. Focus on Maeve.* "You might as well get used to it."

She tenses. "I can't tell if you're joking or not. Since I'm pretty sure you don't actually have a sense of humor, you must be serious. Look around you, Lizzie. Sun and sky and sea are all far more interesting to look at."

She's wrong. They're not interesting—they're terrifying. An endless horizon is an invitation for oblivion, and I enjoy life too much to allow the damned sea to take me. More than that, she *is* more interesting to look at, even if I wasn't afraid of the water. The weight that pulls her shoulders down is nowhere in evidence. For the first time since meeting her, she seems fully *alive*.

She's resplendent.

CHAPTER 8

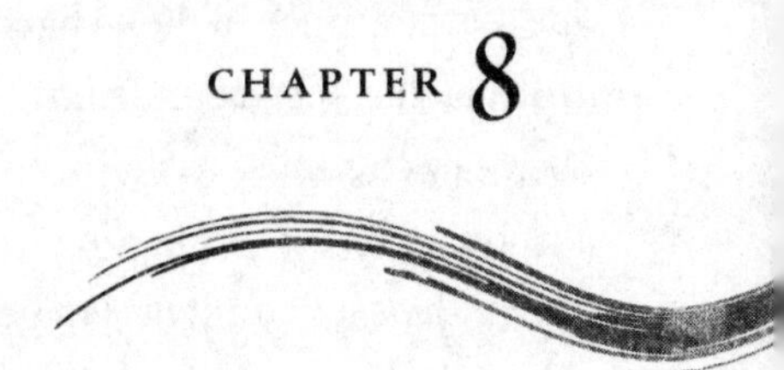

Maeve

I DIDN'T REALIZE HOW MUCH THE CREW OF THE *AUDACITY* shielded me until there's no one around except Lizzie. No one to distract me from her viciously good looks. No one to dampen her intense energy. She's so quiet. On a crowded ship, it was easy to convince myself that I wasn't aware of her presence. It wasn't true, but I had the comforting lie.

Within the first twelve hours on the tiny boat, I'm jumping every time she shifts. I try to quell the reaction, but it's impossible. Her presence is just so *intense*, even when she's just sitting there. And it just gets worse as the hours tick by. I try to distract myself with focusing on sailing, but things are going smoothly. The wind sends us skimming along the surface of the waves. The sun is bright and warm, a pleasant weight against my skin. The world sprawls out before the boat, rife with possibilities. If I was by myself, I might even be enjoying the experience.

Except that's not the truth, is it? Not with the ache in my chest and the knowledge that I'm running out of time.

Whenever despair threatens to take hold, I call on the memory of Lizzie's fingers digging into my chin. It should infuriate me that she touched me so harshly without permission, but the truth is that she grounded me when I needed it the most. The memory continues to do so, not fading in the least as the hours tick on.

By the second night, I'm going out of my skin wondering when she'll need to feed. I've seen what that looks like, or at least the aftermath. Poet certainly seemed pleased with the results. How will it feel to have her teeth pierce my skin, her mouth draw the very blood from my body? The question drives me from sleep over and over again. I've never been particularly careless when it comes to choosing bed partners. There were a few in Viedna as I reached adulthood, exploration and experimentation that faded to friendship over time. I've indulged with sailors a handful of times, but the warnings of my grandmother and mother played too heavily in my mind to ever fully let go. We might not be actively hunted for our pelts in current times, but the community in Viedna has a long memory, and the fear that we'll go back to the bad old days lingers. So I was careful . . . until Bronagh.

And look how that turned out.

"Maeve."

I startle and the rudder slips from my grasp. It's just as well. We have the wind guiding us in the direction we need to go, so I'm mostly hanging on to it to keep my hands busy. But without that to focus on, there's only Lizzie. She sits on the bench across from me, her elbows propped on her knees, her posture perfectly relaxed. The intensity of her gaze gives lie to that relaxation, though. She never truly unwinds.

I'm slightly ashamed that I notice at all. "What?"

"You said three days. We're on day three and I don't see land in sight."

I might have slightly underestimated the time it will take to get to Khollu. I was picked up only a day off the coast of Viedna last time, so I hadn't had a chance to realize that when sailors say it takes three days to get from one island to the other, they are talking about in the massive ships with a full crew. Thankfully, the food I have stashed is enough to last upward of a week, but that doesn't help Lizzie. "We might have another day or two."

She pinches the bridge of her nose. "I'll need to feed in the next day or two. I should have done it already, but I've been taking smaller bites to keep things cordial with the crew on the *Audacity*."

It takes everything I have to maintain a neutral expression and keep my anticipation buried deep. Smaller bites, more frequent feedings. "So you'll feed on me."

Lizzie pauses, the moment flavored with hesitation. She doesn't look unsure, more like she's considering the best angle to approach this conversation from. "It might be helpful if you understood what that entails."

"You bite me. You drink my blood." I aim for irreverence, but I don't quite manage it. My voice is a little too breathy, pitched a little too high. We'll have to get close for her to bite me. Her *mouth* is going to be on my skin.

Her lips shift into something almost like a smile. "Yes, but there is a side effect to my bite. If you're not prepared for the experience, you might find it . . . disconcerting."

She's usually so direct, it makes me suspicious that she's

dancing around this subject. I can't tell if she's teasing me or if she's playing the part of a hunter circling her prey. I clear my throat. "I saw Poet after your . . . feeding. I think I've got the gist of it. I'll enjoy the bite. Simple enough."

Her deep brown eyes flare red, but her expression remains neutral. "Does it make you nervous?"

Of course it makes me nervous. Obviously I would prefer to have a pleasurable bite rather than a painful one, but at least pain would override my senses and drown out the reality that *Lizzie* will have to press against my body to get access to my blood. I've been very careful to keep a decent amount of distance between us, to not touch her by accident. Which is telling in and of itself, but I'm not ready to examine that yet.

Lizzie straightens and takes a moment to glare at the sun overhead as if it's personally insulted her. "It's not just pleasure, Maeve. When I bite you, it will make you orgasm. All bloodline vampires have that side effect, but it's particularly potent because of the powers of the Bianchi family. My family. It's an involuntary physical reaction, and you have nothing to be embarrassed about."

She says it so analytically that I want to laugh. Just a physical reaction. Nothing to be embarrassed about. Except I will be *orgasming* because of something she's doing to me. Maybe it's not too late to dive into the depths and see if I can find something else for her to feed on. Surely that danger is better than the vulnerability required to let her bite me.

But that's the coward's way out. We might have days left before we reach Khollu. I know I can go several days without food if absolutely necessary, but it would weaken me considerably.

Skipping drinking blood will likely do the same to her, but it might be worth it if she can feed on someone in Khollu. Except no it won't, because that means more time wasted, and I need her at full strength to deal with Bronagh when we find him. Not to mention she might get the wrong idea.

I have no problem with vampires as a whole, at least the kind of vampire that Lizzie is. She's not rampaging and slaughtering anyone in her path. In fact, her control appears to be downright legendary for the great violence she's obviously capable of. It will be a bite, plain and simple. Controlled. Calm. No actual danger to me. Easy. Simple.

I've been thinking too long already. I can pretend I'm being forced into this by our circumstances, but I've been curious about her bite ever since seeing Poet come out of our shared room. Best of all, even if an orgasm makes me question things, it won't make Lizzie confused about our relationship. Her first cutting remark will slam me right back to myself. "We might as well get it done. Do it."

"Such a noble sacrifice you're making," she says softly, a hint of something in her voice that almost sounds like seduction. Surely I'm imagining things. She's thinking about my blood, not about *me*. "Come here, Maeve."

I take a moment to strap the rudder in place and then nervously shift to sit beside her. She smells good. Too good for being trapped on this boat for three days. Much better than I must smell. Oh gods, what am I doing? I can't let her get close to me when I stink. In a panic, I shove my arm into her face. "Here. Do it."

This time Lizzie doesn't bother to hide her amusement. Her

lips curve and her eyes flicker crimson. "Biting you there will hamper your ability to move through your day. Besides, I prefer something a little more . . . traditional."

Again, I picture Poet after the feeding with Lizzie. There were no visible bites of her neck or arms. I've spent far too much time thinking about where Lizzie may have bitten her, which vein she chose. There's a particularly juicy one in the upper thigh . . .

But there's no way we're doing *that* right now. Or ever. I'd need a bath and a bottle of alcohol to even consider it.

"Fine." I start to tilt my head to the side, but Lizzie catches the back of my neck in a strong but careful grip. She guides me to turn away from her, to lean back against her. I have to fight my body's instinctive desire to tense, to pull away.

"There's nothing to be nervous about." This time, she actually laughs. "Just relax."

"I'm not nervous."

"Liar." She speaks against my neck, the sensation sending little tingles along my skin. Lower. "Breathe, Maeve. I promise this isn't something to be endured. You'll enjoy yourself."

At this rate, there's a good chance I might just die of embarrassment before she ever gets around to biting me. I tilt my head to the side a little to give her better access, holding my body in a tense line. "Just do it."

I expect her to strike like a snake, quick and vicious. I'm so busy anticipating that moment of pain that I jolt when her lips brush the sensitive skin of my throat. It's not quite a kiss, but it's not *not* a kiss, either. It scrambles my brain as I try to analyze and reason away why she would bother to ease into the bite instead of just feeding.

Then her lips part and her teeth sink into my skin. The pain is quick, sharp, and gone in an instant, pleasure blooming in its wake. I melt against her. Oh. *Oh.* The first pull seems to connect directly to my clit, a sizzling warmth that makes me squirm.

She wraps her arms around me almost tenderly, holding me close. I shiver. It's not intentional. My body has taken over and my brain is shorting out. Lizzie uses one hand to cup the back of my neck and wraps the other around my waist, holding me at the perfect angle for her to continue to drink. It feels good to have her hands on me, but it's not enough. I want her to touch me *everywhere.* Fingers digging into skin, tongue and teeth exploring, her entire body wrapped up in mine.

Even without actual physical stimulation, pleasure builds with each swallow she takes of my blood. My hips shift, seeking friction. *Touch me, touch me, touch me.* I grab her arm banded around my waist, desperate to guide her hand between my thighs, but she's so incredibly strong that I can't move her. Even that denial heightens my desire.

My orgasm draws closer and closer. All the talk of involuntary physical reaction feels laughable now. It's a wonder Lizzie doesn't have a crowd of admirers chasing after her, offering their throats and thighs. How can they not when it feels so good?

There's no space to feel embarrassed. Only to *feel*. My body flushes hot, blood seeming to gather in my breasts and pussy. To center around my clit. She's not even touching me. That thought circles again and again, and each pull of her mouth shoves me toward a world-ending orgasm. All with her holding me in an almost friendly manner. Later, maybe I'll die of embarrassment, but right now I can't do anything but accept that I'm about to orgasm in the vampire's arms. I have a faint thought to try to fight it, but by the time I even consider it, it's too late. My pleasure crests in an undeniable wave that rolls over me, drawing a cry from my lips.

I find myself reaching back, my fingers in her hair, holding her mouth to my skin, even as she gentles the bite and drags her tongue over the puncture wounds. I'm shaking and I can't seem to stop, the aftermath of the orgasm almost as intense as the orgasm itself.

I had intended to suffer through these bites as a necessity. She's my partner in this endeavor, which means she needs to be fed. But as she eases back and straightens my shirt with an efficiency that's almost clinical, I have to clamp my jaw shut to prevent myself from asking her to bite me again. Right now.

This is the kind of pleasure that one could get addicted to. Worse, it leads me to a very dangerous fantasy of how much better that orgasm would be if she was actually touching me . . . if she was biting me somewhere else.

"The wounds will close quickly. You might be light-headed for a little while, but you're not human, so I expect it will pass quickly." She still has one arm banded around my waist. If she weren't already touching me, I would have missed her tiny shiver. "I've never tasted a selkie before."

It must be the orgasm muddling my thoughts, because there's no other reason I would allow the question to leave my lips. "What do selkies taste like?"

"I don't know what the others taste like, but you're . . . salty." She inhales deeply, inhales *me*. "There's a depth of flavor there, something familiar and yet not at the same time."

My brain is slowly coming back online, and that's the only

reason I'm able to stop my next question before I speak it. *Is that a good thing?* It doesn't matter if it's a good thing or not. I'm currently her only source of food. I just need to be grateful that I don't have to suffer through the experience.

I'm a little woozy as I shift back to my spot and take up the rudder again. I want to blame it on the blood loss, but she only took a few mouthfuls. No, what's scrambling my senses is her proximity and the pleasure she dealt me.

I'm in trouble.

Lizzie stretches out and makes a sound that I *know* isn't sexual, but my body responds all the same. I'm helpless to do anything but stare at the long line of her. Her shirt rides up a tiny bit to reveal a slice of pale skin. Gods help me, but my mouth waters at the sight. I want to taste her. To see if she's just as salty and layered as I am, or if there's a sharp edge to her like I suspect. To discover what kinds of sounds she makes when she comes.

Foolish thoughts. Downright suicidal thoughts if I'm being honest. We're partners; the very last thing we need is to complicate things with sex. The only reason we're sailing together is because I need my skin and Lizzie needs her jewels. Once we've fulfilled those conditions, I'll return home and so will she—to an entirely different realm.

I'll never see her again.

The thought should bring relief, but there's only a strange sense of loss. I barely know this vampire, and yet I'm drawn to her all the same. She's not like anyone I've ever met, and I feel like I've barely scratched the surface of her. That's a good thing . . . or at least it should be.

Without meaning to, I lift my hand to my chin and press my

fingers to the exact same spots she did back in Viedna. The memory of her holding me, commanding me back to myself, washes over me. Only this time it's accompanied by her mouth on my skin, her teeth piercing me. With *need*.

I'm in a whole lot of trouble.

CHAPTER 9

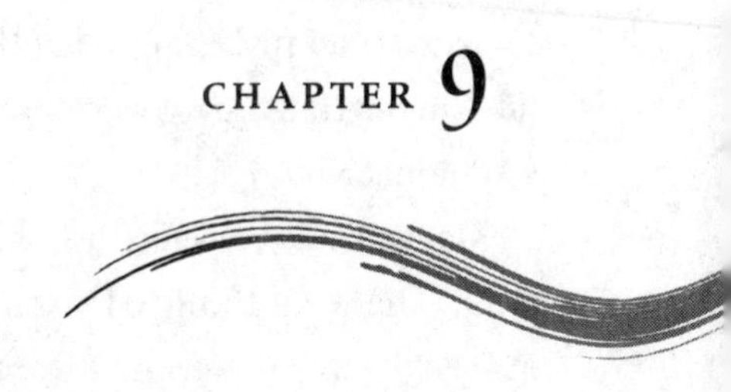

Lizzie

BITING THE SELKIE WAS A MISTAKE. SHE TASTES EVEN better than I could have dreamed, her blood as full of mystery as her inky eyes. Even thinking about it now, hours later, my fangs throb in wanting. Worse in some ways, she came so sweetly. *Desperately.* With cute little whimpers and shudders that tempted me to let things get out of hand.

I need her help for a prolonged period of time; otherwise, I'd already be planning a full seduction the moment we find a bath and bed.

I'm such a fucking liar. I *am* planning a full seduction the moment we find a bath and bed. We're adults. We can enjoy each other and go our separate ways at the end of this. Sex is a perfectly natural outcome when desire sparks so fiercely between people. There's no reason not to give in to it.

No reason except Maeve acting skittish ever since she came back to herself. I can't quite decide if her racing heart is because she wants more . . . or because she's afraid of me in a way she hasn't been since we met.

To distract myself, I nod at the bag she tucked away. "Why did you have a go bag packed when you'd already escaped the island once?"

Maeve makes a face, but we have nothing better to talk about. There's nothing to look at but the endless blue of the sea, and *that* is not something I want to focus on for any length of time. I've historically enjoyed the sea—from shore. The soothing crash of the waves, the early morning mist that kisses my skin, the way the sun glints off the surface as it sets behind the horizon. It's so much different on the water. The sun is unrelenting, the surface creating a mirror that means there's no escaping the bright rays. Salt is *everywhere*, crusted on my clothes, my skin, my hair. I hate it.

Better by far to focus on Maeve.

She finally sighs. "I don't really want to talk about it."

"Then would you rather talk about how pretty you are when you orgasm?" I'm not flirting with her. I just want information, and this is the best way to get it. There's no way she wants to discuss what happened between us when I bit her. Which means I'll get the information I'm seeking. That's all.

Sure enough, her skin deepens to a bright crimson and she looks everywhere but at me. "You are incredibly frustrating."

"People have said worse."

"I can only imagine." She pokes at the rudder, but unless she dives over the side of the boat, she's not getting out of this conversation. Finally the selkie sighs. "The bag isn't mine. It's a community thing. We have them stashed all over the island."

I examine her words from several angles. "To escape the Cŵn Annwn or monsters?"

"*Monsters.*" She makes a derisive noise that wrinkles her cute little nose. "My people have been in Threshold since before the Cŵn Annwn showed up. So have the peoples of *all* the islands. Do you know what stories we pass down?"

This anger feels like it's following a known path, the way a river carves its way through a mountain. "What stories?"

She clenches her fists. "Cautionary tales to give predators wide berth. Because that's what these so-called monsters are—predators acting according to their nature. The Cŵn Annwn have killed more than any predator they hunt, and they've done untold damage to communities who tried to push back against their rule. No monster has done *that*."

Earlier, she said that the selkies have no use for ships and boats because they do their own hunting in their other forms. Which means that there is no easy escape from the island unless they want to swim. If I were hunting selkies, I would merely wait on the surface until they ran out of air and then pick them off like fish in a barrel. They are still mammals, after all. They have to breathe air.

"The go bag?"

"Viedna isn't very large, so people think that what they can see is all there is *to* see. There are caves that stretch for miles and miles. There is fresh water, but not much in the way of food if you're not a fan of mushrooms. Some of the caverns have actual supplies, but near the other entrances, we keep bags. Just in case."

Interesting. I'll admit that I fell into the same trap of assuming that the small island is exactly as it appears to be. "Do the stashes belong to the rebellion?"

"Some of the smaller ones, but that's only because the village elders gave them permission to hide people passing through."

I still have a lot of questions about the rebellion. I know what Nox says. I know what Evelyn and Bowen say. But in their own way, they each occupy a privileged and unique position within the ecosystem of Threshold. They are part of the Cŵn Annwn. The boogeyman that terrifies communities and monsters alike when they sail into port.

That's not the role Maeve has played. "How were you recruited?"

Once again, she seems like she doesn't want to answer me. Once again, she does anyways. But she surprises me. "I'll answer your questions if you answer mine. One for one."

I consider her offer. I don't particularly want to share details about myself with this woman. We're already in a situation of forced intimacy, and it's only going to get more complicated as time goes on. I don't often bite the same person repeatedly, especially if they're not already intimately acquainted with how bloodline vampires work. It's far too easy for them to get the wrong idea. Their blood might taste good, but I'm not feeling the same level of pleasure that they are from the bite.

Unless we're in the middle of having sex when I bite them.

Allowing Maeve closer is a risk. For her. Maybe I shouldn't care about it . . . Actually, I *don't* care about it. She can make her own decisions. If she wants to know more about me, then that's her problem. My logic feels a little flimsy, but I ignore it and press on. "If you insist."

"You've already asked me about my bag. I want to know about how you came into Threshold."

I blink. I expected her to ask about the jewels, or perhaps

about Evelyn. That seems to be what everyone is focused on since they've met me. No one asked what it took to get here. "I came the same way that everyone else seems to. I walked through a portal."

Maeve gives me a stern look. It's cute. "You're not honoring the spirit of the agreement, Lizzie. Tell me the story."

I could push back, but I'm curious about her. If I don't play along with this little game of tit for tat, then I won't get answers to my questions. That's the only reason I give her the full story. "Evelyn demolished the portal in my home that she entered Threshold through, so that way was closed to me. I'm still not sure *how* she made it to Threshold, since that portal wasn't supposed to work like that. It took me two weeks to figure out that she hadn't exited somewhere else but was caught in the in-between. There was another month of hunting down the truth of what that means." During that month, I was convinced Evelyn was dead, torn apart in the space of nothingness. I should have left off the hunt, but I needed closure. I used the excuse of attempting to reclaim the family heirlooms, but I breathed a deep sigh of relief when I finally got the truth.

She wasn't dead. She was in Threshold.

A space between realms. One that is entirely survivable if you are clever and resourceful, both things that Evelyn is in spades. "From there, it was only a matter of finding the actual portal to Threshold. It seemed too risky to attempt what Evelyn did—using a portal meant to travel within our realm and frying it—so I took a more traditional route. It moves, so I had to figure out the exact time and location when it would appear so that I could step through." For Evelyn, only a week or two had passed since she fled my house. For me, it took nearly a year to reach Threshold. Each day, my anger at her grew until it was a fiery thing inside me overwhelming all else. And even in a fit of rage, I couldn't kill her.

My mother would be so disappointed.

"You must have been very driven to find your ex-girlfriend."

I don't dignify that with a response. Instead, I turn back to my original question. "You have your answer. How did the rebellion recruit you?"

Maeve leans back against the side of the boat. Unlike when she was sharing information about the cave system on her island, she seems significantly more relaxed with this topic. "They didn't. It kind of happened by accident. I knew Nox because they were one of the few Cŵn Annwn I could stomach when they stopped by on their way north. Or south. All sailors invariably end up in my family's tavern, drinking themselves under the table. Once I reached adulthood, my mother would often send me away during the nights when those sailors were Cŵn Annwn."

Easy enough to read between the lines. If there's one thing so many of the crews of the Cŵn Annwn do, it's abuse their power. Maeve is stunning and draws the eye wherever she is. It would only be a matter of time before one of those bastards decided to take what she wasn't offering. "And then?"

"On one of those nights, I saw Nox slipping out of the village. I followed. They met up with a shadowy figure not far from where we found this boat. I was close enough to hear their conversation, and when they inevitably caught me, they decided to recruit me instead of killing me."

A risk, but as ruthless as Nox is, they have a soft spot for broken toys. And innocence. Maeve may think that she's broken right now, but she firmly lands in the latter category. "So you put yourself in danger, interacting with the Cŵn Annwn, because of Nox?"

She gives me a wan smile. "That's two questions."

Frustration threatens to take hold, but we're having a conversation without sniping at each other, and she's readily answering my questions. I suppose it's not too much to ask that I continue this little game. "Fine. Ask."

"Tell me about your family."

"That's not a question at all."

She raises her brows. "Are you dodging giving an answer?" Intrigue colors her tone. "Fine, I'll play by the rules properly. What is your family like?" She exaggerates the lift at the end of the last word. Little brat.

I almost give the pat, neat answer that I provide whenever I'm forced into this kind of conversation. There are only seven bloodline families in my realm, and though vampires engage in varying levels of secrecy, everyone in the paranormal community knows of our existence. At least in theory. So when they come across us, there are inevitably questions. Not even fear is enough to completely drown out curiosity. It's inconvenient.

But when I answer, it's the truth that slips from my lips. "My father is dead and has been since I was a small child. My mother rules the family with a bloody iron fist. She's taught me everything I know. My younger brother is the family fuckup. He was supposed to be my right hand, a built-in support for the day when I take over, but he's always chosen to go his own way." Currently, his own way is giving my mother fits of rage, possibly because he's finally beyond her reach. He's created a sickeningly cute little polycule with Mina, Rylan, and Malachi . . . all of whom are members of other bloodline families. Not even my mother would risk war by daring to cross so many powerful vampires.

"You almost sound like you envy him."

I glare. "That's also not a question."

"Lizzie."

"What's the point of playing a game if you don't follow the rules?" Granted, I'm more than happy to discard whatever rules don't serve me. Though, from the look in Maeve's large eyes, I'm not going to escape this subject on her next question. In an attempt to distract her, I say, "Who took your pelt?"

Instantly, all relaxation banishes from her face. I watch her close down in real time, her expression shuddering and her spine straightening. "His name is Bronagh."

I open my mouth, but she beats me there. "Why are you so resentful of your brother?"

"I don't want to answer that question." I don't mean to say it. This game started as an attempt to get more information out of her, to understand the enigma that is Maeve, and yet I feel like I'm the one being stripped bare. She sees more than most people. Even Evelyn never really asked me about Wolf. Or my family, for that matter.

Maeve smiles slightly, the twist of her lips bittersweet. "Then I think this game is done, don't you?"

It should be. It's a smart idea. I don't know how situations continue to slip out of my control time and again. It's never been a problem before. Usually when I'm backed into a corner, I just kill my way out. Or I avoid a fight altogether by virtue of my reputation. Neither of those has been an option for too many of the uncomfortable situations I've found myself in since I came to Threshold. They certainly aren't an option now.

More than that, I want to know about the bastard who took her skin. I want to know the story of how it happened and why. I can barely acknowledge the motivation behind that desire for knowledge. It's not mere curiosity, though that would be significantly less complicated. No, the sensation inside my chest when I think about him is furious . . . and almost protective.

That fucker put the bruised look in Maeve's eyes. He hurt her, carved out a piece of her, and took it with him when he left. Unlike most exes, he did it literally.

I want to see what Maeve is like when she's not mourning a lost piece of herself. I want to know what kind of woman she is when she's at peace. Whatever that looks like.

A deep breath does nothing to settle the jagged pieces inside me that grind together when I think about my brother. "Wolf has never cared about our mother's expectations. He moves through life driven by desire and . . . love, I suppose. He doesn't seem to feel the same pressures I do. He doesn't conform. He doesn't break himself until he's unrecognizable, all to fit a mold created by our mother. I suppose I *am* jealous of him. It makes me hate him sometimes. I've certainly hurt him enough over the centuries. But nothing seems to stick. He endures whatever punishment my mother decrees and then moves on. I don't understand it." The words feel sharp in my throat. Painful. I've never admitted this out loud, not to anyone.

I wait for Maeve to point out that I make my own choices, too. That I am choosing to conform to my mother's demands, just like Wolf is choosing to push back. That I bow to duty over love every single time. It's how I lost Evelyn, after all. It's how I've lost the person I might have been if I was born into a different family, was taught by a different mother.

There's no point in mourning that version of myself. She was weak, so she had to die. It was the only way I could live. There's certainly no point in wondering if this selkie staring at me with fathomless eyes would have liked that softer version much better than the one who sits before her, heart cold and hands drenched in centuries' worth of blood.

And yet . . . I can't help but wonder exactly that.

CHAPTER 10

Maeve

I DIDN'T EXPECT THE THREAD OF PAIN IN LIZZIE'S VOICE when she talks about her brother and family. I certainly didn't expect to read between the lines to the abuse she must have suffered to fulfill the expectations of her mother. Shame coats my throat. I'm guilty of making assumptions about her, of following the lead of Nox and the others on the *Audacity* and believing that Lizzie walked from the womb with a cold smirk and a desire for violence.

Maybe she did, but that doesn't change the fact that the person she is today was formed from a lifetime of experiences, and if the heaviness of her words is any indication, many of those experiences were horrific and violent.

I know what it's like to live under the expectations of others, but attempting to find common ground is a recipe for disaster. At best, she'll laugh in my face. At worst, she'll assume I pity her and hate me for it. Knowing that keeps me from trying to comfort her, but the desire is there all the same.

Before I can do something foolish, she clears her throat. "How did you lose your skin?"

I knew the question was coming. Honestly, I'm surprised no one asked me before. Nox chose not to on purpose. They know better than anyone what Threshold can take from you. But once I agreed to this journey together, it was only a matter of time before Lizzie would want to know about the theft that set me on this path.

Even so, it feels strange to take a deep breath and try to formulate my thoughts into something that isn't shrieking in rage. At myself. At him. At the entire situation.

She answered honestly when I asked her a truly invasive question. I can do nothing less. The pain in my chest is a living thing as I clear my throat. "I spent a good portion of my adult life avoiding entanglements with sailors and the Cŵn Annwn. Once Nox recruited me, I stopped leaving the tavern when the tide washed their ships in. I learned to flirt enough to get them to spill information and to avoid advances in a way that didn't bruise their pride." And I was *good* at it, too. I was able to pass plenty of information about shipping routes, plans, and even a few secrets to the rebellion.

But I was so incredibly lonely.

I can't bring myself to admit *that* aloud. Instead, I say, "Bronagh is incredibly handsome and incredibly charming. His ship has a trading route through Khollu, Viedna, and the handful of smaller islands within a few days' travel, so I saw him a lot. He noticed me."

He noticed me. So much in those three little words. So *little.* Shame is a live thing inside me. I should have known better than to trust him. I should have known better than . . .

"Keep going." Lizzie's words anchor me, drawing me out of my shame spiral. At least a little.

It still hurts to talk. "I thought he was courting me. He's from Khollu and so he was already making the trip down to Viedna once or twice a month. He started bringing me gifts, slipping them to me when no one else noticed." More accurately, when my grandmother and mother didn't notice. They would've put a stop to the situation immediately and likely would've known the danger he presented. But the illicitness of our interactions only made him more attractive to me.

I was a fool.

I look out at the horizon. "I thought I was in love. In hindsight, I just liked the attention. I liked that someone looked at me and saw something special instead of just a barmaid on a backwater island. It made me reckless." Bronagh, on the other hand, obviously had a plan. It wasn't the first time we had sex that he stole from me. It wasn't the second or third time, either. It was the moment when I truly trusted him, when I snuck him into my room. When I let him close enough to hurt me.

Which is exactly what he did.

I swallow hard. "We had a monthlong affair, and when I woke up one morning, he was gone and he'd taken part of me with him."

The theft hurt. Of course it did. It always hurts to lose part of yourself, to have it carved from you with selfish actions. But for *him* to be the one to do it? It made me doubt every instinct I have. I truly believed that he cared for me, and the entire time he was only manipulating me to get what he wanted. Shame is a toxic emotion inside me, and I can admit now that it was probably intentional on his part to make me feel this way. Shame and humiliation ensured I wouldn't go to others for help, that I would try to do it on my own.

Which meant I was certain to fail.

"I see." Lizzie examines her fingernails. They're long and sharp, and I'm honestly not certain how she managed to keep their shape while working on the *Audacity*. "When we take back your skin, we'll take his heart, too."

She says the words so casually that it takes my brain several beats to catch up. I blink. "You mean that literally."

"That wasn't a question, so I'm not going to answer." She drops her hand and gives me an intense look that makes me fight not to squirm on my bench. "I won't offer you sympathy because it'll only make you feel worse in this moment. I certainly won't give you pity. Even if you never recovered your pelt, you would be fine eventually. Instead, I offer revenge."

She speaks with such confidence that I almost fall into the trap of believing her. That eventually this awful feeling in my chest will go away even if I fail. I shake my head and make an attempt to turn the conversation into safer territory. "Are you sure you're not offering sympathy because you're shit at sympathy?"

Her grin is quick and fierce. "That, my dear selkie, was a question." Her grin widens as I sputter out a protest. It's half-hearted at best, because I like this break in her cold persona. She leans forward. "And to answer that question, I *am* garbage at sympathy. I prefer to be a creature of action. If someone hurts me or those I care about, I cut them down without mercy. It provides closure, which I think is more useful than soft words and gentle hugs. Besides, I'm good at killing people. I'm not good at comfort. And I prefer to spend my life only doing things I'm good at."

I haven't known this woman long, but that's such a purely Lizzie answer that I laugh. "That's one way to go about things." A spare tear escapes from the corner of my eye, and I wipe it away quickly, hoping she didn't see. But of course she did. She seems to see everything. "Personally, I think a gentle hug or a soft word can go a long way."

She shrugs. "There are other people better suited to provide that sort of comfort."

It's enough to make me wonder if she was never offered comfort that way, so that's why she doesn't know how to give it. Given what she's said about her mother, it seems likely. I can hardly imagine growing up without an abundance of love. I may have avoided telling my mother and grandmother about the mistake I made that cost me everything, but it's not because I think that they'll condemn me. They would *never.*

But it would hurt them to know that I'm hurt, and I want to spare them that if I can. *What about your absence?* a little voice inside me whispers. *Doesn't that hurt them, too?* I push the thoughts away. It's too late to worry about now. I'll make things right when I return home. Hopefully.

Lizzie tilts her head back and sighs. "What's your mother like?"

It's nothing more than a repeat of my question to her, in slightly different form. But it's also an intentional pivot away from challenging topics. A relief, even if it's only temporary. Does she realize that she's being kind in this moment? Impossible to say. I think she might be better at comfort than she realizes, but I'm not about to point it out. I have a feeling she wouldn't take the observation well.

"She's the best mother I could have ever asked for," I finally say.

"Details. Obey the spirit of the game."

I try to tuck my hair behind my ears, but the breeze immediately flips my curls around my face. I huff and give up. "My father was never in the picture. He didn't die or anything dramatic like that. At least I don't think he did. I suspect he was one of the sailors who passes through. My mother never really wanted a relationship, but she did want a child. And so she had me." It's so easy to picture her in my mind's eye. We have the same coloring, pale skin with freckles, wild curly red hair. She's built leaner than I am, but only slightly. "I've never doubted for a moment that she loves me. She's always there to lean on. She is one of those people that's very good at warm hugs and kind words."

Lizzie has resumed her blank expression, but there's something in her eyes that looks almost bleak. "She sounds . . . nice."

"She is, but she's not a pushover. You can't be if you're running a tavern. The people who cross her only do it once. When my mother draws a line in the sand, the entire village backs her up. It's only happened a few times over the years, but it's memorable all the same. She's terrible at baking, but she can brew the finest beer you've ever had. And she sings in the evenings when she cleans up after we've closed the doors. She's got a lovely voice, though I couldn't tell you if that's because she excels at music or if it's just because I love her."

That carefully blank look on Lizzie's face is morphing into

curiosity again, and I know exactly what she'll ask next. Which is why I ask my own question in a rush. Reckless with the desire to avoid where we're headed. "Do you still love Evelyn?"

Just like that, the curiosity snuffs out of Lizzie's deep brown eyes. "I'm bored of this game. I'm going to take a nap."

I watch in stunned disbelief as she reclines back on the bench, somehow contorting gracefully into the space, and closes her eyes. There's absolutely no way that she falls asleep so quickly, but it only takes seconds for the rise and fall of her chest to settle into a gentle cadence.

I suppose that's one way to get out of an argument question. It's absurd, but I suppose it's better than throwing herself over the edge of the boat and diving deep until I've forgotten what I asked. I've used that method to exit uncomfortable conversations a time or two in the past. Impossible to speak when you're in your seal form and beneath the waves.

Does she realize that her abrupt end to the game is answer enough? She obviously still cares very deeply for Evelyn, and why not? In the days that I sailed on the *Audacity*, Evelyn quickly became a bright spot in the experience. She's beautiful and bubbly and quick-witted, and she doesn't bend when it comes to things that she cares deeply about. What's not to love about that? She's certainly clever enough and powerful enough to ensure no one would steal something valuable from *her*.

In fact, Evelyn is the one who does the stealing. I watched it happen half a dozen times. She'd be talking or flirting or making jokes with one of the crew members or Nox or Bowen. Her hands move when she talks, and most of the time, they wouldn't notice that those movements resulted in her slipping an item off their person and into her pocket. The first time it happened, I almost said something, but before she moved away, she gave a sheepish grin and returned the stolen article.

And she returned it every single time.

She's interesting to me in a way that I don't know what to do with. There's something almost like jealousy in my chest, but that doesn't make a bit of sense. What do I have to be jealous of? I certainly have no designs on Bowen. The man's terrifying, and his joining the rebellion has not made him less so. Even when he's trying to be kind, there's something about him that's so rigid it makes me worry he'll trample me if I step out of line. Perhaps not intentionally, but it happens all the same.

Except I'm not being honest with myself, am I? It's not Bowen I'm jealous of. It's Lizzie. Because this vampire that I don't quite understand and yet am drawn to all the same is someone who intrigues me on a level that I'm not prepared to deal with. Even if I was, her heart is obviously with another person. That person might no longer be hers, but it means she has no room for anyone else.

I would be a fool and a half to pursue anything with Lizzie. It would only end in heartbreak. And I've had enough of that to last me a lifetime.

CHAPTER 11

Lizzie

I DON'T MEAN TO ACTUALLY GO TO SLEEP, BUT WHEN I wake up, it's to a world gone strange. Wind lashes my face. The sky is no longer an irritatingly perfect blue but a worrisome gray tingeing on purple. Worst of all, the boat is seesawing hard enough to make my stomach take up residence in my throat.

"Lizzie!"

I sit up and immediately wish I hadn't. There isn't a bit of land in sight. There isn't *anything* in sight . . . but the storm barreling down on us in the distance. I can actually see the sheets of rain angling from the clouds to the sea. "No."

"Lizzie, I need you." Maeve doesn't appear afraid, but her mouth is tight and her skin has gone paler than normal, her freckles standing out in stark contrast. "We have to lash down the supplies, and I need the sail taken down. If the winds are as bad as they look, it's liable to snap the mast, and then we're in real trouble."

As if we're not in *real trouble* right now.

My fingers bite into the wood of the bench. In the few seconds it's taken me to process what the fuck is going on, the storm is closer. How can it possibly move so fast? Forget worrying about the mast; the first big wave will tip us, and that's the end. Or the water will fill the boat faster than we can bucket it out, and we'll sink. I can't move. My mind is shrieking and my body is locked. "We're going to die."

Maeve glares. "Not if I have anything to say about it. Help me."

But . . . I can't. Fear is a live thing inside me, expanding to fill my skin to the brim. I thought I knew its shape before now—I cut my teeth on the sensation in the pit of my stomach and the way my mouth goes dry and my thoughts numb. This is different. That was a trickle of sensation. This is a tsunami.

Maybe it truly is a tsunami in the most literal sense.

Rain lashes my face. Too cold. Too strong. Too *much*. "I can't," I barely manage to say.

Maeve looks like she's about to curse me, but then she really seems to *see* me. Her brows draw together, and she lets go of the rudder long enough to take the few short steps needed to crouch next to me. "Lizzie, look at me."

"I am looking at you."

"No, *look* at me." She takes my face in her hands, her grip too tight with panic. "I need you. I understand that you're afraid. I am, too. But I can't do this alone. Please, Lizzie. Strap down our supplies."

Her words barely beat my fear away long enough for me to draw a shuddering breath. Maeve needs me. She's practically begging me. I've fought hundreds of enemies—thousands, even—without balking. What is this storm but another enemy?

The logic is flimsy enough to be laughable, but my muscles

unlock enough for me to nod. "Okay. I'll strap down the supplies." Somehow.

It still takes me two tries to get moving. The boat felt small to begin with, but it's pathetically tiny now that it's rocking violently back and forth with rain pattering the floorboards. There's some rope tucked away in the corner of the little enclosure, and I wrestle it over the crate and pack, doing my best to fasten them in place. We are only a day away from Khollu, maybe two, based on Maeve's estimates. But she can't last that long without fresh water, even if she theoretically could without food.

No, we are not losing a single damn supply. Not on my watch.

It takes forever and far too little time to finish my task. I turn to find that Maeve has rolled the sail down and lashed it in place. There's an inch of water at our feet. We look at each other across the short distance, and for the first time, I see fear on her face. True fear.

Strange that this quells my own. That's something to examine later—if we survive this nightmare.

She has to yell to be heard over the screaming wind. "If too much water comes aboard, we'll sink."

There is a single small bucket rattling around. I snatch it up before she has a chance to. If I stop moving, fear will take hold again. "I got it."

"Lizzie—"

"I got it."

She looks like she's about to argue but finally nods. "We can't lash ourselves to the ship. If it tips or breaks apart, we need to be able to swim and not be dragged down in the wreckage."

I stare at her too long. "If it . . . breaks apart." For some reason, *that* outcome had never occurred to me. Tipping, sure. Sinking, of course. But being ripped apart? I shudder and grip the bucket hard enough that I feel it creak in my hands.

"It probably won't." But she casts a worried look at the storm. It's almost to us. The fact that it isn't overhead and my stomach is still twisting itself in knots over how violent the waves are is . . . worrisome.

Yeah, worrisome. Not piss-your-pants terrifying. Not at all.

I bend over and scrape the bucket over the bottom of the boat, whisking up as much water as possible. The movement really does help. I learned a long time ago that putting one foot in front of the other, literally or not, is the only way to get through the most fucked-up experiences. And so I set my entire being into ensuring that this fucking teacup of a boat doesn't sink.

Maeve is doing something to the rudder, but I can't spare the energy to focus on her right now. If I falter, I'm going to freeze up, and that will be the end.

Time ceases to mean a single damn thing. My world narrows down to an endlessly repeating sequence: bend, scrape, straighten, toss. Over and over and over again.

I don't see the wave coming. All I hear is Maeve's scream of warning and then the boat is tipping, tipping, tipping. No amount of grace or balance is enough to keep me out of the furious water. I spin to the selkie as the boat flips entirely, throwing us into the sea.

There's barely time to suck in a startled breath before I'm plunged deep. The few times I've had cause to be in the ocean, it was deceptively calm. Serene almost. That's not this ocean.

Another wave slams me into the overturned boat hard enough to rattle my brain in my skull. I barely have the presence of mind to stab the wood with my nails, digging deep enough to keep me attached to it.

Unless the next wave rips my arm clean off.

"Lizzie!"

I twist, searching for Maeve in the darkness. There's no fucking light. Even with my superior ability to see in the dark, I might as well have a bag over my head. I can't concentrate enough to search for her with my power, but even if I could, it would be a lost cause. The water is too damn cold, and it's likely sucking the warmth right out of Maeve's body more efficiently than a vampire ever could.

Then she appears beside me, a waterlogged angel. "Lizzie," she gasps. "The straps."

I don't think. I release the boat to loop an arm around her and keep her head above water. The result is *both* of us sinking. Maeve shoves me off her and claws her way to the surface. I manage to follow, sputtering out salt water. "Hey!"

"You're going to get us killed," she snarls. My sweet selkie is nowhere, replaced by a furious woman who looks like she wants to drown me herself.

My selkie.

I must have hit my head harder than I thought if I'm calling her that, even internally.

Maeve half crawls onto the overturned boat and yanks something out of the side of it. Some kind of opening? She motions impatiently for me to come closer, as if it's the easiest thing in the world.

The rain chooses that moment to pick up, trying to drown

us from above. I can barely see Maeve through the sheets of water falling from the sky. Fuck Threshold. Fuck sailing. Fuck nature entirely.

I battle my way back to the boat. Every part of me hurts, which I wouldn't have thought possible. It's only been a few minutes, but the sea has beaten me more efficiently than any fight I've ever been in.

Maeve grabs my upper arm with more strength than I expected. She hauls me to the side of the boat and drags my hand up to . . . a strap. That's what she was pulling out of the side of the boat. A fucking strap on its underside.

I glare at her. "You knew this was going to happen!"

"Shut up and hang on." She tilts her head back, her curls plastered to her face. "We just have to outlast the storm and we can flip the boat back over."

She's . . . entirely unfazed.

I want to yell at her some more, to expel the awful energy inside me that tastes just like fear. But that won't do a damn thing. So I cling to one of the two straps on this side of the overturned hull, expecting to be ripped away at any given moment by a particularly strong gust of wind or a rogue wave.

Through it all, I watch Maeve. The tight line of her lips is the only sign of stress. She's got her head tilted back as if she can drink in the entire sky, her brows relaxed and her eyes shut. It's almost as if she's enjoying this, just a little. I want to hate her for it, but she looks so damn good while doing it. And she may have saved my life, because even as my strength flags, the angle of the strap around my wrist keeps me above water.

I barely register the storm leaving. One moment the waves are slightly less violent and the next we're floating on a relatively calm surface, and the rain feels more like mist on my skin than a deluge trying to shove me under the surface.

Maeve leans her head against the boat. "Take a breather, and then we're flipping it over."

Just like that.

Damn it, I can't help but admire her a little in this moment. She handled that crisis significantly better than I did. She's *still* handling it better than I am.

I drag in a salty breath and make a face. I'm pretty sure I'll never be dry again. "Why wait? Let's get this bitch flipped now."

CHAPTER 12

Lizzie

THE LESS SAID ABOUT THE THREE DAYS BETWEEN THE storm and washing up on the shores of Khollu, the better. What little luxuries we had were consumed by the waves, leaving only the bare food and water Maeve had strapped down. Neither of us has been much for conversation in the meantime. The trip was something to be endured as we fought our way in the general direction Maeve was certain we needed to go.

It would be convenient to blame our strained silence on nearly dying, but it wouldn't be the truth. I knew better than to play a game of questions, knew better than to attempt to know this woman better. I'm leaving Threshold, and I don't make a habit of crushing innocents, regardless of what my reputation says.

But Maeve intrigues me. More than that, I recognize the loss in her. I've never had something of such importance stolen—my family heirlooms hardly apply, though my mother might see it differently. It's not just the loss of Maeve's pelt that has harmed her; Bronagh broke her heart with his betrayal.

That's monstrous, even to someone like me.

Catching sight of Khollu on the horizon is a welcome relief. As we row closer, battling the becalmed conditions that Maeve feared when we left Viedna, I get a better look at the island. It could be a rock sticking out of the sea, and I wouldn't give a shit as long as it has a hot bath, but it's rather beautiful.

It's significantly larger than Viedna. At first, I think the color is a trick of the light, but as we get closer, I realize the island really *is* purple, courtesy of a thick forest that stretches along what bits of it I can see. Great, sprawling trees with leaves that look a bit like flowers, all in half a dozen shades of violet. It's . . . pretty.

It also makes my face itch as the wind shifts to blast us with a floral scent. I wrinkle my nose. "What the fuck?"

"You'll get used to it—or so I'm told," Maeve says wearily. "Help me row. I want a bath."

"Agreed." I readjust my grip on the oar—somehow not lost in the storm—and put my back into rowing us to the island as quickly as possible.

I'm pleased to note that there are half a dozen larger ships anchored in the bay. Plenty to choose from—and all are large enough that I should have an actual bunk to sleep in and possibly even access to a shower. Even better, not a single one of them has the crimson sails that mark Cŵn Annwn vessels.

It would be better to circle away from the bay and approach stealthily, but I don't give a shit. Maeve doesn't, either. We're too intent on getting off this damned boat to worry about being sneaky. For once, I don't even flinch when it's time to hop into the water to haul the boat onto shore. It's not as if my boots were dry in the first place.

My nose won't stop itching, and I rub it furiously with the back of my hand. "How long does it take to get used to the smell?"

"Um." Maeve ducks her head and pulls the boat a few inches higher onto the beach.

Suspicion flares. She's absolutely avoiding my gaze, and I don't like it. "Speak, selkie."

"Usually by the first month from what I hear."

A *month*?

I sneeze. "I'm going to burn this entire fucking island to the ground."

"Of course you will. First, why don't we find a room and bath?"

She's patronizing me, but the offer is a good one. It would be too much effort to try to start that large of a fire, anyways. Everything is so *damp* in Threshold. I allow her to lead me away from the beach, down a winding path that's roughly wide enough to drive a car—if Threshold had cars. There are a few crews unloading crates, but they don't seem to pay much attention to us after an initial curious look. "We lost everything in the storm. We can't pay for a bath or a bed or even dry clothes." I've never considered myself to be particularly morose, but being damp for days on end will do that to a person.

"Let me worry about that."

The sinus pressure gets more intense as we squelch our way down the path and to the village proper. It's cold here—just as cold as back in Viedna, and as we walk, the gloomy clouds overhead open up and it starts *snowing*.

"I hate this place." It should be illegal to have seasonal allergies *and* snow.

"Bath, Lizzie. Think of the bath."

Since arriving in Threshold, I've visited dozens of islands with the crew of the *Audacity*. With few exceptions, they're astonishingly mundane. Familiar even. Most of the population is humanoid to some extent, and apparently, while humans may flourish in a number of climates, there are certain consistencies among them. Gravity being one. Some of the islands are more fantastical, but Khollu appears to be of the former variety.

The snow is normal enough. It's odd that the trees are so vibrantly purple, which seems like it should be a thing reserved for spring, but what do I know? I'm hardly a horticulturist. The air tastes like air. It's all very normal for a realm that isn't mine.

The village itself is formed of short domed buildings that seem designed to make the most of the heat within. I bet they do an excellent job of keeping the heat *out*, too, during the summer. We stop in the little square—or whatever the circular equivalent of a village square is. Even without knowing the written language, it's easy enough to pick out the businesses that every one of these islands seems to have: tavern, inn, and a shop to resupply at.

I glance at Maeve. "Bath." My hair is so tacky from the sea, I'm sure it's standing on end. And I'm surprised I don't crunch every time I move from the coating of salt on my skin.

She makes a face, wrinkling her nose in a way that I shouldn't find charming but I most definitely do. "I promised you a bath, and a bath you will have." She hesitates. "Let me do the talking."

"As long as there's hot water and a bed at the end of that conversation." I follow her to the inn.

"Hello." Maeve approaches the small pale man behind the counter. He's perhaps four feet tall with a massive green beard that curls almost playfully. There are rings and small items braided into both his beard and the equally green hair that reaches his shoulders. It's . . . charming. How irritating.

Maeve leans on the counter and gives him a sweet smile. "Ralph, right?"

His smile doesn't dim, but his expression sharpens a little. "I'm good with faces. Know everyone who's been through my doors since I took over this business from my parents. I've never seen you before."

I tense, but Maeve just laughs charmingly. "You've got a good eye. No, I've never been to Khollu before, but we have a mutual friend."

If anything, his eyes narrow further. "Why do I get the feeling you're about to ask for a discount?"

"Nox sent me," she says simply.

Just like that, his irritation fades away. He looks at Maeve with new interest, pausing to give me the same cursory glance. "How is that one? Pain in my ass if I do say so myself."

"Still a pain in the ass. Still fighting the good fight, if you know what I mean." She holds out a hand. "I'm Maeve. My family runs the tavern in Viedna."

"*You're* Maeve. I see. I've heard plenty about you from our . . . mutual friend." He nods. "Well, I suppose I can put you up in a room, but it's going on their tab. If you're lying, I'll let them hunt you down for repayment."

I glance between them. Surely he'll take more convincing than *that*? Maeve barely mentioned Nox and didn't even use a code word or anything as far as I can tell. But there's a bath in my near future, so I stay silent.

Maeve smiles, all sweetness and charm. "I don't suppose you'll throw in a bath and a meal or two for the cause?"

He snorts. "Can't very well have you ruining my mattress with . . ." His gaze flicks over our filthy clothing. "I'll have my girl bring up something to change into. It's not fancy, but it'll do in a pinch. That's the best I can do."

"We appreciate it greatly. *All* of us."

The room we're led to isn't much to look at, but it's clean and has one narrow bed. There's barely enough space to fit the copper bath that the innkeeper hauls in. He has more strength than I would've anticipated, and it makes me watch him warily. I should know better than to underestimate someone based on their appearance. I certainly don't look like someone who could lift a small car, and yet I'm more than capable of it.

Neither Maeve nor I speak while we wait for the bath to be filled. Once again, I'm reminded of how spoiled I've been on the *Audacity*. Nox provides indoor plumbing and hot showers, so I've never had to worry about how someone heats the water when there's no faucet. It's definitely not an experience I look forward to repeating.

The innkeeper straightens with a huff. "There. The tub is spelled to clean the water and keep it at a reasonable temperature. Give a holler when you're done." He walks out the door and closes it behind him without waiting for a response.

"You can take the first bath. I'm going to look around," Maeve says carefully.

I grab her wrist before she takes more than a single step. "Don't think for a second that you're leaving this room without me."

She rolls her eyes. "I'm hardly going to go steal a ship on my own and sail off without you."

That wasn't what I meant. It never even occurred to me that she would leave me behind. But we're in a new place filled with strangers, and if there's one thing I've learned in the last couple weeks, it's that the dangers of Threshold are infinite. Maeve is practically human, which means she's practically defenseless. Gods, I met her when rescuing her after she was taken *captive*.

"We stay together." Admitting that I'm worried about her feels too vulnerable. I'm not even sure how I feel about that worry. Maeve is no pushover, and she's got that spine of steel, but she's soft right down to her center. If she wasn't, that bastard of a sailor never would have had a chance to take advantage; she would have seen him coming a mile away. People will look at her and see a mark. I won't let it happen.

She glares at where I hold her wrist, but I don't drop my grip. Finally, she sighs. "You're being intentionally difficult and I don't understand why."

"It's basic survival skills, baby. We stick together and watch each other's backs." I can't help the hint of flirtation that weaves its way into my words. While I don't normally hold myself back from taking what I want—and I sure as fuck want Maeve—there's too many factors in play to be so careless with this woman. Her skin. My jewels. Our timeline. The last shouldn't make a difference, and yet it is something that I'm considering all the same.

"Whatever you say." She jerks her wrist out of my grip and walks over to the bed but seems to think better of sitting on the clean sheets a moment before she sits down. "Take your bath, Lizzie. I promised you one, and frankly, you stink."

"Surprised you can smell me over your own rankness."

"Yes, yes, I'm aware." She waves a hand in my direction as she moves to the small window that looks out on the purple trees. Just seeing them makes my nose start itching, so I turn away.

I should let her take the tub first. It would be the kind thing to do, but I'm not fucking kind, and if I don't get clean right this second, I might start screaming. Or I might truly set fire to those fucking trees. I sneeze again. "Damn it."

"Lizzie."

"I'm going, I'm going."

I'll need to eat soon, too. It's been long enough since I bit Maeve that hunger is a hollow pit inside me and creates a fine tremor in my hands. I had initially planned on finding someone in the village to feed from, but as I pull my shirt over my head and hear Maeve's sharp inhale . . .

The only person I'll be feeding on is this adorable little selkie.

I'm willing to go hungry for a little while—until she comes to me. In the meantime, there's no reason not to hedge my bets a little, to press my fingers to the scale in my favor. I peel off my pants and do away with my undergarments. I glance at Maeve out of the corner of my eye to find her pale skin has turned a deep crimson.

Oh yes, she's watching.

I almost forget about the show I'm putting on as I slip into the hot water. I don't mean to let out a little moan of pure pleasure, but there's nothing like a hot bath after a hard journey. I dip under the water and scrub my fingers through my hair. The salt water feels like it's crusted on my skin and into the strands, and I forget all about seduction as I grab the soap and begin to scrub it from my skin.

As I lift my hands to my hair, Maeve's voice sounds from behind me. "Let me."

I was so distracted, I hadn't noticed her moving closer. That should concern me, but concern feels very far away as I hand her the soap and she sets to work washing my hair. Her touch is light yet firm, and if I didn't know better, I would think that she's merely doing a favor for a friend.

I do know better, though. My power is in the blood, and I can practically feel her racing heart against my palm, can sense the blood gathering as her desire grows, can hear her quickened breathing that she tries to suppress as she massages my scalp.

Patience is the only virtue I acknowledge, and it's the only thing keeping me from pulling her into the tub with me to see what we can do about this mutual attraction. If Maeve was anyone else . . . But she's not anyone else. She'll come to me on her own, and when she does, this wanting will be worth the reward of having her in my bed.

Even so, desire is a slow pulse inside me. Neither of us rushes, and Maeve certainly takes her time ensuring that every inch of my scalp and hair is clean. True to the innkeeper's promise, whatever spell the tub contains keeps the water crystal clear and at a perfect temperature. I could stay in here for hours, but as much as I'm enjoying a return of creature comforts, I fully intend to reciprocate the favor Maeve bestowed on me.

I rise, droplets spilling down my naked body. Her sharp inhale is music to my ears. I hold out a hand. "Would you pass me a towel?"

Maeve stares for several beats too long before she gives herself a shake. "A towel. Of course." She grabs one of the fluffy towels we've been provided and passes it to me.

"Your turn." I twist away and begin drying myself off. As I suspected, it takes her a little while to work up the courage to strip, even though I'm not actively watching her. That doesn't mean I'm not achingly aware of the slide of cloth against her skin and the soft footsteps as she moves to the bath and slips inside.

Her little moan has me turning, an offer to wash *all* of her on the tip of my tongue. There's a knock on the door before I have a chance to. I swallow down a curse and wrap the towel around me to answer it.

A short woman—obviously related to the innkeeper, judging by her stout figure, pale skin, and deep green curls—stands there with a bag. She holds it up. "Here you go. There'll be food served downstairs in about an hour."

"Noted." I take the bag, finding it heavier than I expected. I'm aware of Maeve listening, so I clear my throat. "Uh, thanks." I close the door and waste no time digging through the bag. There's two sets of clothing for each of us, and the sizing looks pretty accurate. "Who is this guy?"

"He's with the rebellion." Maeve rests her head on the side of the tub. "Most people I send north go straight to Khollu—to Ralph—and the reverse is true with him sending folks south through Viedna."

I figured it was something like that, but it's still a hell of a lot of faith to place in a near stranger. "That doesn't change the fact that we're fucked when it comes to resupplying."

"Have a little faith, Lizzie." Her eyes slide shut. "Why don't you get dressed and go explore the village? It will burn off some of that nervous energy."

"I don't have *nervous energy*."

"You won't after you take a walk. Try not to draw any attention to yourself."

I glare at the clear dismissal. One step forward, two steps sideways. She truly is cagey, but I don't hold it against her. Not when I'm enjoying this strange little dance we're doing, circling each other warily. I permit myself a small smile. "Trying to get rid of me so fast?"

I should have known better than to attempt to look my fill of her. The moment I do, I forget how to breathe entirely. This woman was made for the water. The bath barely covers her large breasts, and I'm delighted to discover that her freckles seem to extend over her entire body. I have the overwhelming desire to trace them with my tongue. Her curly hair spreads around her like particularly pretty seaweed. I've always seen selkies depicted as lean, pale skinned, and dark haired. I much prefer Maeve to those paintings.

Her blush spreads from her upper chest over her throat and takes up residence in her round cheeks. She holds my gaze as I stand there, only a towel, some water, and a crossable distance between us. The moment spins out, and I find myself holding my breath, waiting for her to invite me back into the bath.

But when she speaks, it's to reiterate her request. "Please, Lizzie. I just . . . I need a minute. Several minutes."

Truth be told, after being trapped in a small space for nearly a week, almost dying in a storm, and finally being clean, I *do* need to stretch my legs. Just a little. I dig through the bag to find a pair of pants and a tunic-like shirt. There are even boots. The innkeeper truly did think of everything.

Even so, I don't want Maeve to get the wrong idea. I'll allow a little distance—for now. I pause with my hand on the doorknob. "This thing between us isn't over."

Her smile is a little shy and a little wicked. "I know."

CHAPTER 13

Maeve

I SHOULDN'T HAVE TEASED THE VAMPIRE BY WASHING HER hair, but it's so rare that I get the best of Lizzie that I couldn't resist. More, I wanted to touch her, wanted the excuse to see her unwind even the smallest amount. Getting a bath helped *my* disposition dramatically. A meal will help it even more.

As I dress in the clothing Ralph's daughter provided us, my gaze is drawn again and again to the single bed in the room. I hadn't been sure that Ralph would actually give us a room, but we had no backup plan. The storm took everything but our lives. Thankfully, the loyalty to the rebellion allowed us this room, clothing, and food. It won't get us a ship, but I suspect Lizzie's plan is to murder her way aboard one of them. I'll need to come up with an alternative, but I'm too tired to think about it now.

But I'm *not* too tired to think about sex, apparently.

We're no longer crusted with salt. The bed may be small, but it's clean and comfortable enough. Tonight, there's nothing standing between us and the possibility of *more.*

I want Lizzie. I can admit that to myself now, even if it makes me slightly uncomfortable. My heart still aches from the loss of Bronagh, from his betrayal, but Lizzie is safe in her own way. She's not going to ask me for more than I'm capable of giving. She doesn't even like me that much, though I have no doubt that she wants me just as much as I want her. It's there in the way she watches me when she thinks I'm not looking—and sometimes when I *am* looking. Maybe she needs the escape just as much as I do.

The dress Ralph provided fits me perfectly. Lizzie has returned from her walk, and she does seem more relaxed, her agitation smoothed out. Though every time she sneezes, she glares out the window as if she can track down the tree personally responsible and rip it out of the ground by its roots. She's wearing a loose set of pants and a tight shirt that shows off the lines of muscle in her arms and shoulders. I have the intense urge to take a bite out of her.

"We need to get you food." She turns for the door, not leaving me any room to argue.

Or at least that's obviously her aim, to use momentum to maintain the upper hand. I cross my arms over my chest and wait for her to notice that I'm not following her. It doesn't take long. She barely has the door cracked when she stops.

She turns back to me, exasperation written across her gorgeous features. It's almost enough to make me smile. "Yes, Maeve? You obviously have something to say."

"What about you?" Although I've been watching Lizzie

closely even while on the *Audacity*, she never seemed to show up for mealtimes. I'm not certain if her brand of vampire needs nourishment other than blood, but even if they don't, it's been three days since she ate last. Surely it's nearly time for another bite?

"I had thought to have my meal after dinner. This place is plenty large enough that there's bound to be a sailor I can coerce into volunteering." She motions for me to precede her, but I don't obey. Lizzie curses. "Do you have a problem with that?"

"I want you to bite me again." The words come out in a rush, tumbling over themselves in their effort to be brought to voice. "Not someone else. Me."

She eases the door shut and leans against it. She blocks the only exit from the room, but I don't feel even the least bit in danger. Lizzie crosses her arms over her chest, mirroring my body language. "Explain."

I have half a dozen excuses ready to go. We don't want to draw attention to ourselves, and vampires are rare enough in Threshold that people will take note if she claims a victim here. Even if the "victim" lives to see dawn and has several orgasms in the process. People notice her. Lizzie has taken no vows; the last thing we need is for the Cŵn Annwn to turn their bloody eyes our way. At least when we sailed with Nox, there was some measure of protection. Lizzie could dress in crimson, pretend that she was actually part of the crew, and no one would think to question it.

Out on her own with only me as company? It's an entirely different situation. One wrong word will mark her as someone not native to Threshold, someone to be hunted by the Cŵn Annwn for dodging their laws.

But while all those things are true, they're not the reason I want her to bite me and only me. It still takes more courage than I could have anticipated to draw myself up and speak the truth. "We're stuck together until we see this thing through and reclaim the things stolen from us."

"Yes," she says slowly.

The next part is harder to get out. "I'm not imagining the mutual attraction between us."

Her eyes flare crimson for a heartbeat before returning to their normal color. "No, you're not imagining it."

Again, my skin betrays me. I can feel the blush spreading in response to her easy agreement. I gather my courage once more. "There's no reason we can't enjoy each other for the duration of our time together."

"Enjoy each other." Lizzie pushes off the door and prowls toward me, each slow, intense step closing the distance between us. "I'm sure you have a firm idea of what it is you're asking for, Maeve. Let's hear it."

The way she says my name. A promise and a warning, all wrapped up in seduction. Allowing myself to voice my desire is a mistake. We need to be focused, both on our surroundings and on any potential enemies that we may come across. We could miss clues if we're too busy thinking about fucking each other.

None of that stops me from stepping to the line she's drawn in the sand. "You feed from me exclusively. We share each other's bed, and I don't just mean for sleep."

"You don't know what you're asking for, my sweet little selkie." Her smile is downright predatory. "Sharing my bed isn't something everyone walks away from."

"Evelyn did."

Just like that, the spell being woven between us snaps. I hadn't even realized Lizzie was lifting her hand to touch my face until the moment she drops it without making contact. She steps back. "Yes, I suppose she did." She moves to the door and wrenches it open harder than necessary. "You're a fool, Maeve. It seems you have a habit for chasing those who aren't good for you. But I suppose I'm a fool, too, because I'm not going to tell you no."

That isn't a no, but it's hardly an enthusiastic yes. My stomach chooses that moment to grumble and remind me that it's been days since I've eaten and even longer since I've had a proper hot meal. That ends the conversation as thoroughly as my bringing up Evelyn did.

Lizzie narrows her eyes. "No more arguing. You need to eat." She does one of those faster-than-the-eye-can-follow movements. One moment I'm standing there, considering whether it's worth it to continue arguing, and the next she has her arm around my waist and moves us both into the hall, closing the door neatly behind us. She doesn't give me a chance to argue here, either. She sweeps us down the stairs to the small common room that the inn offers.

It's been weeks now since Bronagh took my skin. He may have stopped here to visit home, but he's probably gone by now. If we can't figure out where—and soon—then we might have to stay on Khollu and wait for him to return. If he doesn't have my pelt, then we'll have to force him to tell us who he sold it to and . . . The sheer task ahead of me makes me want to curl into a ball and sleep for ten years. Wasting any more time is a mistake, and yet . . . I just want a moment to pause and exist without having to search and fight and scramble.

There's no way that Lizzie is aware of the exhaustion weighing down my bones, but she guides me to the little dining room off the entrance to the inn. It's dim and quiet, only half of the handful of tables filled and the people present speaking in low voices. Each table has a little fey lantern, the magic giving off a soothing blue light. It's nice.

She urges me into a chair in the corner with my back to the wall and strides away to find the innkeeper. Within a few minutes, she sets a steaming bowl of stew and a small loaf of dark bread in front of me. She glares. "Eat."

She's gone again before I can dredge up a response, whisking away quickly enough that if I didn't know better, I would assume she's waited tables at some point. But that's impossible. She may have only given scant details about her family and upbringing, but every move she makes speaks of money and possibly even nobility. This woman was born into power and privilege; she wears it on her skin as her birthright. There may have been a cost for that privilege in the form of her monster of a mother, but performing manual labor? It's an absurd thought.

I take a bite of the stew, and am delighted to find that it's better than I expected. The spices are familiar to me, similar to what we have in Viedna, and the hearty root vegetables warm my stomach better than a raging fire.

I'm so focused on my meal that when someone sits down across from me, I just assume it's Lizzie. "Are you sure you don't want to try some of this?"

"My darling Maeve, always so willing to offer up that which you can't afford to lose."

My spoon drops from nerveless fingers. I know that voice. It used to fill my dreams with the possibility of a happy future and then became a specter that haunts my nightmares. I knew I'd have to face him again, but it's too soon, too unexpected. Surely I'm imagining his charming voice, too close.

Except when I finally gather the courage to lift my head, it *is* him.

Bronagh looks exactly the same as the last time I saw him. So much has changed that it seems wrong that he hasn't as well. He's built like so many sailors, lean with a sinewy strength that I used to admire. His dark hair reaches his shoulders in a careless wave, and his skin is darkened by the countless hours in the sun. He looks good, and I hate him for it.

"Have you come looking for me, then?" He leans his elbows on the table and reaches over to snag my loaf of bread. I watch numbly as he takes a bite of it and then hums under his breath. "They always have good shit here."

"What are you doing here?" I had imagined dozens of different ways the reunion would go when I finally found him again. How I would be powerful and strong and vengeful as I took back the thing that he stole from me and made myself whole again. How I would be cold and composed and completely unaffected.

Instead, I'm sitting here trying not to cry. Seeing him has all of the betrayal and fear and pain washing over me in waves that threaten to drown me.

"I always spend a week at home in between doing my trading rounds. You know that." He chews and swallows before he answers me. "But the better question is what *you're* doing here. We saw you row in with that sad excuse for a boat. Really, Maeve, it's pathetic."

Knowing that he witnessed that humiliating entrance

makes my face burn. At least I've had a chance to bathe before talking to him. Having this conversation in crusty clothes and reeking would have been so much worse. "You know why I'm here."

"I guess I do." He tosses the remainder of my loaf back onto my plate and sits back with a groan. "Khollu isn't safe for someone like you, Maeve. Run along home. It's where you belong."

I cannot believe his words. How *dare* he tell me to run home, as if I have any home to run back to. My mother and grandmother will mourn the loss of my pelt as much as I do, and I would spare them that if I could. More, I would spare myself the shame of admitting how careless I've been. That I let someone as selfish and horrible as Bronagh close to me, ignoring the indications that he might not be what he seemed. That he might not care about me the way that I desperately wanted him to.

"Give me my skin back."

He smiles as if I'm a child throwing a temper tantrum. "I can't do that, my girl. I worked so hard to get it." He must see the confusion on my face, because he laughs harshly. "Or did you think I really wanted you? Silly woman. You were a mark, plain and simple. And you made it oh so easy for me." He pushes back from the table and rises slowly, his shadow falling over me and washing away the heat of my meal. "You're a good girl, and that's why I will give you this single warning. Go home, Maeve. There's nothing here for you, and if you continue on with this nonsense about getting your pelt back, you won't like what happens."

I open my mouth to reply, but I never get a chance. He shudders and hits his knees, blood erupting from his mouth. Panic alights his pale eyes. *Oh my gods, oh my gods, oh my gods.* What's going on? As if in answer, the air sizzles intensely enough to make my hair stand on end for a heartbeat before he blinks out of existence.

He teleported away.

I shoot to my feet, which is when I see Lizzie standing in the doorway, two mugs of beer in her hand. Her eyes glow crimson and her upper lip curls in a snarl, revealing sharp teeth. In an instant, she's at my side, though she didn't appear to rush. She sets the mugs on the table. "So that's Bronagh."

"That's Bronagh." I'm shaking and I can't seem to stop. I plant my hands on the table, but it does nothing to center me. I look up, staring into her crimson eyes. "Was that *you*?"

"Yes." She glares at the space where he stood before he teleported. "You should have told me he's able to teleport. I would've gone about things differently."

I want to kiss her and shake some sense into her at the same time. "You can't kill him, Lizzie! We have to find my skin first."

"Wrong. I'll kill him and *then* we'll find your skin." She holds out her hand. "Let's go."

CHAPTER 14

Lizzie

THOUGH I WANT NOTHING MORE THAN TO CHASE DOWN the bastard who put that look on Maeve's face and rip his heart from his chest with my bare hands, the innkeeper isn't particularly happy with the outbreak of violence in his establishment.

"I can't have you attacking the locals. The only reason the re—Nox's goals *work* is because they're done in secret. What you did to Bronagh was not secret."

I open my mouth, ready to tell Ralph that he'll share Bronagh's fate if he keeps up with that bullshit, but Maeve stirs enough to place her hand on my arm. She does it instinctively, the touch light with warning, and the intimacy of it stops me short.

Which gives her the opportunity to smooth things over. "What happened with Bronagh has nothing to do with Nox. It was personal. He stole something from me."

The innkeeper grimaces. "I believe it. That boy has been bad news ever since he started up that *business* of his, but that still doesn't mean I'll allow you to murder him in the middle of my dining room."

"Come on, Ralph. He wasn't murdered. There isn't even any blood on the floor. It was a little disagreement that got out of hand." She looks shaken down to her core, her freckles standing out starkly, but she still manages a sweet smile. "It won't happen again. You have my word."

He sighs. "It would be best if you didn't stick around for very long. I'd love to continue to help you, but I can't afford for you to endanger what I have here. You understand."

"I do. We'll wrap up our business in a day or two and be on our way, and you'll never have to see us again." She lays her hand on his forearm, all sweetness and innocence. "I promise."

She's good. Even freaked out and shaken, she's handled the innkeeper with grace and a heart-wrenching sincerity. He holds up his hands and takes a step back. "Just finish your meal. I'll make sure no one bothers you again."

"Thank you."

I consider the exit, but Maeve didn't eat enough. More, as soon as Ralph hurries away, she seems to wilt. I actually put out my hands to catch her, but she doesn't need the help to get back to the table and sink wearily down into her chair. She picks up her spoon and pokes at the stew listlessly, her eyes dimmed. "You can't kill him, Lizzie," she says softly.

"You'll find that I can do exactly that." I kick one of the chairs around the edge of the table so I can sit at her side. "The real question is: Do you think I scared him enough that he'll risk running immediately or wait for high tide?"

"He's back aboard the *Serpent's Cry*. With his crew around

him, he'll convince himself that there's nothing to fear. I doubt he'll run at all. This is his home." She sets her spoon down. "I'm really not hungry anymore. Let's go."

We pull on dark cloaks that Ralph provided and slip out into the night. I immediately sneeze. "I fucking *hate* this island."

Maeve laughs softly, though it's strained. "Yes, you've mentioned that a time or two."

Across the square, the tavern is still filled with the voices and music and bright lights, but we skirt the edge and stick to the shadows. I hold my cloak to my face, but it doesn't stop my intermittent sneezes as we slip through the buildings to the edge of town. The trees' floral scent clogs the air, making it impossible to smell anything else. I don't like it. They even block out the moon overhead, which makes my skin prickle. Too close. Too claustrophobic.

I breathe a sigh of relief when we emerge from the forest on the far side of the bay from where the docks are, near where we left our boat. Or I try to. Despite my best efforts, I sneeze, and then sneeze again. The air still tastes like strange flowers on my tongue, at least until the sea breeze chases it inland. I rub furiously at my nose. "Don't laugh."

"I wouldn't dream of it."

I glance at our boat. It hasn't been nearly long enough since we were trapped aboard. I don't want to go near it, but we'll need it for what comes next.

I crouch next to Maeve near a boulder on the rocky shore. We both have excellent night vision, but even I'm having a hard time picking apart the ships bobbing gently in the distance. They each have a handful of lanterns, but it does nothing to differentiate one ship from its neighbors.

"Tell me about his ship."

Maeve draws in a ragged breath. She seems diminished from the woman I've come to know, and my fists clench with the need to fight something and revert her back to the steel-spined, quick-witted woman who told me she wants to spend the rest of this journey in my bed.

Bronagh escaped because I acted impulsively. And okay, fine, she may have a point about killing him before we divine the location of her pelt. If he's finished his trading circuit, it might already be gone, but it seems risky to sell a pelt within a few days' travel of Viedna. Surely he'd be looking for a buyer with deeper pockets, which means going farther afield. He hasn't had a chance to do that yet.

Her pelt is on his ship. I'd stake my reputation on it.

"His ship is the *Serpent's Cry*. It's technically a trading vessel, but I think they might be doing some smuggling below the radar of the Cŵn Annwn. I never had proof one way or another, but some of the comments that Bronagh has made suggested that." She draws in a careful breath. "He liked to brag. I thought it meant he trusted me, but it turns out he just liked to hear himself speak."

I have the strangest urge to wrap my arms around her and pull her close. I'll settle for painting his blood across the deck of his ship. It will make both me and Maeve feel better. I'm sure of it. "It would be better not to wait until morning to attack."

"Attack." She lets out a bitter laugh. "*How* are we going to attack, Lizzie? I can barely hold my own in a fight against a single person in this form, and you don't have Nox as backup. It will take us time to row out there, time in which they'll see us coming. If they don't shoot us on sight, they'll be ready for us when we attempt to come aboard. We'll die."

I reach out and catch her chin. "Maeve."

"No. You don't get your way this time through sheer force of personality," she grits out. "Sometimes reality has to be taken into account. And the reality is that we are outnumbered. *Vastly* outnumbered. At least half the crew have some kind of powers that will turn the tide in their favor even if you somehow managed to cut your way through them. More than that, just because Bronagh is a monster doesn't mean his entire crew is. I'm not going to condone a wholesale slaughter."

"Pity. A wholesale slaughter makes things simple."

She glares and wraps her hand around my wrist. "Are you making a joke right now?"

I ignore the question and release her, turning back to face the water. "There's no reason to throw out a good resource. We need a ship to sail where we're headed next. The two of us can't manage a ship of that size. Therefore, we'll need a crew. The one on board will do nicely."

She curses under her breath. "They're *his* crew and *his* ship. Beyond that, he's not even the captain—he's the quartermaster. Killing him will do nothing."

"Killing him will make me feel better, and I think you'll feel better, too." I hold up a hand before she can sputter out another protest. "I hear what you're saying. Bronagh is the quartermaster. The crew has some powerful people on it. Now listen to what *I'm* saying. If your pelt isn't on that ship, then we need that ship to get it back. If it *is* on that ship, it's *right there*."

My plan leaves something to be desired, but there's no help

for it. We're running out of time. I agree with Maeve that Bronagh won't turn tail and run simply because we came to Khollu. But he's arrogant enough that he won't expect an attack tonight, and after my little indiscretion at the inn, he won't be at full strength. "Does he have any powers beyond teleportation?"

She curses under her breath. "No. Or at least I don't think so. That's the only one I'm aware of."

That doesn't really mean anything at all. Since he obviously intended to get close to Maeve and steal her pelt, he was hardly going to share all his secrets with her. Or any of them. It's fine. He didn't see me coming before. He's not going to see me coming this time, either.

Teleportation is a fearsome magic and damn near unstoppable—except for one key factor. The person teleporting has to concentrate on their destination during the teleportation process. It's only a matter of a fraction of a second, but it's a weakness that can be exploited. I've certainly done it in the past. It's a trick of timing.

"None of this changes the fact that we can't even get out there. We might have a chance on the boat in the dark of the moon, but there's too much light right now. They'll see us coming."

"Maeve, we've talked about your lack of imagination. We're two beautiful women. They have no reason to think we're up to no good." I stand and slip out of my cloak. Maeve watches in what appears to be horror as I unbutton my shirt nearly to my navel.

"Lizzie." Her voice is choked. "If you're trying to seduce me, this is hardly the time or place."

A surprised laugh slips free. "Seeing a partially naked woman is enough to cause most people to hesitate. They don't immediately assume attack, which gives us the element of surprise."

"Imagine that." She clears her throat. "You're really not going to listen to reason, are you?"

"Maeve." I take her shoulders. "I'll protect you. It will be fine. We're so close to getting your skin back. Trust me."

"You are the most infuriating, murderous woman I've ever met. This really isn't how I imagined we'd be spending the night together." She smiles a little. "Okay. I trust you. Let's go get the boat."

If that bastard wouldn't have interrupted our meal, maybe I would be stripping her right now, pulling back the fabric to reveal her soft, lovely body. Trailing each revealed inch of skin with my mouth. Strategically biting her so that she comes apart so many times she loses track.

I *will* have her in my bed. Whether it's simply because she likes the way my bite feels or because she's running from the sensation of helplessness resulting from her skin being stolen, it doesn't matter to me. I want her. She wants me. That's enough.

Maeve wades into the icy water next to me as we shove the boat out. It's not until the water reaches our chests and we haul ourselves into the boat that my brain decides to whisper about all the ways that this is a terrible idea. Not because of the sailors waiting for us. No, it's the inky water that hides all manner of sin and monsters. Something could be just inches below the boat and I'd never know.

"Lizzie? Are you okay?"

I belatedly realize that I've stopped rowing and pick up my pace. "I'm fine."

I can't quite see Maeve's expression in the darkness, but she nudges me with her shoulder. When she speaks, her tone is the carefully casual one of someone who knows that I'm freaking out and has decided not to comment on it. "This bay is heavily patrolled by the Cŵn Annwn. Since it's one of the main trade routes from south to north, they stop in regularly to ensure that nothing has taken up residence in the water that might endanger the ships or the people."

It's obvious she picked up on my nerves. Embarrassment heats my skin. I told her I'd protect her, and here I am, shaking as we row over water we've already crossed when arriving on Khollu. "I'm fine." *At least we don't have to swim.*

"I know."

We continue rowing, making good time to the first ship. Maeve peers up at it. "This isn't it."

As we row carefully around that ship and on to the next, the cold starts to seep into my body. I should have fed before we started this process. I curse myself for my hesitance to bite Maeve again before we reached Khollu. I'm not at full strength, but I don't have to be. We're not battling a ship full of the Cŵn Annwn, each more powerful than the next. These are sailors.

I fully intend to scare the shit out of them until they cower and piss themselves and beg me to become their captain.

At the second ship, we hit pay dirt. Maeve's soft sound is confirmation enough, but she whispers, "This is it."

I don't tell her to stay in the boat while I handle this. I already know she won't. I just need to keep her close and ensure she's safe during this process. "Up we go."

The boat bumps lightly against the ship, and I hold my breath as we wait to see if anyone noticed. We never would have managed to get so close to the *Audacity* without the lookout catching us, but obviously this captain runs a looser ship. Bad for them, good for us.

Maeve grabs the edge of the ship, steadying us. "Lizzie, if I didn't know better, I'd say that you were downright chipper at the thought of killing a bunch of people."

"Not a bunch of people. Just two." The captain and the quartermaster. I'll have to convince one of the crew members to become quartermaster after I stake my claim, which is an annoying but necessary step. There's all the nonsense about a vote, but I'm not going to let that stop me from taking what I want. What I need. A ship. A crew to sail it to my destination. Even better, it's a trade ship, so no one will blink twice at it sailing about this realm.

"I think you're trying to be comforting, but there is nothing comforting in planning to murder two people."

Then there's no more breath for speaking as we haul ourselves up the side of the ship. The *Serpent's Cry* is not quite as large as the *Audacity*, but it's obviously built to carry cargo rather than weapons. There are only a handful of cannons . . . which makes me realize that the *Audacity* has no cannons at all. I suppose it's not necessary when nearly every single crew member can function as a cannon themself.

We reach the railing with little problem, and I shift to the side so Maeve can perch next to me. There's a couple people milling about. The majority of the crew are in their bunks below, sleeping the night away. That won't do. I need witnesses for what happens next.

Love or fear. Mother's lessons really do come in handy for a hostile takeover. I need to scare the shit out of these people so they won't dare stab me the moment I turn around. "Maeve, I need you to listen carefully and do exactly as I say."

She listens as I detail my plan, her eyes getting wider and wider. "It will never work."

"It will. Trust me."

For a moment, I think she'll continue to argue, but she finally exhales slowly. "Okay, Lizzie. I trust you. I just hope that trust doesn't get me killed."

CHAPTER 15

Maeve

"YOU KNOW," LIZZIE SAYS IDLY. "THIS IS THE THIRD TIME I've snuck aboard a ship with the intent of murder. What a strange coincidence. I think I like this life of piracy."

"The *third* time." Obviously one of those was saving me, but when did it happen before? It's not something I need to be asking right now when we're hanging from the side of the *Serpent's Cry*. But it seems like information I probably should have had before we started this desperate plan.

"Seems to be becoming a habit." She glances at me, her eyes glowing crimson. Lizzie is having the time of her life. She's not exactly smiling, but she seems lit up in a way I've never seen before.

"Again, Lizzie, you absolutely cannot murder everyone on this ship."

"Killjoy." She nudges me with her elbow, and I swear she grins, but the expression is there and gone again so fast it's hard to tell for certain. She's enjoying herself, no doubt about it. She's downright giddy.

"Lizzie—"

"If you keep saying my name like that, I might forget what we're about tonight." She leans in close and speaks softly in my ear. "I haven't forgotten our earlier conversation. We'll definitely be discussing *that* after we're done here."

As if climbing aboard the *Serpent's Cry*, murdering our way to the captaincy, and scaring the crew into joining us is as simple as popping into the store to pick up some salt. A task with no risk, one that's almost boring in its mundaneness.

I can't do this.

I'm not made for adventure and grand journeys and murder. I might want to rip Bronagh's face right off with my teeth, but that is the exception to the rule. It's also more a violent fantasy than an intent to harm. I know the basics of fighting, but that's not enough for me to survive what comes next.

"Maeve." Lizzie's hand closes on the back of my neck, firm and heavy. "Breathe."

I hadn't even realized that I'd stopped. I draw in a jagged breath and then another. It doesn't quite stop the shaking in my limbs, but at least I'm not about to fall off the side of the ship.

Still, it's on the tip of my tongue to call the whole thing off. I never get the chance. Lizzie goes still, a predator about to pounce. "There he is."

And then she's moving, hauling herself over the railing and onto the deck. I scramble after her, but I'm too damned slow. All I catch sight of is a surprised look on Bronagh's face before she strikes. It happens so fast that my brain blips. Surely she didn't just take off his head with her bare fingers. Surely the head in question isn't bouncing across the deck to stop at my feet. Surely this is all a bad dream.

But it's not.

The blood touches the toes of my boots, and that horrible image is enough to get me moving. The crew that's awake are already sounding the alarm, and Lizzie darts toward the nearest one, the blood painting her hands sharpening into claws. I knew she could control blood, but for some reason, it never occurred to me that she could turn it into a *weapon*. The claws are easily several inches longer than her fingers and absolutely deadly.

I don't stop to think. I just react on instinct. "No murder, Lizzie!"

She's moving fast enough that I shouldn't be able to see her pull her strike, but I witness it all the same. Instead of beheading yet another person, she hits their neck with the edge of her hand. They go down instantly. Then she's next to me, nudging me aside none too gently as another of the sailors swings a broadsword into the place where I just stood. "If you don't want me to murder people, then you're going to have to defend yourself." She kicks the sword out of their hands, sending it flying off into the night. Somehow, she's not out of breath. "If someone so much as scratches you, I'm going to rip out their spine. Your choice, Maeve."

I blink. She delivers the words in a casual conversational tone as if we're sitting down to dinner instead of in the middle of a fight for our lives. Except it's not really a fight for our lives, is it? Lizzie moves through the sailors on deck, knocking them out before they have a chance to do more than turn in her direction. I would think that she had killed them, but the chest of the one nearest to me rises and falls steadily.

She's holding her punches. For me.

"Maeve! Get moving!"

I dart forward just as another sailor rushes out from belowdecks. This one is familiar to me, one of Bronagh's friends. I don't hesitate to shove him over the railing and into the water. It's not as smooth or as fearsome as the way that Lizzie fights, but it gets the job done.

I rush to the hatch that leads belowdecks and slam it down. It takes a few seconds to find a sword to shove into the thing to hold it shut. None too soon, either. Cries rise up belowdecks and hands shove at the hatch, making the sword rattle.

In the midst of the chaos, the captain appears. I've dealt with Captain Ean more than a few times over the years. He's fair enough in his trades, but he's an asshole and a half who lets his crew run rampant whenever they make port. For that, I'll never forgive him.

Recognition rolls over his features as he takes me in. "You!"

He charges me, but Lizzie appears behind him like a vengeful ghost and wraps her hand around his throat, drawing him up short despite the fact that he's twice her size. "Uh-uh. Drop the sword."

For a moment, it seems like he might try to fight his way out of the situation, but she tightens her grip on his throat, her blood claws pricking his skin, and he relents immediately. The sword falls to the deck with a clatter that makes me jump even though I expected it.

"Good." She's practically glowing in the moonlight, and there isn't a single part of her that's bored or uninterested now. She's grinning widely, flashing fangs. "Now, my dear Captain, I have a question for you. It's very important, so listen closely."

"You're going to regret this."

She laughs lightly. "On the contrary, this is the most fun I've had in ages. But *you* may regret it for the short time you have left to live. So let's get down to business."

He goes pale beneath his suntanned skin, as he seems to finally register the headless body on the deck. "What have you done to Bronagh?"

"He took something that doesn't belong to him. I'm sure you understand that the original owner is not pleased with that theft." She shakes him a little. "Where's the selkie skin?"

He doesn't even try to pretend he's unaware of what she's asking about. "In my cabin. We couldn't find a buyer locally, so we were heading to Lyari at the end of the week. Nobles love shit like that, and they're willing to pay a hefty sum."

Of course they are. A selkie pelt brings exceptional bragging rights. There are legends that such a thing can be used to control the selkie themself, but they're nothing more than folktales. If that was ever a power our skins held, it isn't one any longer.

"Very good," Lizzie practically purrs. "Now you have a choice, my dear Captain. You can help us track down the *Crimson Hag*—"

He makes a shocked sound. "The *Crimson Hag* is a Cŵn Annwn ship. Chasing it down is suicide. I won't do it."

"Pity." Lizzie isn't surprised, and neither am I. There was no way he was ever going to bow to our plan, but a part of me had hoped to be proven wrong. I don't like the man, but that doesn't mean I wish him dead.

Unfortunately, it's too late for that. A hand appears in the center of his chest, and my eyes refuse to acknowledge the fact that Lizzie just shoved her hand through the rib cage of a grown man. He slumps to the ground without a sound, his blood pooling out to join Bronagh's.

"Damn it, Lizzie. You didn't even give him a chance to change his mind."

"He wasn't going to. You know it and I know it. I was merely saving us time." She examines the heart in her hand, and my horrified brain is certain that it beats a few times before going still, as if it's not quite aware that it has left the safety of its body. "Let the rest of the crew up. They have their own choices to make."

I stare at the scene around us, at the crew members who are softly groaning as they regain consciousness, at the beheaded body of the quartermaster and the heartless body of the captain. It's gruesome and terrifying, and Lizzie stands in the middle of it, her pale skin bathed in red. She looks like some otherworldly creature that appeared from a nightmare, one intended to seduce and then traumatize.

But keeping the crew locked up indefinitely isn't an option. This will be our one chance to get what we need. I reach for the sword with shaking hands and pull it free. Then I step back, putting a decent amount of distance between me and the crew members, who will no doubt be furious.

But when they emerge from belowdecks, it's cautiously and with fear in their eyes. The *Serpent's Cry* doesn't run a particularly large crew. The captain was always cheap, so he kept it bare bones. There are scarcely a dozen people who file onto the deck and stare at the carnage.

"Your captain and quartermaster took something that did not belong to them. It's a mistake they won't make a second time." Lizzie tosses the heart and catches it idly. "I have need of this ship and this crew to reclaim something that was also taken from me. Cooperate, and whatever riches we find along the way will be yours. At the end of our search, you can elect your own captain and sail off to do whatever the fuck you want. The best part is that you'll be alive to do it. Deny me and . . ." She tosses the heart again. "Well, I don't have to tell you what will happen."

The crew exchanges looks. At some point, this will become a problem. When they have time to think and let their anger grow instead of being overridden by fear. But in this moment, no one protests.

Lizzie smiles slowly. "I thought you might see things my way. Pick your new quartermaster. We sail at high tide."

Things happen quickly after that. There's some arguing before the crew puts forth Alix as the new quartermaster. They're a bird person, their feathers a dozen shades of black, and they seem reasonable enough. It's about the best we can ask for.

We're shown to the captain's cabin as someone provides a few mops and buckets of seawater to clean up the mess on the deck. The moment I step through the door, the sensation of the missing piece of me becomes almost overwhelming. Lizzie says something, but my ears are clogged to anything but the call of my pelt. I rush through the captain's cabin, digging through chest after chest before finding one tucked in the corner. And there it is, neatly folded on the top.

My pelt.

I reach for it with shaking hands but stop just short of touching it. This hasn't been an easy journey, but at the same time . . . it's been too easy. I expected for weeks and weeks to pass as the search stretched out and became frustrating and hopeless.

"It's there, Maeve. Take it." Lizzie sounds carefully distant, the fervor in her voice having died down now that we no longer have an audience. The blood is gone from her skin even though I'm nearly certain that she didn't stop to wash it off. That's a strange little mystery for another day.

I take a deep breath and pick up my skin. It's as warm as my own body, and the urge to wrap it around myself is nearly overwhelming. But not here. Not like this. "I need—"

Lizzie is there in an instant, wrapping an arm around my waist and guiding me through the door and out onto the deck. The sailors watch us with fear in their eyes and no little amount of curiosity. Now that the time has come, I'm almost afraid to wrap the skin around myself. What if it's no longer part of me? What if it rejects me? I've never heard of such a thing, but that doesn't mean it's impossible.

"You won't know until you try." I hadn't realized that I'd been speaking aloud, but Lizzie's voice is very soft and careful. As kind as I've ever heard her.

Later, perhaps, I'll be grateful for how carefully she's handled me in this situation. Right now I can only imagine what happens next. Before I can think of all the ways this could possibly go wrong, I wrap my skin around myself.

And I am whole once more.

CHAPTER 16

Lizzie

I'VE SEEN SHIFTERS CHANGE THEIR SHAPE PLENTY OF times. It tends to be gruesome business, bones breaking and skin splitting as their bodies go from one version of themselves to the other. It's not like that at all with Maeve. She drapes the pelt—a fur with a gray dappled pattern—around her body, and it's as if my eyes go blurry for a moment. One second, the woman whom I'm starting to have incredibly complicated feelings for is standing in front of me. The next, a massive leopard seal crouches in front of me.

I'm hardly a zoologist, but even I'm aware of the various types of seals and where they come from. But when I think of seals, I think of the cute little brown-furred ones with doe eyes. Prey. The kind of animal that falls victim to superior predators like orcas. Now *that* is an animal I can get behind; they even play with their prey.

Maeve isn't that kind of seal at all.

She's massive, for one. She has to be upward of a thousand pounds and easily fifteen feet from nose to tail. She blinks at me, and though the rest of her is unrecognizable, those inky eyes remain the same. We stare at each other in charged silence as I try to understand what the fuck my heart is doing right now.

And then she throws herself over the railing in a shockingly agile movement. There's a splash down below, and only silence follows. I step to the railing and look down to see her pale form circling the ship and then diving deep. The happiness in her movements almost makes me smile.

Then she dives deeper, and I can't see her at all any longer. I grip the railing and search the dark water, but it's just that . . . dark water. No seal. No Maeve. She said there was nothing to fear in these waters, that the Cŵn Annwn drive out—or, more accurately, murder—anything that takes up residence. She's fine. She's not being torn apart just out of sight.

But she . . . doesn't surface.

Seconds tick into minutes and then longer. I can hear the crew shuffling about behind me, but I can't seem to move. There's no sign of her. No matter how many times I search the gently rolling waves, that truth doesn't change.

Even when the sun crests the horizon, bathing the world in light and turning the water into something only slightly less opaque. Still no Maeve.

She's . . . gone.

I stare at the water, wondering how I got this all so wrong. I'm ruthless to a fault. It's the only way I know how to be. How did I not use our bargain to *my* advantage? I should have insisted we go after my family heirlooms first, and then I should have been the one to leave her behind with her needs unsatisfied. I must be a fool, because I honestly didn't expect her to abandon me the moment she reclaimed her stolen skin.

I also didn't expect it to hurt so much.

I finally drag myself away from the railing and turn to find several of the crew members watching me covertly. It's tempting to snap at them to mind their own damn business, but showing even that much reaction is broadcasting my weakness in an invitation to be exploited. So I stare them down until they find somewhere else to be.

All except Alix, the bird person. To hear Evelyn tell of it, there was one of their people aboard the *Crimson Hag* as a medic, a delightfully delicate person whom Evelyn was naturally taken by. Alix is hardly that. Their beak is curved like that of a predator. They may move on two feet, but somehow they still give the impression of diving down to clutch up helpless prey. It would be impressive if I wasn't feeling like I might vomit.

They stand next to me, watching me out of the corner of their large pale eyes. "This likely won't go well for you."

"Why don't you try again?" I say mildly. "The last person who threatened me ended up with their head bouncing across the deck."

"I'm not threatening you. I'm merely stating a fact. One of my people tells me you're hunting the *Crimson Hag*. It might not be captained by Bowen any longer, but that doesn't make it any less formidable an opponent. It's suicide."

I find myself looking back at the water and curse silently. Surely I'm not this much of a fool to be staring at the waves and waiting for Maeve to reappear? What am I? Some forlorn housewife whose spouse has gone out to sea, never to be seen again? Ridiculous.

It takes more effort than it should to turn to Alix and give them the majority of my attention. "I don't have a death wish. Battling them at sea would get us all killed. I simply need to find them so I can retrieve something that belongs to me. As soon as we locate the ship, your task with me is done." It would be more convenient to keep them on until I find a portal home, but I have no interest in being stabbed in my sleep. The threat of that is already too prominent. If Alix believes they'll gain what they want—the captainship—the moment I accomplish my task, they're less likely to cause problems.

"It's a risk."

"Life is a risk." Despite my best efforts, I can't help looking out into the water again. It's fully morning now, which means it's been hours since Maeve disappeared beneath the surface. "It's your choice whether you bring the crew in line or I murder them all and find a new crew that's more willing to work with me."

They huff out a strange cawing laugh. "Heard and understood . . . Captain. The *Crimson Hag* doesn't sail south all that often, so our best bet is to head north to Drash. There should be better information there."

I would almost rather sail directly to the damn capital and wait them out there, but that's a fool's game. In the way of established dictators everywhere, the Council that rules Threshold is complacent in the extreme. They rule with an iron fist, but they've done it for so long without being challenged that they don't think they *can* be challenged.

That will work in the rebellion's favor—it already has. Not that such things matter to me. I won't be around to see the rebellion prevail or fail, whichever the future holds. As soon as I reclaim my family jewels, I will return home and . . .

Go back to how things have been for the last century. Rising to meet my mother's every demand. Scheming and plotting and killing to further my family's power. There was a time when such things excited me, but when I think about it now, there's only a heaviness in my chest.

What is wrong with me? I don't *doubt*. Such emotion is for lesser beings. I've always had a direction in life, I've always had a goal to strive toward. I fully intend to be matriarch of my family at some point. The problem is that without Wolf and me being good little breeders with the proper partners and producing pureblood heirs, what family *is* there? Vampires live long enough that it might as well be forever. It will be centuries before there's even a chance my mother might perish. Or before I become fed up enough with her control and stage a coup.

But what then? Wolf is enjoying his ridiculous little polycule, and though they've popped out three children, those children are of mixed bloodlines. Somehow they've gained the power of all three fathers—as well as their mother's glamour and seraphim magic. They will undoubtedly change the vampire world when they're of age, might even challenge the pureblood mentality that my mother clings to so fiercely.

That's in the distant future, though. She wants to grow our family's numbers *now*—which means she expects me to be the one to move forward with those plans. I have no desire for children. I never have. Even if I did, there is no guarantee I could become pregnant. Bloodline vampires may live damn near forever, but that means that we don't breed easily. We're lucky if we get one babe a generation. The fact that my mother had two was a small miracle, at least until we became the disappointments that we continue to be to this day.

What's *wrong* with me? I don't think like this. There's no room for doubt when it comes to my mother. She carved that part of me out a very long time ago—just like she carved out every other alleged weakness I possessed.

I belatedly realize that Alix is still waiting for a response. I can't afford to let my guard down now. Their ambition will work in my favor, but only as long as they fear me. "To Drash it is, then."

"Very well." They turn and move away in a strange little hop-flutter movement that's not quite walking and not quite flying.

With them gone, there's nothing else to focus on. Nothing except Maeve's absence.

What if she didn't leave intentionally? What if the bay isn't nearly as safe as we were led to believe? What if she fought and died below the surface and I had *no fucking idea*?

I grip the railing hard enough for the wood to crack against my palms. If I didn't know better, I would assume that Maeve had cast a spell on me. There's no other reason for me to be unraveling this quickly over such a short acquaintance. Yes, I want her. Of course I do. She's gorgeous and soft and stubborn to a fault. But lust is a simple emotion for all that it can be overwhelming. What I'm feeling right now isn't simple. I don't understand it.

"Lizzie."

She's back. There's no thought of tempering my response. I spin and rush to where Maeve has just climbed over the railing several feet away and stands before me, her clothing and hair dripping wet, with a bag in her hands. She grins. "I figured we needed our things."

I don't stop to think. I throw my arms around her and pull her close until she squeaks. "You're here."

"Of course I'm here. Where else would I be?" She gingerly pats my back as if she's not sure what to think of me. And why would she be? I am not acting normal right now. "Are you okay?"

"I'm fine." It still takes several beats before I'm able to release her and step back. I clear my throat, but my heart is racing far faster than it needs to. "You seem . . . well." Better than well. There's a vibrancy to her that I didn't realize she was missing. It's pure joy, and it draws me to her even more than she did to begin with. I want to sink my hands into her hair and claim her mouth, to channel that joy into pleasure. To claim *her.*

I glance at the sky; dawn has long since passed. There's a thousand reasons to be less reckless, but I can't think of a single one of them right now. I scoop up the bag, Maeve's soaking wet skin, and grab her hand. "Come on."

"Where are we—" She makes that delightful squeaking noise again as I haul her across the deck to the captain's cabin and through the door. The place reeks of aftershave and some kind of herb, but I don't care. I haven't known Maeve that long, but it feels like I've been waiting forever to get my hands on her properly. I can't wait any longer.

I slam the door and lock it and then press her against it, molding my body to hers. "Do you feel the same as when we last spoke?"

Understanding dawns in her inky eyes. Quickly followed by

desire hot enough to scald me. She worries her bottom lip, and it's everything I can do not to close the rest of the distance and soothe that spot with my tongue. "I still want you, if that's what you mean," she finally says.

I barely manage to hold myself back. All I want to do is ravish her, but some lines are sacred. My voice is ragged when I finally manage to speak. "If that changes, no matter where we are or what we're doing, this stops."

If anything, she softens even further against me. "I know."

There's no reason to hesitate any longer. I dig my hands into her curly hair and angle her head so I can take her mouth. Maeve tastes like the sea, salty and enticing enough to drive me to become a sailor and never touch dry land again. To lose myself in her in a way that I've never wanted to do with anyone else before.

Then her hands find my hips, urging me closer yet, and there's no space for thinking anything at all. I kiss her like I've wanted to for far too long. Tongue and teeth and the lightest of nips. Not quite a bite, but pleasure shudders through her body all the same.

We're doing this. We're *finally* doing this.

I'll fucking kill anyone who interrupts us before we're done.

CHAPTER 17

Maeve

MY BODY BUZZES WITH THE COMBINATION OF BEING whole once more and Lizzie's hands on my skin. She's so incredibly strong, yet she touches me like I'm spun gossamer. Considering the violence she's capable of—the violence she craves—this is a gift that I barely know what to do with. It would be all too easy to allow myself to believe that she treats me like this because she cares.

That belief is a trap.

This is the culmination of the lust that's spawned between us. Nothing more. Nothing less. I can enjoy myself as long as I keep my expectations reined in.

"Maeve." Lizzie's voice is rough in my ear. "If you don't want to—"

"I do," I blurt. I grab the band of her pants and jerk her closer yet. "I really, really do."

"Then obviously I need to pull out all the stops to keep you from mentally wandering." She laughs softly. "Come on. I'd love to fuck you against a door later, but that's not what we're doing the first time."

She eases away from me, and I have to bite down the protest at the loss of her body against mine. I can't help that my brain is constantly spinning. Especially now. Especially in this situation, with this person. The last partner I had was mopped off the deck outside. A fitting punishment, perhaps, for his betrayal, but it's the betrayal in question that has me all twisted up. I trusted him, and he didn't hesitate to use that trust to rip out a piece of me with his bare hands.

Lizzie yanks all the bedding off the bed and tosses it on the floor. "The mattress is clean. That's good."

I don't ask how she's able to tell. I can smell the truth of her statement. I still watch with wide eyes as she digs through one of the heavy trunks against the wall until she comes up with clean bedding. "Lizzie—"

"I am not fucking you on a bare mattress like a college kid." She picks up her pace, moving in a blur around the bed as she makes it. Then she kicks the used sheets farther away for good measure. "One last thing." Lizzie walks to me and plucks my pelt from where I'd dropped it at my feet.

I bite down my instinctive protest. I'm between her and the door. If she thinks to—

But all she does is fold it neatly, using far more care than she did with any of the blankets or sheets to date, and set it gently on the nearest closed chest. She turns to face me, and I don't know what my expression is doing, but it makes her stalk slowly to me. "That was the smallest of kindnesses. Don't look at me with your heart in your eyes, Maeve. That's not what this is."

"I know," I manage. If I think too long on how much such a

small kindness affects me, I might get depressed. Lizzie has never been less than honest with me about her intentions and plans. At the end of this, she leaves and I go home. There is no future that contains the two of us side by side.

I don't know what drives me to keep speaking, to risk the pending pleasure. "But could you pretend?"

Lizzie blinks. "Baby, that's not a good idea."

It's not. It's a terrible idea. But I'm so raw from everything that's happened, and it's only been *three weeks* since the fledgling future I'd been dreaming of with Bronagh was ripped away. That future was never going to happen, and our relationship was never as deep as I wanted it to be, but the hurt is still there.

The . . . doubt . . . is still there.

"Please, Lizzie."

She crosses to me slowly, once again cupping my face and placing her thumbs along my cheekbones. The fact that these same hands were stealing the life from two people a few hours ago—one of whom I almost fancied myself in love with—should make me flinch away. Instead, I lean in to her touch and close my eyes.

Her sigh is so soft as to be nearly soundless, a tiny puff of capitulation. Then her mouth is on mine and there's no hesitation to speak of. I expect a light and teasing touch, or maybe a dose of the frenzy that had her dragging me into this cabin in the first place, but the kiss is neither.

It's a seduction, pure and simple.

Lizzie expertly coaxes my mouth open and delves inside. She explores me as if she has all day, as if this kiss is the thing she's been most looking forward to, rather than everything that comes after. I barely register us moving, but a few moments later, she's guiding me back onto the bed and following me down.

I know I asked for this, but I've wanted this woman almost from the moment I saw her, and we're moving too slowly. "Lizzie, please." I grab at the hem of her shirt, intent on getting it off her as quickly as possible.

She catches my hands. "Don't rush me."

I start to wrestle off my clothes. "I don't want to rush, but I want to be naked with you."

Lizzie makes a choked noise. "I suppose I can't argue that." She pushes back enough to allow me to shimmy out of my dress, and then she strips fast enough to leave me breathless. Or maybe it's the sight of her. She reminds me of the sharks that migrate into our waters every fall; Lizzie is a streamlined killing machine. She's perfectly made, her small breasts topped with rosy pink nipples, her muscular thighs flexing as I lick my lips. Her long dark hair is a wild mess around her face, which only makes her feel more real. And she's all mine, at least for now.

She hooks the back of my knees and drags me to the edge of the bed, pushing my thighs wide.

Her eyes flare crimson. "You are so fucking beautiful." She leans down and presses her face to my stomach, inhaling deeply. "And you smell good enough to eat."

My skin flares hot. "Lizzie." Considering she's a vampire, I don't know if that's a threat or the hottest thing anyone has ever said to me.

She moves down my body, kissing and nipping lightly, seeming determined to learn every inch of me. I can't stop shaking. Most of my past sexual encounters have been just that—

encounters. I was hardly going to bring them to my room—at least until that ill-advised final night with Bronagh—and even at my most lust-stricken, I knew better than to go aboard their ship. So we made do with hurried, secret moments when we could find them.

I don't know what to do with this. I don't know how to act when Lizzie is licking my inner thighs, her grip holding me open for her pleasure. Or my pleasure. Or both.

"Maeve." She exhales directly over my pussy, making my whole body clench. "Is there a reason you're acting so skittish right now? Do you not like this?"

I takes me two tries to find my words. "I like this *very much*."

"Hmm." She squeezes my thighs lightly. "Then why are you so tense?"

I really do not want to answer her, but she's not moving, and I've known Lizzie long enough to know there will be no winning a standoff. So I gather my courage, take a deep breath, and confess. "I've never done this before."

She's silent for a beat. Two. Three. "You don't mean sex."

I stare at the wooden ceiling and wonder if my skin can actually catch fire from humiliation. "I don't mean sex. I mean . . . this."

It's only because her mouth is so close to my center that I feel her exhale shudder out. "You mean no one has ever licked this pretty pussy."

"Yes," I choke out. "That's what I mean."

"Do you want me to stop?"

"I think I might die if you don't keep going."

She makes a sound that's dangerously close to a purr. "I

know I shouldn't give a shit about being your first, but I do. It makes me very, very happy. Relax, baby. Let me take care of you." Then her mouth is on me and . . .

"Oh gods!" I don't make a conscious decision to dig my hands into her hair and lift my hips. My body simply takes over. I've enjoyed most of the sex I've had, but this . . . I could have been doing *this* this whole time? "Don't stop. *Please* don't stop."

She doesn't. Lizzie explores me with her tongue, wet and slick and so dangerously pleasurable that I may come apart before she ever makes it to my clit. Then she presses the flat of her tongue there, and I *do* come apart.

My orgasm is quick and leaves me breathless. So breathless that it takes me several heartbeats to realize she hasn't stopped. She keeps licking me, keeps driving my pleasure higher and higher. I don't know if I come a second time or if it's just a new wave of the first. It's too good. Too much. Too *everything*.

"Shh, shh, baby, I've got you." She moves up my body, kissing my stomach, my breasts, my chest, before taking my mouth.

She tastes of me and her, a combination I might spend the rest of my life craving. That's a worry for another day, another night. I cling to her, drowning myself in her kiss even as she hooks the back of my knee and draws my leg up, bringing us closer together. I realize her intention right away. It allows her thigh to press against my pussy. She's so smooth and hard and guiding me to grind on her.

I break the kiss to gasp. "I can't. Not again."

"You can, baby." She's never sounded sweeter than she does in this moment, drawing more pleasure from my body than I could have dreamed. She kisses me again. I allow myself to sink into her touch, her taste, the desire she coaxes from me with the confidence of someone who truly cares. Of someone who could love me.

I know it's a lie. I don't care. It's a gift and one I am greedy for.

But it's not all I'm greedy for.

I barely wait for the most recent orgasm to fade before I move. The only reason I manage to successfully flip her is because I surprise her. It's so vindicating to see Lizzie on her back, her dark hair spread around her, skin flushed with desire, lips plump from kissing *me*.

She gathers my hair away from my face as I descend her body to settle between her thighs. Her pussy is just as perfect as the rest of her, and there's something about seeing her so wet and knowing it's for *me* that makes my head spin.

I lick my lips. "Tell me if I'm doing something wrong."

Her laugh is a little rough. "You won't do anything wrong."

Sweet of her to say so, but I've never done this before. I want to make it just as good for her as she made it for me, but it's hard to focus with the scent of her arousal muddying what remains of my thoughts. I drag my tongue over her experimentally, but at the first taste, I forget all attempts at being strategic.

She tastes *amazing*.

I lick and suck and delve into her with my tongue. Distantly, I'm aware of Lizzie's breathing going ragged and sweet little moans slipping from her lips, but I'm too intent on tasting every bit of her.

At least until she tightens her fist in my hair and nudges me up to her clit. "Stop *teasing* me, baby."

I love that she's started to unravel because of *me*. I'm going to love it even more when she comes all over my face. It takes me a few tries to figure out the motion and pressure that makes her thighs tighten around my head and her body shake. I've never felt more powerful in my life than the moment when Lizzie moans my name as she orgasms.

I crawl up her body and ease down beside her. I'm grinning and I can't seem to stop. "That was amazing."

She opens her eyes. They're still a glowing crimson that makes me clench my thighs together despite my best efforts. Lizzie knows. She smiles slowly. "We're not done yet. Not by a long shot."

CHAPTER 18

Lizzie

I HAVE NEVER SEEN JOY LIKE SEAL-MAEVE SWIMMING. SHE spends a good part of the next day in the water beside the ship, her large dappled form cutting through the waves with ease. She twists and dives and rolls.

I can't stop watching her.

It's tempting to lie and tell myself that I'm just ensuring she doesn't break our bargain and bolt. It's not the truth. The truth is that this woman has gotten beneath my skin despite all common sense. It started well before us having sex yesterday—and all through the day and night—but that definitely contributed. Learning her body, knowing that I'm the first person to taste that sweet pussy? More, I can say that I was merely being soft because she asked me to, but the truth is that it felt right.

It still feels right. Everything about her does.

How many times have I considered the traditional selkie's story since we met? Always from her point of view, from the selkie who lost a key part of themself and exists in a state of mourning and bitterness. But now that she's whole again, it's hard not to look at it as the sailor who saw something so beautiful that he couldn't stop himself from wanting to possess it. Even knowing that their relationship, such as it is, is doomed from the start.

She will always leave. What draw can a human—or a vampire—hold when the sea is her first love?

When the sun is high in the sky, I force myself away from the railing and move to the helm, where Alix confers with the navigator, Rin. Ze is a lizard person similar to the one who tried to kill Evelyn on the *Crimson Hag*. No relation, I'm told. Not that it would matter. I've already promised Maeve that I won't murder anyone else on the crew unless I'm actively provoked, and her definition of "provoked" is significantly narrower than mine. Besides, I'm not in the habit of slaughtering people simply for their bloodlines. At least people who aren't vampires.

My family has been feuding with the other bloodlines for time unknowing, but my generation exists in a state of cautious peace. All of us are too paranoid to really believe we won't get a knife in the back; we're just not actively hunting each other the way our parents and grandparents did.

But there are no other bloodline vampires in Threshold. No one worried about continuing their family lines and bolstering their power. No one ready to attack me for being born as a Bianchi. There might be plenty of people in this realm who would be happy to murder me, but it's for reasons that are entirely new and fresh. It's . . . freeing.

Rin looks up as I approach, the movement quick and almost uncanny. Ze flicks out zir tongue. "Captain," ze says cautiously, "we're about a week out from Drash."

A week. A few days ago, that kind of delay would have sent me climbing the walls. Now, it feels like too short a time. Every day we get closer to finding my family heirlooms is a day closer to never seeing Maeve again. It may take time, but once I reclaim the jewels, I can go home. The thought should fill me with joy, or at least relief, but all there is in my chest is an aching emptiness where my heart should be.

What the fuck is *wrong* with me?

"Lizzie!"

Maeve hauls herself over the railing, having shed her skin in motion. Beneath it, she's wearing pants and a shirt that hug her shapely body. The pelt drapes over her arm, dripping over the deck as she rushes to us. "We have a problem."

Alix and Rin exchange a look, but it's Alix who speaks. It's always Alix who speaks when it's the two of them. "What problem?"

"There's a water horse following us," says Maeve.

"Shit." I breathe. "You're sure?"

"As sure as I can be," Maeve says.

Alix curses, but I'm still staring at Maeve in confusion. "A water horse? Like a kelpie? But we're in the middle of the sea." I was under the impression those creatures stick to lakes and rivers, the better to lure in their victims from dry land. There are no victims around here . . .

Except us.

The thought chills me despite my best efforts. Now that we're back on a proper ship, I've managed to get my unease about sailing back under control. But if this water horse acts like the legends I'm familiar with, it will latch onto its victim and drag them down, helpless and unwilling, until the sea rushes into their lungs and . . . I shake my head roughly. "We need to move faster."

Rin eyes the sails and lifts zir hand to test the wind. "Can't outrun them in these conditions."

My stomach drops at how resigned ze sounds. No, damn it. I am not some helpless victim in waiting. "So we fight." My voice is steady despite how fast my heart is beating. Thankfully, I'm the only one who can read such things.

Every eye turns to me, and none of them look particularly happy. Alix shakes their head. "If it's desperate—or hungry—enough to come after a full ship, then we're in trouble. We're smugglers, not the Cŵn Annwn. We don't hunt monsters, and we're not equipped for it."

The small hairs on the back of my neck rise. I can't see the danger yet, but knowing that it's coming is enough to make my heart beat harder and my thoughts clear. "You're smugglers. Which means you're aware there's always a chance of trouble. You're prepared for it. That's exactly what this is—trouble."

Rin's tail twitches nervously. "The best smugglers don't draw attention to themselves and never need to fight." Ze gives Maeve an apologetic look. "Sorry about your skin, though. We didn't know that Bronagh was going to take it. Apparently he had a buyer interested."

She waves that away with her usual grace. "I have it back and Bronagh is dead. There's nothing to apologize for."

"All the same." Rin glances back past the stern to where the ripples have gotten more prominent. "Might not get a chance to apologize again, and I like you, selkie."

"Um, thanks. I kind of wish you saying that when we're about to be attacked didn't feel like a goodbye."

"No one is going to die," I snap, though Rin's words catch my interest. A buyer. Maeve mentioned in passing at one point that there used to be a market for selkie pelts. If this person specifically wanted one, they may try again. Once we find my heirlooms, we should hunt them down and remove the threat they represent. In the meantime, I have a more immediate danger to deal with. "Except for the water horse. I'll kill it. Simple enough." I hope.

Again, they exchange a look. I'm getting heartily tired of being tiptoed around like I'm a foolish child. I glare. "Stop looking at each other and speak. Why don't you think I can kill it?"

Maeve clears her throat. "In a fair fight, you could without issue. But water horses don't fight fair. It will come over the railing and take someone below, dragging them down until they drown. It will do that enough times to get the food it requires, and then it'll feast."

The shiver of fear working its way through me tries to gain strength, but I muscle down the reaction. Yes, the thought of being dragged to the depths is a terrifying one and my personal nightmare. But this is just one creature, magical or not. It doesn't even have claws and fangs. It's a fucking horse. Granted, I've never seen a kelpie, because they were hunted to extinction a long time ago. I know the stories, though—my family keeps excellent records. "I'll rip its heart out before it has a chance to."

There's a shout from the crow's nest, and we all turn as something emerges from the waves behind us. It's a black horse, just like I expected, but the closer it gets, carving through the waves to race on top of them, the more I see that the similarities are superficial at best. Four legs, a strong body, an arching neck, all a deep blue that's nearly black. A mane and tail that stream out behind it as it closes the distance between us and it. What was I saying about fangs and claws? It has both.

Not to mention that it's bigger than even a fucking Clydesdale, with the body type of a thoroughbred. Fighting that thing will be a godsdamn bitch. I wish I had my rifle with me. That would put an end to this with a single bullet between its eyes.

"Get everyone who's not exclusively required off the deck." I speak softly. Everyone is so tense, a harsh word might make them panic. Might make *me* panic. Damn it, *no*. I am a hardened killer, and I will not quail in the face of an overgrown herbivore that thinks it can be a predator. "It has to come on board in order to take a victim. When it does, I'll deal with it."

Alix clears their throat. "It might not be that simple. This is . . ."

Maeve makes a sound that is part laugh and part pure desperation. "This is *what*?"

"This isn't any normal water horse." They shudder. "It's too big. And the color is wrong. I've been warned about this one, but I'd hoped to never see it in person. This motherfucker sinks ships."

The charge seems impossible. Surely one singular creature could not sink a ship, even if this isn't a warship like the Cŵn Annwn sail. But Alix isn't joking, and Rin's scales have gone from a nice healthy green to something closer to yellow with zir fear.

I have to keep them talking, keep them thinking. If I don't, at best they're going to be useless; at worst, they're going to get us all killed. Having to mop blood off the deck will upset Maeve, so I'd like to avoid that outcome. "You obviously know plenty about this creature. How would you have dealt with it under normal circumstances?"

"We wouldn't be traveling this route in the first place. But if we had to, we would get our air-user to bolster the wind until we outran it. It might be a monster, but its stamina doesn't last forever." At my askance look, Alix shrugs. "Our captain was the air-user. You killed him. Therefore we have no air-user. This water horse is going to sink us, and then it can eat the crew at its leisure."

"Yeah, that's not going to work for me." I bend over to pull off my boots. After some consideration, I don't bother to take off the rest of my clothes. If it gets me into the water, then I'm fighting a losing battle and my clothing making it challenging to swim will be the least of my problems. "The order still stands. Clear the decks."

"Lizzie," Maeve says. "Don't. We'll find another way."

I catch the back of Maeve's neck and pull her into a rough kiss. "Go into the captain's quarters. I need to be focused for this fight. I won't be if I'm worrying about you."

"But—"

"Please, Maeve."

She seems shocked that I said please, and even with everything going on, it strikes me that I've never said that word to her before. Maeve looks back into our wake, where the water horse is closer than ever. There's something in her expression that I don't like, but surely she knows she can't fight that thing. I'm the best chance of taking it down. We're already running on a tight crew, and we can't afford to lose any more people. Not without slowing us down.

Finally, she says, "I'll go into the crow's nest. That's my only compromise." Before I can tell her that that's a ridiculous plan and I want her safely shut away, she rushes to the netting. She drapes her pelt over her shoulder and scales up to the crow's nest, moving faster than she has a right to. As if she can outrun my words.

"Captain."

It's only been a couple days, and that title sits ill at ease on my shoulders. I take a deep breath and turn to the back of the ship. "Keep our course."

"Yes, Captain." Rin and Alix huddle back behind the helm. There's little protection on either side, so I resist the urge to head toward the back of the boat to meet the water horse. It won't attack from that direction, anyways. Not if it's as clever as Rin and Alix seem to think. If I was hunting a ship like this, I would come over the side.

Even as the thought crosses my mind, the horse dives beneath the water. I find myself holding my breath, waiting for it to surface again, but it doesn't. Seconds tick by, tension coiling tighter and tighter. I drag my nail along my inner arm and will the blood to cover my hands, forming claws. The sharp pain clears the rapidly circling thoughts in my head. We might be in the middle of the ocean on a ship with a predator circling, but I *know* this feeling. The moment before a fight for my life. Only one of us will see the sunset, and it's damn well going to be me. I take a breath and dig my nail deeper into my forearm, forcing more blood out and lengthening the blood claws as much as I can without making them brittle. It's a fine balance, and one I've spent years perfecting.

I'm a fucking killer as much as this water horse is. More, because I bet I've lived longer.

It still takes effort to steady my breathing, to strive for a slice of calm before the attack. Usually, I'm fighting for my life, for my family's honor, out of sheer boredom. That's not the case today. If I fail, over a dozen people die. If I fail, *Maeve* might die.

Unacceptable.

"Jugular is likely my best bet," I murmur to myself. "Those hooves are too dangerous to fuck with." I'll need to find a way to flank it or come over its back. It's been damn near fifty years since I've been on the back of a horse, and that one didn't have claws and fangs. I don't look forward to this experience.

"Lizzie! Starboard side!"

Maeve's voice has me snapping around, and not a moment too soon. The water rises unnaturally there, up and up and up, cresting as the water horse bursts free of the surface. Water splashes over the railing in a wave that nearly takes me off my feet. I stagger and curse as it lands among us, the weight of it rattling the boards beneath my feet. I knew that it was huge, but its size is even more gargantuan than it appeared at a distance. It's damn near twice as tall as I am, its body deceptively muscular and its claws twice the size of the blood-coated ones on my fingers.

How the fuck am I going to kill this thing?

Come on, Lizzie. You kill it the same way you kill everything else. Rip it open until it stops moving.

On instinct, I whip out my magic, intending to bring it to its knees so I have easier access to its neck. But instead of feeling the familiar sensation of taking hold of another being's blood... my magic finds nothing to latch onto. What the fuck?

No time to wonder what this freakish creature has running through its veins. It charges toward the helm, intent on Alix and

Rin. "Oh no you don't." I sprint to meet it, heading it off before it can snatch my navigator.

It sees me coming and changes course, the pounding of its claw-hooves making the deck shake beneath my bare feet. I gather myself and spring up, aiming for its head. If I can wrap my body around it then I can—

It pivots, moving even faster than I'm capable of in midmotion. Certainly faster than I can counter. Instead of meeting its head, I land sprawled across its back. That's fine. I can work with this. I just need to—

It's magic takes hold and pins my arms and legs to either side of its broad body. I fight against the invisible bonds holding me in place, but there's nothing to fight *against*. *Trapped*. I thrash as much as I'm able, but it's as if I'm glued to its muscular back. It twists, and I know where it's headed before it takes its first step. "No!" Not the water. Not the depths. Not the thing I fear most in the world.

As if sensing my fear and feeding off it, the massive kelpie screams in triumph and it leaps over the side of the ship, taking me with it. I don't even get one last look at Maeve in the crow's nest before the water closes over my head.

CHAPTER 19

Maeve

My breath turns to stone in my lungs when the kelpie takes Lizzie over the edge and into the water. *She's going to die.* More than that, she'll be terrified when it happens. I can't let her go. Not yet. Not like this.

My body takes over. There's no time for my brain to provide all the ways this is suicidal. There's only motion. I throw myself from the crow's nest with every bit of strength I have, propelling myself well outside of the range of the ship and drawing my skin close around my body as I fall. My stomach is in my throat. I'll only get one chance at this.

I shift in the air, my body growing and morphing. It feels like stretching after spending hours in a cramped space. Even now, even with panic screaming through my mind, there's a sliver of joy in the ability to do this.

I dive into the surface of the water face-first, my body narrowing to take advantage of the momentum of the fall.

I fully expected the water horse to drag Lizzie into the

depths, but it's a handful of yards below the surface. Just deep enough to drown. She's trapped on its back, its magic holding her in place despite her struggles. And she *is* struggling. Blood saturates the water around them as she drives her fingers into the water horse's side again and again. It's not nearly enough.

She has a few minutes. Maybe a few seconds.

I charge through the water in their direction, pouring every bit of strength I have into pure speed. The water horse is easily twice my size, but it's distracted with the vampire attached to its back. More than that, its horse shape is made for running on hard surfaces. *I* am made for the deep.

I'll only get one chance to strike unchallenged before it's an all-out fight. I have to make it count. I dive deeper, coming up from below, where it won't expect an attack. Lizzie sees me first and her crimson eyes go wide. There's no time to reassure her. No time for anything.

I hit the water horse in the stomach hard enough to spin it toward the surface. Even over the roaring in my ears, I hear its pained cry. It's so *fast*. It turns almost instantly and lashes at me with its hind claws. I dodge out of the way easily. This is a fearsome beast, but *I am not prey*.

I twist around it, distracting it as best I can as I wait for another opening. I can hold my breath for a prolonged period of time, but I don't think Lizzie is able to. She's a vampire, but vampires are mammals just like humans. She can't go without oxygen indefinitely. Not like the water horse can.

I charge again, though this time I don't have quite as much speed behind me. It doesn't matter. My entire body is a weapon and my teeth are just as sharp as the kelpie's. I dodge another kick and rip into its hindquarters. It screams in pain again, but it hasn't released Lizzie.

Blood clogs the water. It's in my mouth, thick and coppery and *not enough*. I have to save her. We're running out of time. Distantly, fear clamors that we're going to draw bigger and more fearsome predators if we're not fast. There's no time to worry about that now. I have to save Lizzie. We have to kill the water horse, or at least drive it off and save the crew and the ship.

Overhead, the *Serpent's Cry* continues to cut away from us, the crew running for their lives. Of course they are. They're not warriors. They owe no allegiance to us. They're hoping that the water horse is too busy murdering us to come after them. I don't blame Alix and the rest of them for that choice, but I have no interest in dying today. Or letting Lizzie drown.

The kelpie spins to face me, its fangs snapping closed inches from my side. I barely twist out of the way in time and slap it with my tail.

It startles back and shudders. I get a glimpse of Lizzie wrenching herself off its back, its magic obviously waning as its distraction increases. But instead of pushing off and rushing for the surface, she clings to its neck and drives her fingers into its throat. The water horse lets out a shriek that I can feel in my bones, but I don't stop to feel sorry for it.

It's us or the kelpie.

I dive for the back of its neck, using my bigger body to knock Lizzie free as I sink my teeth into the top of its spine and twist and spin and wrench as hard as I can. Once, twice, a third time. On the fourth, its spine snaps and the creature goes still. I push it farther down into the depths, hoping that any other predators in the area will go after the body instead of us.

I sweep back up, coming beneath Lizzie's flailing body. She wraps her arms around me and I swim as quickly as I can to the surface. Her gasping breath is music to my ears. We *survived*. But we need to get out of the water, and we need to do it now. It's not safe. The dead water horse will draw other predators, and we need to be well away from here when that happens.

I'm not able to speak in this form, but Lizzie eases her grip on me so that I can swim easier and tow her to the ship. It takes a matter of seconds. But the entire time, I'm paranoid that something will rise from the depths and attempt to take a bite out of us.

As we come even with the *Serpent's Cry*, I fully expect the crew to ignore us—or try to finish what the water horse started. But Rin leans over the railing and tosses down a rope to trail in the water before us. Lizzie wastes no time wrapping it around her waist. Ze pulls her up onto the deck with quick movements, far stronger than zir lean body suggests. Less than a minute later, Lizzie is back safely aboard the ship.

Now it's my turn.

It wasn't until I'd regained my skin that I realized exactly how much I'd lost alongside it. How much strength and speed, how much confidence. Even now, days later, I'm not entirely certain how much of that was actually physical or mental. Regardless of the cause, I'm easily able to scale the side of the ship and vault over the railing to land on the deck at Lizzie's side. She's on her hands and knees, coughing up water.

She's breathing. She's *alive*. That's all that matters.

I crouch at her side, my hand hovering over her back. I don't close the distance, don't try to help beyond offering my presence. Both because I don't know if she'd accept it and because I don't want to weaken her standing with the crew. If they become even a little less scared of her, we might be in danger.

After a few moments, she sits back on her heels and clears her throat. Her wet hair is plastered to her face, her cheeks are gaunt, and her eyes are glowing a bright crimson. "Like I said, I'll handle it."

That's certainly one way to put it. I lift my brows, but she's very pointedly not looking at me. A giant splash makes us all jump, and I look back in time to see something massive breach the surface, the water horse's body in its giant jaws. My mind shies away from identifying exactly what that creature is.

I clear my throat. "Maybe it's best we pick up the pace as much as possible."

"Good idea." Alix doesn't point out that we were already at the maximum speed possible without magical aid. They just go back to the helm and start shouting orders at the crew emerging from belowdecks. Everyone is wide-eyed and shaky, but they go about their jobs with quick efficiency.

Living in Threshold means coming face-to-face with a wide variety of creatures that want to eat you for dinner. There aren't many natural predators to selkies in the waters around Viedna, but the sailors and the Cŵn Annwn come through with plenty of stories about the horrors that haunt the deep.

Horrors. Monsters. Things that need to be put down, according to them. More like they're creatures who are predators without any morality of their own. That doesn't make them evil. But, either way, I'm not interested in becoming the snack of a predator of the deep.

I move closer to Lizzie, and she holds up a hand. "I'm fine."

"I didn't say anything." She's most assuredly not fine. There are brackets around her mouth that I've never seen before and her pale skin is downright waxy. She's not shaking, but she hardly looks steady on her feet. Almost drowning is a terrifying experience for even the most hardened sailor, let alone someone actively afraid of the sea. I don't say it. I have a feeling that Lizzie will snap my head right from my shoulders if I put her fear to words.

Not that I'm going to let that stop me from finding a way to comfort her. "Let's get you dry." I ignore her faint sound of protest and wrap an arm around her waist, dragging her with me to the captain's quarters. The crew very pointedly doesn't look at either of us as I guide her inside and slam the door behind me.

She spins on me and snaps her fangs. "I said I'm fine."

"If you were fine, you wouldn't be throwing a tantrum like a child." If I thought that she would accept softness, I'd give it to her, but she only knows thorns. There's a part of me that mourns that, but I *will* create a safe place for her to land in the emotional aftermath of this experience . . . after I've gotten her out of her wet clothes and checked her for injuries. The vampire heals faster than she has any right to, but that doesn't mean she's uninjured.

"A . . . tantrum." Her voice goes low and deadly. "Just because we've fucked—"

"I highly suggest you stop right there before you piss me off." I cut in. "I know you're scared out of your mind right now, but that doesn't mean I'm going to allow you to take it out on me. Get those wet clothes off and let me check you for injuries."

"I. Am. Fine."

The fact that she keeps saying it and hasn't once questioned whether *I'm* okay only highlights how shaken she really is. Lizzie can be a cold bitch, but she has shown a remarkable amount of caring when it comes to my safety. Sharpness doesn't seem to be working. Softness it is, then. I march over to her and drag her into my arms. She tries to push me away, but only a little.

Her hands finally come to rest on my hips, fine tremors in her fingers. "Godsdamn it, Maeve."

"I'm really glad you're okay," I say into the crook of her neck. "You scared the shit out of me. There was a moment there where I thought I'd lost you forever." The words are almost a confession, almost a declaration that I have no intention of making. Because I *will* lose Lizzie forever. Not to death but to her family and obligations and a realm far beyond Threshold. At least in that scenario, I have the comfort of knowing that she's alive. Not a water horse's meal.

She takes in a breath, and it shudders out in a sound that's almost a sob. Still, she holds herself too straight. As if she's afraid to bend, because that means she'll break. My heart aches for her, for the lessons that she had to learn that told her never to show even the slightest bit of weakness. I don't tell her that she's safe with me. I don't think she'll believe it. I just hold her as tightly as I can until the tension melts out of her body and she collapses into my arms.

"I'm fine," she whispers.

"You will be."

When I'm certain she won't fight me, I ease back and pull off her wet clothes. She doesn't say anything. She just lifts her arms so I can get her shirt over her head and steps out of her pants after I work them down her legs. Passive. That alone is enough to freak me out, but I manage to keep my worry internal as I guide her unresisting body to the large tub in the captain's quarters. It's one of the few ostentatious things on this ship. I was delighted to discover it's similar to the one at the inn, with magically warm and clean water. It's even shielded so that it won't splash out of the metal tub. A useful trick on tumultuous seas, no doubt.

Lizzie resists, digging in her heels as I push her toward the tub. "I've had enough water to last me a lifetime."

"You'll feel better once you get the salt off your skin. Trust me."

She resists for a heartbeat longer and then allows me to usher her into the tub. I watch her closely, waiting for the moment that she relaxes. It doesn't come. She huddles in the center of the tub, her knees drawn to her chest. Which is just a testament of how truly terrified she was.

Best I can tell, Lizzie spent most of her life on land before coming to Threshold. There's nothing quite like the sea to remind you of the fact that you're not truly unkillable. The sea doesn't care about your magic or your strength, and certainly not your stamina. It's the ultimate equalizer. It's perfectly rational to be terrified, but if Lizzie has spent lifetimes being an apex predator, she's not going to be comfortable with fear. She's certainly not going to thank me for pointing out that it's a perfectly reasonable response.

My clothes are already starting to dry stiffly against my body, so I pull them off and drop them in a pile next to Lizzie's. When I turn around, she's slid down in the tub until her chin touches the surface of the water, her dark hair spread out around her as she watches me. "You were brilliant down there," she says softly.

Brilliant. That's not a word I would have used to describe the desperation in my attacks. I've killed for food and I've killed to protect myself, but it's never been a fight like that before. I think my hands are shaking, but it's easy enough to put the aftermath of the battle into the back of my mind when I can focus on her instead. "I wasn't going to let it take you."

"I've underestimated you, Maeve." She smiles a little, though her eyes are still haunted. "I suppose I should thank you for saving my life."

I shift uneasily on my feet. I don't know what to do with this version of Lizzie. I don't know how to comfort her in a way she'll accept. "There's no thanks necessary. Like I said, I wasn't going to let you die."

She lifts a hand. "Come here."

I want nothing more than to go to her, but I still plant my feet and force myself to stillness. "We both just had a big scare. I hardly think that jumping into the bath with you is the right solution."

"Probably not. But it can't hurt."

CHAPTER 20

Lizzie

I DON'T EXACTLY INTEND TO USE SEX AS A DISTRACTION, but I can't seem to stop shaking. The bath cleans the salt from my skin, but it also reminds me how close I came to losing *everything*. The water shakes with my little tremors, giving lie to my determination to be fine. I can still feel the press of the depths against my skin, eager to rush in the moment I lost my last bit of oxygen and my instinctive desire to breathe took over. Can still feel the way the kelpie tensed and twisted against me, its magic holding me helpless. I underestimated the water horse. All my strength, all my cunning, and I was as helpless as a civilian.

If Maeve hadn't come after me, it would be feasting on my flesh right now.

"Lizzie." Even the sight of Maeve, naked and glorious, isn't quite enough to push back the feeling that's shaking me down to my bones. *Fear.* It's been so long since I've felt it that I hardly know its flavor.

No, that's a lie. For far too long, fear was my bread and butter.

It was the only nourishment I was allowed. My mother cleaved to the belief that if she overwhelmed me and Wolf through most of our youth, we would never feel it again. That, at worst, we would become immune, and at best, we would be bosom friends, able to twist it to our will. It's certainly not true for my brother, but I'd mistakenly thought it was the truth for me. *Wrong.*

"How do you stand it?" I don't mean to speak, to expose my quivering heart, but the words come all the same. "Down there. Where there's nothing to see but blue and black. Where anything could be coming for you."

Maeve's expression softens. If I see pity in her eyes, I will flee the room, but there's only a deep understanding. "It still scares me sometimes. But I don't look at the depths as something that finite. It can be multiple things at once. I was taught as a child to respect the sea, and that respect and no small amount of fear reside in me today." She moves closer and takes my hand, holding it between two of hers. "But fear isn't the only thing down there. There's freedom. Beneath the surface, there's nothing constraining me, nothing holding me back. I can fight and twist and play and hunt to my heart's content."

"I don't understand," I whisper. My teeth try to close around the words, my mother's training nearly overwhelming. Never admit weakness. Never give anyone something that they could use against you. But this woman isn't *anyone*. She's Maeve, and there's something about her that makes me feel safe in a way I don't completely understand. In a way that has nothing to do with physicality and everything to do with my heart. It's because of that beacon of safety that I confess my deepest sin. "I thought I was going to die. I was terrified. I stopped thinking strategically—I stopped thinking *at all*. I was panicking."

"Lizzie," she breathes. In the next moment, she's sliding into the tub, wrapping her arms around me, and pulling me close. The water that previously felt almost hostile morphs into something warm and welcoming. Because she's there with me.

I'm falling apart. I don't understand what's happening to me, only that I'm increasingly worried that it might not be reversible. I tell myself to get out of the bath and put on my clothes and go terrorize the crew so I feel more like myself. But I don't do any of that. I cling to Maeve and bury my face in the curve of her neck.

She holds me until the shakes work their way from my body. She doesn't speak. She just strokes a hand down my spine and hums a haunting melody that burrows into my brain and slowly unwinds the fear sinking its claws into me. It still takes far too long before I'm able to draw a full breath.

"They say drowning is the sweetest way to die."

I jolt. "That's a horrible fucking thing to say."

"Is it?" She allows me to ease back and there's no amusement on her face. Only an aching seriousness that makes me want to kiss her.

But I can't let that absurd statement stand. "There's no good way to die, Maeve. Only good ways to kill so you're the one to walk away from the fight."

She shrugs freckled shoulders. "All living creatures die eventually. Some just take longer than others. There's peace in knowing that."

I stare. "The idea of dying doesn't feel like peace. It feels like failure."

"It's understandable that you feel that way. You're one of the most alive people I've ever met, for all that you hide it behind a wall of ice." She smiles softly. "I'm still not certain if my mother lied to me about drowning, or if it's just something that people say because we live in a realm ruled by the sea. She claims that it's like giving in to the inevitable, to the tide, to the elements. The sea feeds us, and eventually we'll feed it right back."

I understand what she's saying in an abstract sort of way. I can rationalize the poetic justice of it, the circular rhythm to life. But it's *abhorrent* to me. Vampires don't live forever, but no one's ever been able to determine if that's because we're incapable of it or just because we're too busy killing each other off. It doesn't matter, because living forever is still the goal. It's what we strive for, the ultimate endgame. What Maeve is talking about might feel peaceful to her, but it makes me want to scream my defiance to the universe. "There is nothing peaceful about being drowned and eaten by a water horse."

Her brows draw together, a line appearing between them. "I am absolutely *not* suggesting that you should have given up and breathed in water. I wasn't going to let you die, Lizzie."

That, more than anything, gives me something besides drowning to focus on. I look at her with new eyes. I've seen her in her seal form for several days now, but I think a part of me still associated her with the helpless little seals back in my realm who are playthings for larger predators.

There was nothing helpless about her in that fight. She was violent grace incarnate, easily dodging the attacks from the water horse, managing to free me, and then snapping its neck in the space of minutes. If we hadn't been yards below the surface with the pressure closing in around me, I would've wished for the fight to go on longer just to witness her beauty. "You were amazing."

She blushes in a way that has nothing to do with the temperature of the bathwater. The rosy glow creeps up her chest and takes up residence in her round cheeks. “I couldn’t let it take you. I wasn’t thinking. I just reacted.”

Really, there’s nothing to do but kiss her. I frame her face in my hands and brush my lips against hers. The first time aboard the *Serpent’s Cry* was a frantic flurry of hands and mouths and bodies. Desire pent up for far too long, spiced with no small amount of fear.

This is different.

She sighs into my mouth and I guide her back against the side of the tub. It’s the most natural thing in the world to press my thigh to her pussy and cup her hips, urging her to grind against me. I want to feel her come apart, I want the abandon of her orgasm and to know that *I’m* the cause of it. I need her surrender more than I need my next breath.

Maybe drowning really is the sweetest way to die.

With that in mind, I kiss my way down her chest, taking the time to lavish her breasts with all the attention they deserve. Her fingers are in my hair, but Maeve makes no move to guide me. It’s as if she knows that I need this. But then, she always seems to know what I need almost before I do. I draw in a slow breath and then descend below the surface of the water, nipping and kissing her stomach and then settling between her thighs. A short time ago, the pressure of air in my lungs, knowing that my next breath was not assured, was a nightmare. Now it’s something significantly more dreamlike.

This is how I reclaim myself. By claiming *her*.

Even with the bathwater all around us, she still tastes like the sea. I lick her, enjoying the way that her thighs tense on either side of my head. Our first time together may have been a frenzy, but that doesn't mean I wasn't paying attention. I know exactly what gets my little selkie off.

I give it to her now. I press two fingers into her and focus on her clit, using the flat of my tongue to stroke her just the way she desires. Who needs breath? This isn't terrifying. This is a choice I'm making, one I will happily make again and again. She'll come before my breath runs out. I'll make sure of it.

It doesn't take long. Maeve moves against me in long, graceful motions, grinding against my tongue as she chases her pleasure with the same fervor that I do. The only thing I mourn is that I don't hear her cry as she comes. I certainly feel it, her pussy clamping around my fingers tightly enough to bruise.

And then I bite her.

Her whole body goes tight and tense, her blood salty on my tongue. I don't take much, just a few pulls, just enough to ensure that her orgasm keeps going and going.

Just enough to ensure that she'll never get over me.

I don't know where that thought came from, and I refuse to examine it as her hands tighten in my hair and she wrenches me back to the surface to kiss me, hard and messy. I can't stop touching her, gripping her big ass, stroking up her spine to clasp the back of her neck, hooking her thigh around my waist so we can get closer. Did I really think one orgasm was going to be enough? Normally I'm not such a fool.

"You make me crazed," she says between kisses. "I'm trying to *comfort* you."

I smile against her lips. "I'm feeling incredibly comforted right now. Aren't you?"

"Lizzie." Her growl makes my nipples tighten. And then her

hand is between my thighs, stroking my pleasure the same way I stroked hers. It's hard to tell because her eyes are naturally so dark, but I swear they darken further. Her lips curve as she relaxes against the side of the tub. She tilts her head to the side, baring her neck to me. "Bite me again."

"Maeve." Since we came aboard the *Serpent's Cry*, she's been eating better than she was in that little sad excuse for a sailboat, but that doesn't mean she's at full strength after going days without food and water in the wake of the storm. She doesn't heal the way a vampire does. If I drink too much, I will harm her.

"Please, Lizzie." She presses a third finger into me, scrambling my thoughts. "Do it when you're right about to come. I want us to go over the edge together."

I make a sound that's almost a laugh, but it feels like desperation. Does she understand what she's doing to me? I can't focus enough to ask. I kiss her hard, even as her clever fingers tease me closer and closer to that edge she promised. Apparently Maeve learned my body just as quickly as I learned hers. Enough to ensure that she knows exactly what I need to orgasm.

She presses her thumb to my clit. Hard. The barest edge of her nail causing a spike of pain that sends me hurtling into oblivion. In that moment, when I'm poised before falling, I strike, biting her neck. Too hard. Too deep. But I can't control myself as I'm spasming through an orgasm. I try to unclench my jaw, but she just keeps stroking me, her cries of pleasure ringing in my ears.

On and on it goes, one orgasm bleeding into another and another. Finally, I'm able to wrench my mouth from her skin, but not before her blood colors the water around us. Too much. Far too much. The cleaning spell can't keep up with it.

What have I done?

"Maeve." Her head lolls as I gather her into my arms. There's a smile on her face, but what the fuck does that mean? "Maeve. Maeve, talk to me."

"Too loud," she murmurs, her voice fading fast. "I'm fine. Everything is fine."

I don't believe her for a minute.

CHAPTER 21

Maeve

I'M HAVING A HARD TIME KEEPING MY EYES OPEN. MY BODY is heavy and there's a faint throbbing in my throat. I can feel Lizzie's distress, and the fact that she's not even trying to hide it indicates how bad this situation is. Worry barely penetrates the lethargy permeating my limbs. "I'm fine." Did I say that already? I'm not certain.

"Godsdamn it," Lizzie mutters under her breath as she sweeps me into her arms and lifts me out of the tub with no apparent effort whatsoever. Vampire strength truly is nothing to underestimate.

She carries me to the bed and lays me down on the newly cleaned sheets. "Maeve. Talk to me."

My neck aches in time with the slow thud of my heart. I'm aware of what went wrong. I knew what was happening while she was biting me, and I didn't care. I didn't want the pleasure to stop. Not mine. Not hers. But last time she bit me, I don't think she took more than a mouthful or two. This time was different.

My pleasure went on and on, cresting repeatedly as she took my throat. "Just give me a few minutes. I just need to close my eyes—"

"Maeve." The snap in her voice forces my lids open despite the exhaustion weighing them down. She crouches next to me, naked and glorious and absolutely perfect. If not for the panic flaring in her dark eyes.

Another time, I might be delighted by the fact that she's actually emoting. Right now, I can't quite bring myself to enjoy it. "Lizzie." My voice is too faint. Distantly, I'm aware that Lizzie might have cause for panic. I heal faster than a human, but only marginally. I can absolutely succumb to blood loss. And she wasn't careful this time. She was too busy coming on my fingers.

"Under no circumstances are you to go to sleep. Do you understand me?"

I study her beautiful face, taking in the tense line of her mouth and the tightness around her eyes. "Are you worried about me?"

She snaps her teeth, which draws my attention to the fact that there's still blood dried on the edge of her mouth. *My* blood. A tremor works through me, and I couldn't begin to say if it's the echoes of pleasure or concern. The concern isn't for me. I feel too good to worry about the consequences of our actions. No, it's all for Lizzie, who's unraveling before my eyes.

I knew better than to escalate things when she was feeling so off-center. She needed comfort, not a distraction. Her control never would've wavered otherwise. And yet . . . there's a small, secret part of me that delights in the fact that I caused her to lose control. *Me*. Maeve.

Not anyone else. Sure as fuck not Evelyn.

"This ship has to have a fucking medic. Don't you dare go to sleep. Keep your eyes open. I will be right back."

"Lizzie." I brush her arm with a listless hand. "You're naked."

She snarls at me, the sound more animalistic than anything I can make, even in my seal form. And then she's gone, only the banging of the door against the wall an indication of her passage. I hear her yelling on deck for a medic. I don't know how to tell her that I don't think this ship has one. Or if they do, it's unlikely the person will be anywhere as skilled in healing as what we'd find on a Cŵn Annwn ship.

I'll be fine. Probably. I've never felt this woozy from blood loss, but I've never lost this much blood before. I tend to keep it inside my body. Bodies are good for that.

My thoughts' strange spiral should worry me, but it feels like too much effort to dredge up any amount of concern.

Sometime later, whether seconds or minutes or even an hour, Lizzie returns, dragging Rin behind her. Ze looks terrified; zir skin is a mottled yellow that edges onto white. The color gets even paler when ze looks at me. "I told you. We don't have a medic. We just do the best we can in between ports."

Lizzie flings zir at me. "I don't give a fuck. Fix her."

"You're the vampire. Dealing with blood loss is something that you've experienced more than I have," Rin snaps. "If she hasn't died already, she probably just needs rest and fluids. Which *you* can give her. You don't need me for it."

I open my mouth to tell Lizzie to dial back her rage. She's terrifying the poor person, and ze hasn't done anything wrong. But the room is swirling strangely in my vision. "I think I'm going to pass out now."

The last thing I see before darkness takes me are Lizzie's and Rin's panicked expressions as they both rush to the bed. Lizzie is, in fact, still naked.

I DON'T KNOW HOW LONG I SLEEP. BUT WHEN I WAKE, MY mouth feels like it's grown fuzz and my head pounds as if someone's taken a knife and pried my skull open. I try to shift, but my body chooses that moment to scream in protest. I try to speak, but all I'm capable of is a faint groan.

Gentle hands catch me behind the head and lift me just enough as they press a cup to my lips. "Drink." Lizzie sounds as exhausted as I feel. That's not a good sign.

But the water is cool and perfect on my tongue, and so I sip it eagerly. Far too soon, she takes it away. When I make a sound of protest, she says, "Go slow."

I finally manage to peel my lids open and immediately wish I hadn't. The low light of the cabin pierces my eyes. "I feel like death."

"Death didn't take you this time."

I manage to twist my head enough to see Lizzie hunched over on a stool next to the bed. She looks like shit. Her hair hangs in tangles, obviously never combed after our bath, and her skin has gone waxy in a way that suggests it's been some time since she ate. Which means it's been some time since I was awake. "How long?"

"Two. Days." She lifts the cup to my lips again, and I carefully sip a little bit more water. "We are *never* doing that again."

It says something about my state of mind that I immediately want to argue with her. Yes, things got out of control, but that doesn't mean that they will every time. We spent an entire day and night together the first time we had sex, and I only woke with a faint headache in the morning. That little pain was far outweighed by the heavy memory of pleasure that still throbbed through my body.

Without thinking, I grab her wrist, panic bleating at the back of my throat. "What do you mean we're never doing that again?"

"You saved my life, comforted me when I was falling apart, and the only thanks I gave you was almost killing you."

I drag in a breath to argue, but force myself to slow down and study her. This woman looks nothing like the Lizzie I've come to know in our short time together. There's no hint of her icy exterior, no suggestion of her perfect poise. She looks almost fragile. Brittle. As if one strong word might shatter her.

It scares the shit out of me. "Lizzie, I'm okay."

Her mouth curves, but not like anything is funny. "It's so purely *you* that you would try to comfort me when you just woke up from a coma. I have been dribbling water and broth down your throat for two days, Maeve. You don't get to tell me that you're okay. We make port in Drash in a few days. The first thing we're doing when we reach the island is take you to a proper medic. A healer."

I don't have much experience with healers beyond those that live in Viedna. Their specialty is specifically my people. Ours is a particular flavor of magic that takes a careful hand to coax. The rules for normal shifters don't quite apply, so we don't tend to go to others for help when there's an injury or sickness.

But all it takes is one look at Lizzie's face to know that any argument will be met with a brick wall. She wants me to see a healer, and so she will drag me there even if I'm kicking and screaming in protest. The very thought of fighting exhausts me, which is enough to make me worry that she's right. That maybe we shouldn't do this again.

No. I refuse to accept that. We only have a short time together, and I'm not about to waste it just because we lost control once. I was an active participant. I could have pushed her away and she would've gone. Instead, I held her closer and drove her pleasure higher, knowing that it fractured her control in the process.

"I'm sorry," I finally say.

She snarls at me. "Don't you dare apologize to me. There's only one person to blame, and it's not you."

We can circle this conversation over and over again, but we're not going to get anywhere in our current positions. Better to get out of this cabin for a little while. To gain some perspective. To remind ourselves why we're here in the first place. I've reclaimed my skin, but Lizzie is still without her family heirlooms.

A perverse part of me wants to do exactly the opposite. Every step closer to retrieving her stolen items is another step closer to losing her. I want to pull her close and do whatever it takes to lose ourselves in each other until we forget all about her mission to reclaim those jewels and return home. Until she realizes that her mother is a monster who doesn't have to maintain a hold on her. Lizzie could be happy here in Threshold, I think.

Maybe she could even be happy with me.

I don't say the words aloud. She won't be receptive to them right now, not with guilt riding her so hard. I suspect that Lizzie has never felt guilty once in her life, and therefore has no immunity to the sensation. Something to unpack later, perhaps.

"If I ask for a bath, are you going to lose it completely?"

She glares at me, but her expression falls into one that I'm more familiar with: complete arrogance. "I won't lose control again."

I examine the gauntlet that she just threw at my feet and tuck it away for later use. Just like our current argument. "In that case, I feel awful, and I think getting clean would help."

My bath is significantly less eventful than the last one, but I do feel like a completely different person by the time I've pulled clean clothes on. Lizzie even takes the opportunity to dunk herself a few times. She looks more like the vampire I know once she's pulled on her pants and shirt and laced up her boots. But the air of brittleness remains.

It doesn't fade as the days tick by and my strength slowly returns. I still feel like I've been run over by a water horse, but I'm steadily improving. Lizzie hovers over me like a mother bird protecting her chicks, though I know better than to point it out or complain. She's worried about me, and even as I start to chafe under that worry, it warms my heart to know she cares.

Three days later, we emerge on deck to find Drash looming before us. I've only read about this place. Its towering cliffs seem to reach into the sky and offer no entrance. We sail along the south coast, and I'm increasingly confused about how we'll reach the port . . . if there even is one. This island is essentially a tower, though one built by nature rather than people.

Alix guides us into an opening that I never would've noticed on my own, so narrow that I could reach out and touch the cliff walls as we pass. After a few minutes, we sail into a remarkably large bay. There are a handful of other ships here, and I exhale in relief when I note that the sails are mundane white. Not Cŵn Annwn. Perfect.

The village itself is built into tiers that rise up along the cliff face, round windows and doors carved into the rock, giving an indication of how many people live here. More than I could have guessed on our circuit of the perimeter. I stare up and up and up, counting easily a dozen tiers reaching well over a hundred feet, nearly to the top of the cliffs.

Rin moves to stand next to me, zir scales a nice healthy green. Ze flicks zir tongue at me in a way I've come to learn is how ze gathers more information about zir environment. "You're looking better."

"I'm feeling better, too." I shoot a glance at Lizzie out of the corner of my eye, but she's got her head close to Alix's and is discussing something in a soft voice. Even so, I feel her attention on me. It's not a heated thing, more that she believes I'll collapse at any moment and is poised to spring to catch me. It's comforting and disconcerting all at the same time. "Thank you for your help before. I know that wasn't easy for you."

"It's fine." Ze shrugs. "The crew likes you quite a bit. The vampire might scare the shit out of us, but it's obvious you hold her leash. We have a vested interest in keeping you alive."

Hold Lizzie's leash? Zir statement almost makes me laugh. There's no one holding that vampire's leash. I can barely keep her from murdering everyone she comes across who slightly inconveniences her. But I don't challenge Rin as we drop anchor and the crew gathers round.

Alix gives out orders, designating four people to stay with the ship and the rest to go ashore. They turn and look at me and

Lizzie. "We have some trading to do here, since we don't come up this way often. We have no intention of leaving without you, so you're more than welcome to do whatever errands you need to while we're here. You can find me in the tavern when you're done with your business."

I glance at Lizzie. Does she realize what progress she must have made for them not to toss us overboard and take off the moment they have the chance? Impossible to say. Her expression is perfectly locked down, even when she looks at me. It couldn't be clearer that she intends to distance herself from me.

Well, that's not going to work for me. I got a taste of what it could be like to really be with her, and I'll be damned before she slams that door in my face out of fear. It would be one thing if she didn't want me, but the barrier now standing between us is guilt and fear. Unacceptable. We have so little time left together that I'm determined not to waste it. I'm going to knock down that barrier the first chance I get.

I'm going to seduce myself a vampire.

CHAPTER 22

Lizzie

I BARELY HAVE THE SPACE TO WORRY ABOUT THIS NEW village and these new people because I'm too busy worrying about Maeve. Drash is more city than village, though I've never been in a city I could see in a single glance. It reminds me of the natural amphitheaters that exist in my realm, but so much more intentional. Later, I'll be curious. Right now, I'm focused on getting Maeve to a healer.

She keeps telling me she's fine, as if she didn't spend two full days unconscious. Vampire blood can heal, but in my experience, there are plenty of supernatural creatures who would rather die than take it. Sometimes there are adverse effects. Sometimes unintended paranormal consequences. I don't know enough about selkies, let alone selkies in Threshold, to risk it. Hurting Maeve more than I already have is unacceptable.

I've never really worried about hurting people before. I don't like the sensation. I hate how helpless it makes me feel. But the alternative is walking away, and that's even more unacceptable.

I cup Maeve's elbow, ignoring her sharp look, and help her onto the dock. Not that she seems to need much assistance, but guilt is riding me hard, and I manage to put distance between us. "Let's find you a healer."

"That is absolutely not necessary." She covers my hand with hers, her eyes concerned. "Have you fed since . . . ?"

"No." I barely left her side for the last five days. I hadn't *wanted* to leave her side. I couldn't shake the fear that if I wasn't there to measure each inhale and exhale, each beat of her heart, that both might . . . stop.

"Lizzie, you have to feed."

I have the strangest urge to shuffle my feet and drop my eyes. Even stranger is the desire to dig in my heels. Hurting Maeve scared the shit out of me. I don't know if I can bring myself to bite her again, but the thought of biting someone else fills me with unease. It's a silly reaction. It makes absolutely no sense. I don't know a single vampire who is perfectly monogamous. Even if they are sexually, they certainly aren't when it comes to their bites. Even being in a long-term relationship with some fast-healing supernatural, there might be times when it's simply not feasible that they're your only source of blood. Now, with Maeve, who almost died because of me, the concept is unthinkable.

So why haven't I asked one of the crew to step in? I could say that most of them are still terrified of me and would rather toss themselves into the sea than allow me near them, but that's not quite the truth. It barely registered that I should ask in the first place. Hunger is a gnawing monster inside me, but it's one that I've dealt with before. Conquered before.

I'll conquer it this time, too.

"Lizzie." Maeve tightens her grip on my arm. "Let's talk about this."

"There's nothing to talk about." I try to pick up my pace, but I pull up short when I realize she's not doing the same. I've never had conflicting urges to conquer and protect inside me. Not even with Evelyn, whom I cared about more than I thought possible. Funny how I have to remind myself of that now. Funny how what I experience with Maeve has eclipsed that feeling in every way. Except it's not funny. Not even a little bit.

I'm thinking myself in circles, and it's making me want to scream. This isn't what I do. I pick a direction and go, annihilating anything in my path. There's no room for questioning, no room for doubt. And yet that seems to be all I'm capable of currently.

It's a testament to how much better Maeve is feeling that she digs in her heels the moment we leave the dock. "If you want me to go to a healer, then we're going to talk about this. Now."

I snap at her, even as my mind wonders what the fuck I'm doing. I'm no animal, to bear my teeth when I'm frustrated, and yet I seem to be devolving with every day I spend in this gods-forsaken realm. I step closer, crowding into Maeve's space. Her regular bathing has washed away the scent of sickness—of weakness—leaving only her. It makes my mouth water.

Back up. Give her some space. I can't quite make my body obey the command. "What's to stop me from throwing you over my shoulder and taking you to a damned healer, Maeve? We both know I can overpower you."

"Yes, you can." She doesn't so much as flinch. "But you're not going to do that. Not with me. Not anymore. So you can agree to talk to me, and I can agree to respect your concern and see a healer, or we can get into a screaming match right here in public."

I glance around. It's midday, the sun a pulsing sphere of fire overhead that makes me sweat, but it hasn't deterred the crowds coming to and from the port. The locals seem to dress in flowing robes and veils that protect their faces from the scorching sun overhead. They mingle with people from dozens of different islands. Sailors are easy enough to pick out in their sun-bleached fabrics and suntanned skins. People from the Three Sisters wear their expensive fabrics and carry an air of pretentiousness. There are others in garb that's unfamiliar to me. People from islands that I have yet to visit.

A month ago, I wouldn't be experiencing the curiosity that flows through me despite my current argument with Maeve. I wouldn't be wondering what their home islands are like or where in Threshold they come from. I certainly wouldn't be having the faintest desire to visit and find out for myself. I hardly recognize myself anymore.

But Maeve is right—we're attracting too much attention. I turn back to her and lower my head until I'm speaking directly into her ear. "Fine. Have it your way. But we *will* be seeing the healer first. If you submit and let them help you, then we'll have that discussion you're so keen on. Do you understand me?"

"As long as you understand that there will be no distracting me from the conversation itself." There's no give in her voice, and the steel I find there sends a thrill through me despite my concern for her.

"So be it." I take her hand and start toward the nearest staircase carved into the cliffside. As we get closer, I'm relieved to see a lift that appears to be powered by magic. Good. Maeve might be feeling better, but if we have to climb more than one level, it will put too much stress on her body. I veer toward the lift, pretending that I don't hear Maeve's huff of irritation. She can be mad if she wants, but I *am* looking out for her best interests. Even if she doesn't appreciate it.

The person at the lift is dressed head to toe in shades of vibrant purple. Only their eyes are visible, deep orange orbs that give little indication to the type of person hidden beneath the clothing.

Conscious of the irritated selkie at my back, I decide not to make matters worse by being an asshole. I can't quite manage a smile, but I keep my tone polite. "Can you direct us to a healer?" After a pause, I add, "Please."

Like everyone else in Threshold, the translation spell I acquired upon entry seems to work with them. They take me in and glance at Maeve. It's everything I can do not to step sideways to prevent them from looking at her. My reaction doesn't even make sense. They're hardly threatening.

They point one gloved finger upward. "Three levels. Go right. Look for the door with roses on the mantel overhead."

"Thanks." Whoever this healer is, they'd better be good. No doubt, the locals keep the most skilled healers to themselves, far away from sailors and tourists. It's what I would do. If I have to, I'll track down one of those fuckers, but it would piss Maeve off more, so I truly hope it won't come to that.

We take the lift up three levels as directed and follow the instructions to the curved doorway with roses carved and painted along the mantel frame. Up until this point, Maeve seemed content to let me take the lead, but as I raise my hand to knock on the faded white wood, she steps in front of me. "I'll take it from here."

"Maeve."

"Lizzie," she mimics my irritation. "If your glaring face is the first thing the healer sees upon opening the door, they're liable to slam it right in your face. Let me do the talking."

"As long as you're honest about how you're feeling and what happened." I'm not used to this guilt. I don't know how to combat it. I don't even know if I have the desire to combat it. I've killed so many people over the course of my life, and never spared a thought to who they were or what their hopes and dreams may have been. Or even who they left behind. I've hurt countless others with the same lack of care.

But there is no lack of care when it comes to Maeve. I catch myself staring at her face, clocking the exact tone of her skin to ensure that she's feeling well. Of measuring the steady beat of her heart for any irregularities. Every time I blink, I see her in that bed, too pale, too still, too lacking in the vivacity that makes Maeve *Maeve*.

Because of me. Because I lost control and almost damaged someone that I have grown to—*No*. There's no use following that train of thought to its natural conclusion.

I step back and allow Maeve to knock gently on the door. A few moments later, a robed figure, this time in light gray, opens it. They have orange eyes as well, though they are faded to a pale color and lined on each side with age. "A vampire and a selkie. What a strange combination. Come in."

Maeve and I exchange a look. There are plenty of paranormals who can clock me at a glance, but her? With her pelt tucked carefully into her bag, she could be anyone. I have the strangest desire to turn around and hustle Maeve away, but after making such a big deal about getting her to a healer, there's nothing I can do but follow her inside.

This, at least, is familiar. I may not recognize all the herbs and jars and miscellaneous paraphernalia in the cabinets lining the walls around the room, but I recognize the sensation of a healer's place. It doesn't matter what the culture, what the variety of paranormal, what the time or space or anything else—all these spaces have a vaguely similar feel. Dim and soothing and scented with whatever herbs are designed to relax nervous patients. Most people find it comforting. It makes me want to crawl right out of my skin.

Vampires heal at an exponential rate. All I need to recover from even a mortal wound is blood. We don't have much use for healers, and there's a complicated history there where a number of them would very much like to poke and prod us to find out if our healing powers can be applied to others in their care.

Personally, I take exception to being poked and prodded.

I stick close to Maeve as we step into the room and follow the healer's urging to sit on the wide stone bench in the center. They move to stand before us and clasp their hands in front of them. It's then that I notice the hands themselves, gnarled with age and containing an extra knuckle on each finger. "I'm Rose. Tell me what brought you here today."

Maeve puts her hand on my thigh before I can say anything. It's just as well. She gives the healer a sweet smile. "My friend here was a little overzealous in her bite and took too much blood. I'm feeling fine, but it would reassure her if you would check me over."

"She was unconscious for two days," I snap.

Rose turns those eyes on me, and it feels like she sees things that I have no intention of sharing. "More than a little overzealous, then."

Shame heats my skin, but I meet her gaze steadily. "It won't happen again."

Rose shrugs. "Young love and lust often make fools of us all. You've seen the consequences of that loss of control." She moves to Maeve and motions with those delicate fingers. "May I?"

Maeve lifts her hand and places it in Rose's. The healer does something that makes the air sizzle around us. Defining the nature of the magic isn't a skill set I have, but I've been around long enough that I can often figure it out from context clues. Not this time. Instead, I watch Maeve closely, watch for any signs of discomfort or pain.

Instead, she looks almost peaceful. When Rose releases her hand and steps back, Maeve even smiles. Rose clears her throat. "It's just as you say. There's nothing else amiss. She just needs plenty of fluids and rest, and a proper meal wouldn't hurt."

Maeve turns to me with a victorious smile. "See, I told you so."

"We can discuss this later." I rise and reclaim her hand. "What do I owe you?"

"Consider it a gesture of goodwill." Rose waves away my offer of payment. "I did nothing but the diagnosis, and that hardly took the time that it cost you to take the lift up to me. You can be on your way."

It's as clear a dismissal as I've ever heard. I start to turn toward the door but pause. "Thank you." The words feel odd on my tongue. "I appreciate you taking the time to help us."

Maeve's smile is brilliant enough to chase away my discomfort at my politeness. Being vicious and cold has always helped me attain my goals. I've never tried being nice. I don't know how. But I've made my selkie happy, and that's more than reason enough to consider doing it again. "Come on. Let's find you some food."

CHAPTER 23

Maeve

IT DOESN'T TAKE LONG FOR US TO FIND A LITTLE RESTAURANT one level down from the healer's residence. Its entrance is a bright yellow with various plates of food and fizzy-looking drinks painted on it. Inside, it's cozy, all domed ceilings and sturdy furniture. The bartender is dressed in a dizzying robe that shifts color depending on their movement and the light. They immediately point us to a quiet table for two in the back corner.

We gave most of the riches in the captain's quarters of the *Serpent's Cry* to the crew to ensure goodwill, but we kept enough that we won't have to worry about paying for things for a little while. If I can find someone working with the rebellion on Drash, I can make that money stretch further, but that's down on my list of priorities at the moment.

I manage to keep my patience until I've eaten the bowl of soup—a delicious mix of shellfish and root vegetables—to head off Lizzie's concern that I have enough nourishment. We need to have a serious conversation, but we won't manage it if we're bickering about my growling stomach.

I didn't expect her to be so protective the moment I got hurt, and I certainly didn't expect it to last days after I woke up. She's *hovering.* Maybe later I'll relish the knowledge that she cares enough to worry, but right now I want to shake her until the Lizzie I've come to know returns.

Once my spoon scrapes the bottom of the bowl, I set it down and give her a pointed stare. "No more putting this off. We're talking now."

Lizzie swirls the wine in her cup, her expression carefully blank. "I'm listening."

I fight not to grind my teeth in frustration. I've been *trying* to talk to her since the moment I woke up. Why listen to reason when she can continue lashing herself with guilt? I don't have high hopes that she's *listening* now. I take a deep breath and strive to keep my voice even. "Don't you think you're overreacting?"

She finally lifts her gaze to mine, her dark eyes going so cold that I shiver. "What part of *you almost died* do you not understand, Maeve? There was a point where you went to sleep and I didn't think you'd wake up again. So no, I don't think I'm overreacting."

I grab onto my patience with both hands and do my best to not yell in her face. "This is a discussion you should have with me instead of making unilateral decisions that affect both of us. You hardly attacked me in the bath. I climbed in of my own volition, and I'm the one who drove you past the point of desire until you forgot yourself. More than that, I *knew* that you were emotionally distraught after your experience with the kelpie, and I still allowed us to get out of control. It took two of us to reach that point, and you need to acknowledge that. I'm not an innocent victim that you attacked in the middle of the night. I chose that, Lizzie. I chose *you*."

"You chose that? You chose *me*?" She lets out a laugh that's too loud and too harsh. It turns the heads of several people in our nearby space, and she leans closer and lowers her voice. "You don't even know what you're saying. Did you know that you would spend the next two days unconscious when you offered up your neck to me?"

Of course not. Of course I had no idea that things would spiral to that level. But if she'd told me that was a possibility, I don't know that I would have cared. I was too far gone—just like she was. If I was anyone else, *I* could have hurt *her*.

Maybe I . . . *did* hurt her.

I stare at Lizzie, taking in the sharp little movements that she makes as she fidgets, the lines bracketing her mouth that haven't gone away even though I'm feeling closer to my old self than ever. How many times today have I thought about the fact that I hardly recognize her like this? It took two of us to get to that point. She ignored that she was taking too much, and I ignored that she was emotionally fragile in the first place.

I clear my throat. "I'm sorry."

She jolts hard enough to rattle our cups on the table. "What do you have to apologize for?"

"If I hadn't climbed in the tub with you while you were off-center because of what had happened with the water horse, I don't think you would've lost control like that. I worried you. More than that, I worried you when you were already in an emotionally vulnerable place."

"You're wrong." She narrows her eyes. "This is something that happens with bloodline vampires from time to time. Biting you feels almost as good as it does to be bitten by me. Sometimes we forget ourselves. Sometimes we hurt people."

I know I should be horrified that she's hurt people, but I'm more concerned with how defeated she seems. "You wouldn't hurt me on purpose."

Her mouth flattens. "I *did* hurt you. Intent matters less than the results. You almost died. It won't happen again."

"But what if I want it to?" The question's out before I can call it back, and I wouldn't anyways. "As I said before, it took two of us to get in that situation, and I think it's more than fair that the two of us come to a decision about how we move forward."

She plants her hands on the table. "You can make all the statements you want, Maeve." She speaks slowly, each word enunciated clearly. "But ultimately it doesn't matter if it took two of us to get to that point or if I am solely responsible, because I *almost killed you* and I will not do it again. You can make your own choices with your safety and health, but you can't force me to bite you."

I want to keep arguing, but it's coming from a selfish place. We had finally reached a point where it felt good to be there. With her in my bed, comfortable enough to do all the things that we both wanted to do. To have newly created distance between us feels wrong. It's only a matter of time before she returns to her realm; I don't want to lose another minute with Lizzie.

If she harmed me, then I harmed her right back. The evidence of it has already been cataloged. If I was a better person, I would allow her to retreat instead of clinging to her with all my strength. A month ago, I would have said I *was* a better person. It turns out . . . I'm not. "What if we compromise?"

She glares at me. "If you're about to suggest that I bite you—"

"I want that, but I understand if you're not ready for it." I keep talking, even when she's obviously about to protest that she'll never be ready. I desperately don't want her to say those words out loud, because then they might be true.

I want Lizzie, with or without her bite. If that means that I have to sit by while other people orgasm as a result . . . it hurts to think about, but she's not mine. More than that, if she was, I would be a terrible partner to demand that she starve herself to appease my jealousy. "Do you still want me?"

"What kind of question is that? Yes, I still want you. That's what got us into this situation to begin with."

Relief makes my shoulders sag for a moment. Hearing her confirm her desire comforts the part of me that's been on edge since I woke up. Lizzie may be a lot of things, but she's not a liar. I can trust her when she tells me she wants me. I want to trust her. "I still want you, too. You need to eat, and if you won't bite me, then you need to pick someone else."

She watches me closely, as if sensing a trap and not being able to define the parameters of it. "You're okay with that? With me biting someone else?"

No. Yes. I don't know. I want to be okay with it if my approval is what she needs. We have such a short time together, and we've already wasted days of it with this nonsense. Granted, I don't think Lizzie would qualify it as such, but I'm not in the mood to admit she might be right.

"I have no claim on you," I finally say, but the words are stilted and wrong.

Lizzie leans forward, expression intent. "Do you want a claim on me?"

Does she understand what she's asking? The implications? Of course I want a claim on her. I haven't known her nearly long enough to justify the strength of my feelings, but I want her at my side in whatever way I can manage, for as long as I can manage. "You're leaving. You were always going to leave."

"Yes," she says slowly. "But there's not a deadline in place. It could be weeks—or months or years. Threshold is large enough to lose a ship for that long and longer. I'm bound to find those family heirlooms and return them to their proper place, but I think we're getting a little ahead of ourselves if we start acting like I'm going home tomorrow."

Every bit of that statement is full of contradictions. She almost sounds like she doesn't want to find the *Crimson Hag* at all, but that can't possibly be right. Her only goal since arriving on Threshold has been reclaiming the jewels stolen from her.

She might care for me—and her reaction to taking too much blood cannot be construed as anything other than caring—but I have no illusions about what that means. She cared for Evelyn, too, and she still chased her across the realms with the intent to kill her and retrieve the stolen items. I can't count on Lizzie's caring being enough to combat the loyalty she feels to her family, no matter how toxic they seem from the little bits she's shared.

I would be a fool to read into her words for anything other than what she intends. Which is to leave. No matter what she says, it won't take years to find the *Crimson Hag*. If we're not able to track them down in the next week or two, then we'll travel to Lyari and wait for them there. All of the Cŵn Annwn are required to stop in at some point during the year to report to the Council. Even if we missed the *Crimson Hag* when we initially arrived, it would be less than a year before they returned—sooner if the Council had reason to summon them.

But I don't say any of that out loud.

Lizzie's fingers twitch as if she wants to reach for my hand but stops herself. "Do you want a claim on me, Maeve?" she asks again.

Some long-buried instinct demands that I do anything to avoid baring even a portion of my heart to this woman, who's destined to break it. But I've never been a coward, and I won't start now. No matter the consequences. I tell the truth. "Yes."

At my soft word, she finally moves, hooking the edge of my chair with her foot and dragging me around the side of the table to her. She laces my fingers with hers and lifts them to her lips to press a soft kiss to my knuckles. "Then we find a way through."

So much contained in that single sentence. I know better than to hope, and yet hope flutters in my chest all the same. It's tempting to seek reassurances, but it wouldn't be fair to ask her for them. Lizzie has none to give me.

Instead, I focus on the problem in front of us. "You need to feed."

"I won't—"

Feed from me. "I know." I hold up a hand. "But the fact remains that you do need to."

Lizzie shifts in her seat. "You know the nature of my bite. I have no intention of taking anyone else to bed, but there's no way to control the side effect. Perhaps I'm getting ahead of myself in demanding exclusivity, but the thought of you with someone else makes me want to bathe the room in blood. And I don't want anyone but you."

Gods, does she know what her words do to me? The longer our conversation goes on, the more of the old Lizzie I see, as if she's drawing her coldness around her like a barrier. Part of me mourns the loss, and yet I find it reassuring all the same. There's still warmth lingering in her dark eyes. Warmth that's just for *me*. Somehow, that makes it all the more special.

"What if . . . we find a compromise?"

"I'm listening."

I take a deep breath. "There must be a brothel or three in Drash. You can explain your needs, and I imagine one of the people there will agree to feed you. If I'm in the room, maybe it won't be so upsetting." There's every possibility that it will be even *more* upsetting to watch someone else come apart in her arms, all while wishing it was me. But if I'm not there, I'll wonder. It's unfair in the extreme—I can acknowledge that—but it's the truth. "Maybe I'm asking too much."

Lizzie's lips curve and her smile warms even more. "I like that you're asking it. I like that you're jealous." She leans in, her breath ghosting against the sensitive space behind my ear. "After I feed, I fully intend to reacquaint myself with every inch of your body. How does that sound?"

I can't quite draw a full breath. My heart thrums in my chest and my skin heats in anticipation. I clear my throat. "That sounds good. Really, really good."

CHAPTER 24

Lizzie

I'M NOT CERTAIN THAT I EVER ACTUALLY AGREE TO Maeve's proposal. One moment, we're sitting close at the dinner table and I'm inhaling her sea scent, and the next, I find myself in a brothel, her hand linked with mine. Like all the other buildings in Drash, the brothel is carved into the cliff face, its doorway painted a deep violet so dark as to almost be black. The designs are subtle, a shade lighter than the violet, all of night-blooming flowers.

As we step inside, the temperature is several degrees cooler than the outside. It's honestly a clever design that doesn't require the use of magic, and a welcome relief from the heat that makes my clothes stick to my skin. The stone insulates from both hot and cold, keeping the building nicely temperate. The main room looks similar enough to brothels everywhere, the lights kept low, sensual music playing low enough to allow for each conversation, and a bar with free-flowing drinks.

The place is packed, most of the low round tables filled with patrons. I identify humans, several lizard folk like Rin, and many who are obviously citizens of islands I have yet to visit. Living as long as I have, I thought I'd seen all there was to see of people, both paranormal and not. Coming to Threshold has more than proven me wrong.

Robed locals move through the tables, some with drinks, some leaning down to flirt with the patrons. Their robes are every color of the rainbow—and some I have no name for—and at least half of them are sheer enough to tease at the bodies beneath the fabric. The glimpses I get show bodies that are humanoid, but the proportions are slightly different, their limbs slightly longer and leaner.

Another time, I might find this whole experience a revelation. Right now, I'm too twisted up inside to enjoy the fact that Threshold makes me feel small in a strangely comforting way.

Maeve watches me expectantly, waiting for me to take the lead. I'm still not sure this is a good idea. I've shared partners in the past, have indulged in all manner of acts with both sex and blood. When you live long enough, the taboo ceases to exist, and "good" and "bad" are purely a metric of what feels good and what the people involved enjoy.

But I don't want to hurt her. Not again. Her solution of me biting someone else circumvents the physical hurt, but that doesn't mean it won't emotionally harm her. It's not something I've ever really worried about with a partner, and now I can't stop analyzing the possibility from every angle. I already dimmed Maeve's light with my carelessness. I desperately don't want to do it again.

"Relax." Maeve brushes her fingertips over my knuckles. "It's going to be okay."

Ironic that she's the one comforting me. It's a testament to what kind of person she is. When we first met, all I could focus on was the strength in her, the unwillingness to roll over and admit defeat. Now? Her softness is just as appealing. She's filled with layers that I want to delve into and discover for myself. I have a feeling I could spend years at her side and still not have plumbed the full depths of what she's capable of.

But we don't have years.

The reminder sours my mood even further. "This is a terrible idea."

"No, it's really not. We need to question people who may have seen the *Crimson Hag*, but we can't do that if you're ready to rip out someone's throat at the smallest inconvenience. You'll feel better after you feed."

She's managing me, but I'm not certain if she's wrong. Hunger is a dull throb inside me, hollowing me out and shortening my temper—which wasn't great to begin with. I slump back in my chair and wave a careless hand at the robed people flitting between tables. "Fine. Pick one and do your negotiations."

She frowns at me. "Don't you want to pick?"

The only one I want is Maeve. Saying as much will only give her the wrong idea. I have no intention of drinking from her again. No matter how much my tongue aches for her taste, it's not going to happen. It's too dangerous. Telling her that will give her hope she can bring me around to her way of thinking. I can't allow it to happen. More than that, I don't want to waste what time we have left together by fighting.

"I'd rather you pick," I finally say. Past partners have preferred not to be in the room if I feed on someone else. The sexual nature of my bite makes it too difficult for them if they're not actively involved. I'm not certain about Maeve's insistence that she's fine with it.

But the truth is that I don't want her anywhere else. I don't want to bite anyone else. At least if she's in the room, it doesn't feel like I'm closing her out and creating more distance between us. It's not something that I've ever had to worry about before, and now it's all I can think of.

True to form, Maeve gives this the same level of consideration she seems to give everything. She chats with a few of the employees of the brothel, making easy conversation even as I grow tenser and tenser. I just want to get this over with, but it feels wrong to rush it after I asked her to take the lead.

Finally, she makes her decision. "Hyacinth, I would love to make you a proposition."

Hyacinth is a lean woman with sheer purple robes that display her lithe form, giving hints of a graceful body while shielding the majority of her from sight. It's an artful display of flirtation that she maximizes to her benefit. She sits on the arm of Maeve's chair, curling one of her red strands of hair around her finger.

I want to bite that fucking finger off.

Hyacinth leans closer, her deep coral eyes lighting up with interest. "I won't lie, the conversation has been lovely, but I'm eager to hear your proposition." Insinuation laces every word, making them borderline obscene. She's very good at her job, and she seems to enjoy it, but it's impossible to say if that's reality or just part of the act.

I want to be anywhere else, but I force myself to sit still and silent as Maeve outlines our request. From the way Hyacinth goes still, it's not a normal one. No surprise there. I haven't encountered any other vampires in Threshold, so there's no reason that a bite being part of the proposition would enter into anyone's mind.

Hyacinth turns those seductive eyes my way. "Is it true? Your bite is orgasmic?"

"Yes."

Maeve gives me a sharp look at the harshness of my tone, but I ignore it. She smiles up at Hyacinth. "What do you say?"

"You understand that this is not a normal request. I need to speak with the owner. We don't typically do contracts for the night, but I suspect that she will want one for this instance. Are you agreeable to that?"

Maeve smiles, the very picture of sweetness. "Of course. Whatever works best."

"I'll be right back."

Hyacinth rises gracefully and weaves through the tables to the bar, where a short woman in robes tends the drinks. The madam, obviously. I don't get a chance to do more than glimpse her before Maeve is scooting her chair closer and leaning against me. "Stop glaring at everyone, or they'll worry you're going to murder her. If they tell us no, there will be no feeding, and we'll be right back where we started."

"Maybe that's for the best."

"Lizzie." The snap in the word turns me to face her despite myself. I blink. She's furious, her brows drawn together and the color high in her freckled cheeks. "Not too long ago, you told me to snap out of my self-pity. Now I'm doing the same to you. We can argue in circles about whether you intended to hurt me and what that means for the future—later. Right now, you need to feed, and Hyacinth is willing. So we're going to go up to that room and you're going to bite her and take just enough blood to sustain you and not hurt her. And then we'll send her on her way, well paid and well satisfied. Do you understand me?"

Warmth blooms in my chest, coursing lower. I might love this woman. Soft and sweet, harsh and commanding. The very picture of contradictions. Right now, she's willing to watch me with another person to ensure that my needs are met. She's practically bullying me to make it happen.

I cup her face with my hand, drawing her closer. "I understand."

Maeve opens her mouth as if she expected me to argue but stops short. She frowns. "Good. Well—"

"Just like I understand that if we're paying for the room for the night, *we* will be utilizing it."

She blinks those inky eyes at me. Her lips part, a perfect rosebud O. "What?"

"I don't believe I need to repeat myself. Do I?" I stroke my thumb across her cheekbone and down to her jaw. It's a tragedy that I haven't had a chance to map the freckles on her body with my mouth. There hasn't been time, or opportunity. After that first night, we could hardly stay locked away in the cabin of the *Serpent's Cry*. The crew would have absolutely mutinied.

And what happened in the bath was just as frenzied.

"The crew is drinking themselves silly right now. In the morning, they're going to be lazing about and moaning over their headaches. I have some thoughts about what happens next, but I need to speak with Alix and Rin first. If we stay in Drash for a few days, it will give us plenty of opportunity to ask our questions. But we don't have to start tonight."

I don't think she quite realizes she's leaning into my touch.

This woman puts her trust in me again and again, despite the fact that I've proven, again and again, that I don't deserve it. I've shared pleasure and comfort with past lovers, but even with the ones who cared about me the most, there was always a thread of fear. An awareness of our discrepancy in power. A knowledge that my true loyalties lay with my family and that if they ever came to a cross purpose, I would murder my partner without hesitation.

But not Maeve. She likely has the most to fear from me, and yet she insists on trusting me. It's disconcerting in the extreme.

Hyacinth reappears, breaking the moment. She sinks into the chair across from us and plants her elbows on the table, all business. A reluctant thread of respect courses through me. It only grows when she speaks plainly. "This is an incredibly unprecedented request. I hope you understand that. The madam is willing to take a risk if I am, and *I'm* willing to say yes if you give me your word that no permanent harm will come to me."

Maeve starts to speak, but I put my hand on her thigh to still her words. "Why would you take that risk? I could kill you, and you'd be too dead to worry about me breaking my word."

"Yes." Hyacinth's eyes twinkle at me, her mirth cutting in a way that feels familiar. "But my fatal flaw is curiosity, and you've aroused it. When will I get to experience something like this again?"

She leans back, her posture perfectly relaxed. "Besides, you'll be required to sign a blood oath, and if you break your word, you'll die horribly. So I'm plenty reassured that I'll see the morning."

"I don't think that's necessary—" Maeve starts.

I squeeze her thigh. "How soon will the paperwork be ready?"

"Oh, we don't do anything as mundane as paper for this sort of thing." She pulls off a purple glove, revealing a smooth hand with an extra set of knuckles, just like the healer's. Her skin is a pale lilac. She flips over her hand, exposing her palm. "A simple exchange of blood will do."

A blood oath is a binding that's inescapable. Depending on the wording, it can be the worst kind of curse. I still can't believe that Evelyn took one for the Cŵn Annwn. I know she thought she could outwit it, and maybe she still will, but I have my doubts. The only thing that's kept them from hunting her to a violent and bloody death is the fact that she's still technically sailing with the Cŵn Annwn. At least until they figure out that Nox isn't the loyal captain the Council believes them to be.

"And the oath?"

"A simple one. You will vow not to cause any irreparable harm to me. If you do, your life is forfeit—and hers as well." Her hand doesn't so much as quiver. "In exchange, I'll feed you through your bite until you're satisfied."

"What happens if my satisfaction is your death?"

Hyacinth actually rolls her eyes. "Now you're just being difficult. Agree or don't. If you're not going to, then you're wasting my time."

I slice my nail along my palm, waiting for the blood to well, and Hyacinth produces an adorable little knife and does the same to her palm. We shake, repeating the oath. The magic courses through me, taking root in a way that makes me shiver. I have no intention of harming this woman, but the threat of a horrible death—of Maeve's horrible death—is almost enough to make me walk out the door and not look back. Only the fact that Maeve won't go with me keeps me seated.

Hyacinth examines her palm and then slides her glove back on. "Now that the nitty-gritty details are taken care of, it's time to have some fun. Follow me."

CHAPTER 25

Maeve

HYACINTH LEADS US UP THE STAIRS TO A ROOM THAT'S decorated in what I'm assuming is her trademark purple. It's lovely, the walls faded and comforting, the bed ridiculously overstuffed, and even a scattering of chairs and a sofa in a makeshift sitting area. She closes the door behind us and motions to the room as a whole. "Wherever you would be most comfortable."

Lizzie marches to the couch and drops onto it with none of her usual grace. I don't know if I'm reassured that she doesn't want to do this or irritated with her for dragging her heels through the whole process. There's a kernel of jealousy beneath my ribs as Hyacinth sinks onto the cushion next to Lizzie, which only complicates my feelings on the whole matter. There's absolutely no way that I am joining them on the couch, so I take the chair across from them.

It's a mistake.

From this angle, they create a tableau of beauty that makes

my chest ache. Hyacinth goes to some cleverly hidden ties at the shoulders of her robes, but Lizzie shakes her head sharply. "Keep it on."

For her part, Hyacinth just shrugs. "Where would you like to feed?"

Lizzie's gaze tracks to me, and whatever she sees on my face, despite my best efforts to hide it, makes her say, "Your wrist will do well enough."

If Hyacinth finds that remotely disconcerting, she doesn't show any evidence of it. But as she slides off her glove, every movement radiates seduction. Her wrist is dainty, and as her robes slide up to reveal her forearm, I get a better look at her skin. Also purple, though it's the kind of purple that's so pale it's almost without shade. It should make her look sickly, but it's just beautiful.

Lizzie gingerly takes her wrist, but her eyes are on me. They haven't left me since this started. It makes me shift in my seat. I don't want to do anything to make her feel more uncomfortable than she obviously already is, but with every second that this continues, I wonder if I've made a mistake in more than my choice of seating.

No. *No,* I can't afford to think like that. Lizzie's a vampire; going without food means she'll be weak when she can't afford to be. If we're tracking the Cŵn Annwn, I need her at full strength. If she's not, she could *die*. She might be destined to leave me, but at least I'll have the comfort of knowing that she's safe and well. If she hamstrings herself to make me comfortable, that's not a guaranteed outcome.

I force my fretting hands still, place them in my lap, and will my body to relax back into the seat. My expression takes longer to get under control, but after a few beats I'm certain I've managed it. "Go on, Lizzie." Even my voice is carefully neutral.

Lizzie's brows draw together, but we've had this argument half a dozen times today, and apparently she doesn't want to revisit it any more than I do.

She strikes, faster than I can follow, her mouth closing around Hyacinth's wrist. I see the exact moment the bite's pleasure takes hold. Hyacinth melts back into the couch, a breathless little sound coming from her lips. Her eyes close and her hips writhe, obviously seeking friction the same way I did during that first bite from Lizzie. Hyacinth is beautiful. Everything about her seems designed to seduce, even the way she orgasms.

But Lizzie isn't looking at her. She isn't marking the way that Hyacinth's breasts heave against the thin fabric of her robes, her nipples at sharp peaks. She isn't watching how Hyacinth rubs her thighs together before finally releasing a whimper and delving her hands between them. She doesn't seem to notice at all.

Because she's watching me.

I mark the color returning to her cheeks, and even though it can't have been more than a minute or two, it feels like a small eternity before she lifts her mouth and runs her tongue over her fang. One last kiss to Hyacinth's wrist heals the woman. Even at this short distance, I can see the puncture wounds knitting back together seamlessly.

"Wow." Hyacinth lifts a shaking hand to her brow. "I know that you told me what to expect, but I honestly didn't believe you. That was . . . wow." Her laugh is musical and downright giddy. "If you ever want a job, I think the madam would pay your weight in gold for that kind of trick."

"I appreciate the offer, but I have other aims." Lizzie is still staring at me, her dark eyes going heavy-lidded. "We paid for this room for the night, no?"

Hyacinth stretches leisurely. "Technically the room comes with me, but I can see that you're not interested."

My throat feels tight and my chest is closing in around my heart. Lizzie still hasn't looked away from me, her attention traps me in my chair, and I can't help the desire that rises in response. I want her so desperately that I can taste it on my tongue.

But when she speaks, her words are for the woman next to her. "I'm not interested . . . in you."

"Yes, I'm aware." Hyacinth waves that away with a graceful flick of her wrist. "Enjoy yourselves, pretties. I certainly did."

"I know. Now get out."

If Hyacinth is bothered by Lizzie's rudeness, she makes no mention of it. She rises and gives a delicious little shiver. "You're one lucky woman, Maeve. You've paid me well for this experience, but I think I might've done it for free if I'd known exactly what it would be like." Without another word, she slips from the room and closes the door softly behind her.

I like her. I enjoyed our conversation down in the main room. But in this moment, I want nothing more than to shove that woman over the railing and lock the door between us. The force of my violent thought staggers me. This isn't how I operate. But then, I've never had to worry about sharing one of my lovers before. We're in new territory and I don't know how to navigate it. I don't know if I even should.

"Maeve." Lizzie practically purrs my name. "Did it bother you to see?"

It's on the tip of my tongue to lie, but what's the point? With her powers, she can measure my racing heart, can feel the blood pooling in my cheeks, whether in embarrassment or in anger. "Yes, but not as much as it bothers me to think about you starving on my behalf."

She holds out an imperial hand, her fingers crooking as she commands me closer without saying a word. There is a part of me that wants to resist for the sake of resisting, but I haven't been successful denying Lizzie since we met. There's no reason to start now.

I rise and cross to her, slipping my hand into hers and allowing her to pull me down to straddle her. She runs her hands over my thighs and catches my hips, pulling me more firmly against her. All of the tension that's been riding her so hard since I woke up appears to have diminished. She's not quite drunk on blood, but she's relaxed and indolent as she courses her hands over my sides to cup my breasts. "I was thinking . . ."

"I'm listening." I can't quite catch my breath, but why do I need to breathe when she's touching me? I press into her palms, but she's already moving, skating her thumbs over my collarbones and sliding her fingers down my arms to take my hands.

"I had every intention of putting some distance between us. It's not safe for you to be with me." She flips one of my hands over and traces the blue veins of my wrist. "But the thought of letting you go makes me want to murder something."

I manage a breathless laugh. "Lizzie, wanting to murder something is practically your default existence."

"Yes, but it's different with you." She releases my hand, and her fingers go to the buttons at the front of my shirt, undoing them slowly enough that I want to scream with frustration. "Everything's different with you. I don't just want to make you come so many times that you lose all track of yourself. I don't just want to bite you because your taste is better than anyone I've ever known." My shirt parts, but she keeps her hold on either side of it. "I want to *keep* you."

I want to be kept by her.

I don't say the words aloud. I can't do that to her, to me. No matter that she seems to be feeling better, it doesn't change the fact that she's still in an emotionally vulnerable state. I am, too, but at least I'm self-aware enough to realize it. Lizzie doesn't seem to be. I doubt she's ever experienced being out of her element the way she has since arriving in Threshold. It's thrown her into a tailspin, and she's clinging to the one steady thing in her life right now: me.

Ultimately, it means nothing. Or, if not nothing, then not *enough*. Not enough to save us from heartbreak. Not enough to keep her from leaving. Not enough, not enough, not enough.

I don't want to ruin this fragile moment between us by saying as much. Brutal honesty isn't always the answer; I have a deep suspicion that it would hurt her. Instead, I kiss her. It's the only thing I can do to stop this conversation from coming to its inevitable end. From us having to admit that we *have* an inevitable end.

She goes still for one small heartbeat, and then she's moving, her hands coursing over my body almost too fast to register. One moment I'm straddling her, mostly dressed, and the next she's divested me of my clothing—and herself of hers as well—and kneels between my thighs, with me on my back on the couch.

I blink up at her, slightly shaken. "You know, there's something to be said for slow seduction."

"Maeve, my darling, this *is* a slow seduction." Her smile flashes fangs, and there's a part of me that mourns the fact that she won't bite me the way that she bit Hyacinth. The way that she's bitten me previously. She may give me her body and her attention, but she fully intends to keep that part of her back. Forever.

I'm horrifically greedy for wanting it. But then, it feels like I've spent so much of my life in a state of wanting. The horizon, the rebellion, love. Every time, at every turn, that wanting has turned on me. But I can't seem to make myself stop doing it. I don't think I ever will.

Lizzie kneels between my thighs, her gaze tracing over me in a stroke that I swear I can feel. I blink. I'm not imagining it; I *can* feel it. Not from her touching me physically, but from her calling my blood to the surface of my skin, spreading warmth in the wake of her attention. It's disconcerting in the extreme, and yet it feels so good that I don't want her to stop.

I lick my lips. "What are you doing to me?"

"Counting your freckles." The warmth spreads over my stomach in a wandering pattern before blooming in my pussy. My clit aches in time with my heartbeat. Lizzie licks her lips. "I think it may take me all night."

I don't know if I can stand another minute of this, let alone until dawn. I start to reach for her, but she catches my wrists easily and presses them over my head. All while that delicious heat continues its path, mapping my freckles. Over my hips, around my thighs, licking over my calves and even the tops of my feet. I shiver and writhe, seeking physical touch, but Lizzie holds herself above me and denies it to me. "Lizzie, please."

"I have barely gotten a taste of you, Maeve. Barely shaved the edge off my desire. We've rushed too many times in the past, but I'm not going to rush tonight. Now, be a good girl and hold your hands in this position."

CHAPTER 26

Lizzie

HYACINTH'S BLOOD STRENGTHENS ME, MAKING MY thoughts clearer. I hadn't realized how much hunger had dulled my senses until I have Maeve beneath me, warm and flushed and smelling of the sea. Strange how the sea itself is one of the few terrors I'll never conquer, but scenting it on Maeve's skin is an addiction I'm not prepared to give up. I contain multitudes, apparently.

"Are you going to be good?"

Maeve sets her full bottom lip as if she's considering it. Her skin is a charming pink that I am dying to drag my tongue over. We have all night. No potentially murderous crew lying in wait. No interruptions. Finally, she nods and presses her arms harder into the pillow above her head.

Only then do I ease back to sit on my heels and just *look* at her.

I've lived multiple human lifetimes, but I've never seen a woman like Maeve. It's more than the composition of her body, the dips and curves and stretch marks and dimpled skin. Or the fucking *freckles*. There's an energy to her that calls to me. It sizzles between us and makes me want to wrap myself up in her—or encase her in me. I don't know. I'm feeling too much to think properly. "You're beautiful."

"Lizzie." Her blush deepens. "You don't have to say that to me. I'm here. I'm naked. I might die if you don't touch me right now."

I trace my fingers over her skin, keeping a careful inch between us. It's the easiest thing in the world to draw her blood to her breasts, to catch it in her nipples until they deepen to a dark rose. I've never seen a prettier color. It's not quite the same thing as nipple clamps, but it will work well enough. "You should know by now—no one can make me do or say anything I don't want to. And I want to say you're beautiful. Don't get shy on me now, baby."

She pauses in the middle of lowering her arms to cover her chest. "You're embarrassing me on purpose." She shifts between my thighs. "What are you *doing* to me?"

"Whatever I want." I lean down and exhale against first one nipple and then the other, causing her skin to break out in goose bumps. I give her a wicked grin. "Do you want me to stop?"

She isn't quite pulling off the glare she's aiming for. Her brows are drawn together, but her lips keep curving. "You're insufferable."

"You say the meanest things." I'm . . . giddy. I don't know how else to explain it. What a strange concept. I don't know that I've ever felt it before. I like it.

I expect Maeve to keep snarking at me. She's cute when she does. I'm so busy watching her mouth, waiting on her next words, that she surprises the hell out of me when she darts up and steals a kiss. It's light and playful—and nowhere near enough.

All of a sudden, I don't feel like playing anymore. I dip down and take her mouth, kissing her the way she deserves: deep and consuming. She makes a sexy little gasp against my lips, and then she's kissing me back. Tongues and teeth, a meeting of two people who are certainly not prey. She nips my bottom lip hard enough to draw blood.

I jerk back. "*Maeve.*"

"Um." She blinks, big eyes dazed. "Sorry?"

I lick my lip, savoring the coppery taste on my tongue. "Don't be." I pull more of her blood to her breasts, enjoying the way she squirms. "I like it. I like *you*." Dangerous words. I know better than to make promises, even vague ones. It's a long way from confessing my everlasting love, but it's still something I've never said aloud to anyone before. "I like you," I repeat slowly.

"I like you, too," she whispers. "Now, no more talking. Kiss me."

It's a retreat, but I'm too off-center to deny her. What would be the point? Liking or . . . more . . . doesn't matter in the grand scheme of things. They're worries for the future; better to not let them dampen our night.

I lower myself down to press my body against hers. She ignores my earlier command to keep her hands above her head, digging her fingers into my hair as she kisses me with a growing frenzy. More, more, more.

There's no warning. One moment Maeve is writhing against me in the sweetest way. The next, she hooks her ankle behind my knee and shoves my shoulders, toppling me onto the floor.

She follows me down, claiming my mouth again before I can protest her underhanded tactics. As if I *would* protest.

I like her like this. I like her all the damn time. When she's vulnerable. When she's strong. Stubborn and flirty and furious and sweet. So many different flavors, and I want to taste them all, again and again.

Maeve palms my pussy. "You tease too much."

I release the blood from her breasts, grinning when she whimpers. "You enjoy every moment of it."

"I do." She presses two fingers into me, sure and strong. "But I like this, too." She curls her fingers against my G-spot. I try to fight the desire out of sheer perversity, but it's no use. She's turned my bones to something soft and warm. The little selkie knows it, too. Maeve keeps stroking me, twisting my need tighter with slow strokes.

"You're so *agreeable* when you're coming," she murmurs against my lips. "No thoughts of murder to be had."

That startles a strangled laugh out of me. "I'll murder anyone who interrupts us."

"There she is, my murderous Lizzie."

I want to be yours.

She kisses me before I can say the words and ruin this thing between us. We might enjoy each other's company. We certainly enjoy having sex with each other. But keeping? It's out of the question. I highly doubt Maeve would have engaged in this affair if we didn't have a built-in deadline. Why should she? A murderous vampire who treats every situation as one that violence can solve . . . I'm hardly a catch for someone like Maeve.

I never had cause to mourn the person I am. There was a time for that, and it's dead and gone, turned to dust in some unmarked grave. If I were any softer, any less vicious, I wouldn't be here today. I've never regretted doing what it took to survive.

But, deep down in some hidden part of me, I almost wish things had turned out differently. That I could be the person she deserves. The kind of woman whom Maeve would want for more than sex and as a vicious protector.

She nips my shoulder, slamming me back into the here and now. "Come for me, Lizzie. I want to feel it."

I love her like this, confident and wicked, her clever fingers winding me up. I drag my fingers down her sides and grip her ass, pulling her closer. Urging her to grind her pussy against my thigh. I'll get another taste of her, and soon. But this is perfect for an appetizer. "Make me."

She laughs. It's light and joyful and filled with a promise I don't know how to fulfill. Maeve presses the heel of her palm against my clit, hard, and there's no holding out. I orgasm, pleasure bending my spine and *almost* making me forget myself enough to bite her. Her throat is so close, perfectly arched and sprinkled with those devastating freckles. I could . . .

I twist and snap my teeth around a pillow. The fabric feels wrong against my tongue, but it's better than the alternative. Was I just wishing to be soft enough to deserve this woman? What a joke. I almost killed her a few days ago, and all it takes is a single orgasm to have me in danger of doing it again.

Pathetic.

Maeve doesn't give me a chance to sink into self-loathing. She drags her mouth down my throat, pausing to give me a tiny nibble that makes my thighs clench, and then shifts down my body and pushes my thighs wide. "Your restraint is admirable." There's something in her tone, something almost brittle, but she dips down and covers my pussy with her mouth before my pleasure-drugged brain can figure out what I've done to upset her.

She eases her fingers out of me and replaces them with her tongue, soft and slick and absolutely decadent. I manage to unclench my jaw enough to free the pillow. Barely. At least she's out of reach of my fangs now. There's still the problem of how I'm going to taste *her* without losing control, but I'll get to that . . . soon . . . very soon.

She drags her tongue over my center and wedges three fingers into me. "You make me so angry and hot, and I just want to punish you."

"Punish me?" I blink down at her. I can't *think*. "I'm going to come again," I gasp.

"I know." Some smugness works its way into her tone. She sucks on my clit and then works it in short, unhurried strokes with the flat of her tongue as she keeps stroking my G-spot with her fingers. By all rights, I should be too sensitized to come again, but one of the perks of quick healing is even faster recovery. We could go for hours if I'm careful with her. Days, honestly.

We don't have days here in this room. We only have until dawn.

"Maeve."

She bands one arm over my stomach, holding me in place as she ruthlessly drives me into another orgasm. My brain actually blips, or maybe I black out. It feels like one moment Maeve is between my thighs, and the next she's at my back, wrapping herself around me and delving her hand back between my thighs.

I shiver. "Maeve, please." I could break her hold easily, could twist and pin her to the ground, could drive her to distraction the same way she's doing to me. I don't. "Let me touch you."

"It made me so jealous to see you bite her," she murmurs in my ear. She parts my pussy and drags the tip of her middle finger over my sensitive clit. "To see her get something that should, by rights, be mine."

My mouth works, but I can't seem to speak. If I was a better person, her jealousy wouldn't make me hotter. I wouldn't take it as some kind of proof of wanting. But I'm not a better person. I grip her arm, not trying to stop her, just hanging on and letting her guide this. "I only want you." I don't mean to say it. I truly don't.

"I know." Maeve cups one breast with her free hand, plucking at my nipple even as she works me toward a third orgasm. "You *have* me, Lizzie." She kisses my throat. "You just have to take me."

Except I don't have her. She's a selkie wife, mine for the time being, but I was always destined to lose her. There's a reason all the stories end the same. I thought it was bullshit, but the truth is undeniable. I'm going to spend the rest of my life chasing the feeling of being with Maeve . . . and I'm going to spend the rest of my life coming up short.

That, more than anything, gives me the strength to move, to turn and kiss her. To focus on giving her even more pleasure than she's given me. "She wasn't you." I speak against her lips as I wedge my arm between us and stroke her pussy. "No one compares to you, baby. No one will ever be you."

"Take me," she repeats. The words have weight, as if they mean far more than sexually. I can't *think*, can't reason through why doing so would be a bad idea.

Nothing can touch us right now, right here. I haul myself to my feet and scoop Maeve into my arms. It's only a few steps to the bed, and I lay her down like a bride on her wedding night. Moonlight filters through the window, bathing her in soft light. "I will, baby. I'll take you all night."

I'll take you forever.

CHAPTER 27

Maeve

HYACINTH *REALLY* LIKED LIZZIE'S BITE, ENOUGH THAT she allows us to sleep well into the afternoon instead of kicking us out at dawn. It's nice to wake in a bed with Lizzie. Really nice. I turn onto my side and study my vampire. Most people look younger when they sleep, but not Lizzie. She doesn't look more innocent, either. But there's still something in her that relaxes. The fact that she trusts me enough to allow me to witness it feels like a gift I'll spend the rest of my life cherishing. Even long after she's gone.

I didn't mean for my jealousy to slip its leash last night. I certainly didn't expect said jealousy to make the sex hotter. My heart feels strangely bruised, but I can't begin to say why. Lizzie has made no promises to me. Yes, her determination not to hurt me seems to suggest she cares, but that ultimately changes nothing.

Except it *feels* like something changed, as if some piece clicked into place, as if we crossed a point of no return that I hadn't noticed. I don't know what it means. I don't even know how to ask if she feels it, too.

Lizzie's a natural predator, so it doesn't take long for her to sense my attention. She blinks her eyes open, instantly awake. "You were watching me sleep."

"Only a little."

She stretches slowly, her gaze tracking to the bright blue sky outside the window. "It's well past dawn." Lizzie sighs. "Shall we take bets on whether the ship has sailed off without us?"

I want to reassure her that Alix wouldn't do that, but the truth is I have no idea. They hardly wanted Lizzie as interim captain, for all that they're getting a promotion as soon as we leave the crew. It would stand to reason that they'd speed said promotion along by leaving us behind the first chance they got. "No bet."

"Thought as much." She gives one last stretch and then sits up. "I think we've abused Hyacinth's hospitality long enough, even if we paid for the privilege. Let's get moving."

I clamp my lips shut on the protest that rises within me. I don't want to get moving. I want to stay in this strange moment of in-between forever. As soon as we leave this room, the real world will come rushing in, reminding me Lizzie will never be mine in any meaningful way.

There's a very real chance that when she leaves, she'll take a piece of my heart with her.

We dress in comfortable silence that grows more tense as the seconds tick by. When Lizzie opens the door and I follow her down the stairs and out onto the street, it almost feels like last night never happened. Until she grabs my elbow and uses her hold to spin me around and press me against the wall.

She steps close, the heat of her enveloping me. "Stop that."

"Stop what?"

"Last night meant something to me, the same way it meant something to you. We have to focus on business now, but that doesn't mean I'm going back to dancing around each other, as skittish as maidens. I've gotten over my guilt. So have you. Let's move on together."

Just like that. Lizzie isn't one to linger on things she finds uncomfortable. I swallow hard. "Okay."

She gives me a look like she isn't quite convinced, but she just takes my hand and leads me toward the lift to descend to the bay. "First, we need to check to see if the ship's still there. The local taverns won't be occupied by more than the hard-core locals at this time of day. We'll find you some food and then figure out next steps from there."

Down in the bay, I'm pleasantly surprised to discover that the *Serpent's Cry* hasn't sailed away without us. In fact, Alix stands on the docks, deep in conversation with two people, their hoods pulled forward on their faces. They look at us as we approach, and the strangers break away, headed in the opposite direction. I stomp down on the curiosity fluttering in my chest. It's none of our business. The most important thing is that Alix is still here.

Alix crosses their wings over their chest and gives us a severe look. "So. You're still alive."

"Is there a reason we wouldn't be?" Lizzie tenses as if she's going to attack. I place my hand on the center of her back, urging her to patience.

They shrug. "A person came by asking questions. Pointed questions. The kind that make people like me nervous."

Now it's my turn to tense. No one should even know we're here, let alone where to start asking questions. "Cŵn Annwn?"

"If they were, they were undercover. Not a crimson piece of clothing in sight. They also didn't feel like those bastards." Alix sighs. "Look, I have no issue with you—at least in theory. I've made some good trades already on Drash, enough that we'll likely incorporate this into our route going forward. But that doesn't change the fact that we're not a vessel equipped to hunt in the way that you need."

It's nothing more than they've said from the moment we came aboard, but I respect them for saying it to our face instead of sneaking off in the dead of night. I tap my fingers on Lizzie's back and move to step in front of her. "So this is goodbye."

Alix's gaze flicks over my shoulder to Lizzie. "That would be my preference. There are enough ships that come through Drash that you should be able to book passage once you know where you're headed."

I can actually feel Lizzie tense behind me, but she stays silent. There's an element of trust there that I'm not sure I know what to do with, but there's no time to examine it now. "We just need our things from your ship and then you can be on your way." It will likely be days before we find any information—if there's even information to be found. A ship like the *Serpent's Cry* requires constant movement to be effective. Lingering too long in one place is a great way to have people asking questions that they don't want to answer.

Alix and the rest of their crew didn't kill us in our sleep. It's the bare minimum, but they could've at least tried. They chose not to. "Good luck on your travels."

Alix visibly relaxes, though they give Lizzie another nervous look. "I took the courtesy of grabbing your stuff before I came to shore." They hold up their wings and take a quick step back. "I wasn't going to toss it. I fully intended to wait until you came looking. It's just my good luck that you didn't make me wait long."

Lizzie is still tense enough that she obviously wants to attack. She doesn't, though. She keeps her silence as we collect our bag and head back toward the lift. Lizzie's jaw is set in a tight line, and her strides are sharp with anger. "I hope you have a good reason for letting them leave without us. We need that ship."

"There are other ships. And don't pretend like the thought of taking over another one doesn't make you a little bit excited."

She shoots me a sharp look. "It would make me more excited if you weren't so cagey about letting me murder the people who stand in our way."

Despite everything, I laugh. "Let's just see how it goes."

We find an inn on the next level up and pay for a night's stay. Then I give in to Lizzie's pestering to eat until she's satisfied I'm not going to pass out from lack of nourishment. By that point, the sun is once again sinking toward the horizon. The taverns will be bustling with the dinner crowd, and then the drinking will begin, which means people won't be watching their tongues as closely.

It's time to begin asking our questions.

I survey our options and decide to start with a tiny tavern on the first level near the docks. It's the obvious choice for sailors just washing in. "Let me do the talking. You scare people." She glares and I point at her face. "Yes, that's exactly what I'm talking about, you get that look on your face like you're going to start ripping out throats, and people get nervous."

"Ripping out throats is my favorite pastime." But she relents immediately. "You might as well tell me the plan of attack."

"Once again, no attacking. No murder. No bar fights. Nothing that's going to make our welcome on Drash shift." I tuck my hair behind my ears. "There's two plans of attack, so to speak. We talk to the sailors. Most of them aren't locals and so pass through, some with regularity and some without, but they'll have the most recent rumors about the Cŵn Annwn. Then we talk to the barkeeps. They see every single person who comes through their doors. If the *Crimson Hag* has been in these waters, they'll know it." The trick is charming them into parting with that information without needing to delve into our dwindling stash of money. I know who the rebellion contacts are on the two closest islands to Viedna, but there was no reason to give me the information about islands farther afield. Especially when it could mean a security risk. I might be able to find whoever locally support the rebellion, but there's no guarantee. We have to make the money last.

Lizzie raises her eyebrows. "That seems deceptively simple."

"Because it *is* a deceptively simple plan. Putting it into action is significantly more complicated. Sailors love to talk, but every person in Threshold fears the Cŵn Annwn. If they think for a second that we mean the crew of the *Crimson Hag* harm, we won't be able to get a single piece of information out of them. Not because they're loyal, but because they're afraid of the consequences coming back onto them and their people."

Lizzie braids her hair back with smooth, practiced movements. It leaves her face on display, and it's almost too much beauty for me to think straight. I expected to be inoculated to her presence after all this time together, but moments like these strike me all over again, and I'm rendered speechless.

Not that she seems to notice. She finishes braiding her hair and frowns. "It's interesting to hear the perception of the Cŵn Annwn from someone who isn't Bowen. I don't understand how someone so disgustingly honorable spent so long wrapped up in such a corrupt system."

From what I gather, Bowen is the exception to the rule. Honorable Cŵn Annwn are certainly not *my* experience. "He didn't choose to be part of their group any more than most people do. And, to hear tell of it, the last captain of his ship, Ezra, was a lot like him." That was before my time gathering information for the rebellion, but when my mother indulges in more than her usual amount of wine, she's been known to wax poetic about Ezra. A member of the Cŵn Annwn with honor? It defies belief. The only exceptions I've seen are people who actively participate in the rebellion. Like Nox.

"I won't pretend to be some paragon, but at least my family doesn't run around terrorizing entire civilizations." She says it slowly, almost as if musing to herself. "The Cŵn Annwn truly are evil."

It's on the tip of my tongue to point out that participating in the rebellion would ensure a significant amount of murder, certainly enough to satisfy her more violent impulses. Surely that's reason enough for her to stay.

But I don't. Even making that comment in jest reeks of manipulation. Lizzie has no interest in the rebellion or staying in Threshold longer than strictly necessary.

What if she asked me to come with her?

The thought slips free before I have a chance to smother it. And then it's there, sitting in the center of my brain and demanding a response. I turn away from Lizzie, angry at myself for even contemplating it. She's not going to ask me to come with her, and even if she did, what would that even look like?

My place is here. In Threshold. Fighting against a corrupt system. Or at least informing for those who are fighting. When this hunt for Lizzie's family heirlooms is over, I'll return to Viedna and resume my place in my family's tavern. I'll smile and charm the Cŵn Annwn who come through our doors and milk them for every piece of information they have access to. And then I'll turn around and report it to the rebellion. And some day, hopefully within my lifetime, we'll take down the Council and the corrupt crews and establish a new, just system in Threshold.

With such a higher purpose, it is the height of selfishness to even consider leaving.

Not to mention the fact that Lizzie hasn't asked me to come with her and shows no indication of doing so. I'm living in a fantasy, and it's only hurting my own feelings.

"Maeve?"

I clear my throat, swallowing past the burning that takes up residence behind my eyes. I have the rest of my life to mourn the loss of Lizzie. I'm not going to start while she's still with me. When I turn around, I have my smile firmly in place. "Let's get started."

CHAPTER 28

Lizzie

THERE'S A SADNESS ABOUT MAEVE THAT I DON'T UNDERstand. She's trying to hide it from me, too. I almost pull her aside and hash it out right then and there, but she's a blur of motion, dragging me along behind her to the first tavern on our list. Drash is large enough to house half a dozen taverns that seem to be making good business off sailors, tourists, and locals alike. The city may feel different than any of the others I've visited since arriving in Threshold, but the first bar Maeve leads me to is familiar enough. There must be some universal law that says all dockside taverns must have low light, sticky floors, and a clientele that smells ripe from spending so long at sea. This one is no different.

Maeve is right that I'm not particularly skilled when it comes to charm, so I order a round of beer for us and sit back and watch her work.

She's a master at it. I can see why the rebellion recruited her, because people of every gender and age immediately melt upon exchanging words with her. If I were a different person, jealousy might flicker through me in response to how they flock to her, bees to a particularly intoxicating flower.

What am I saying? *Of course* I'm fucking jealous. Watching her dole out those smiles, flirting, and just being generally kind makes me want to wrap her in a cloak and haul her out of here. I've never been overly territorial, but I want to keep all that sunshine just for myself.

I'm in trouble. There's no two ways about it. Last night more than proved my feelings, even if I've been in denial ever since. Honestly, the trouble goes back even further. I'm not sure when she crept beneath my barriers, but she's taken up residence and I don't have the heart to eradicate her. Or the desire to. I like spending time with her. I like the fact that I'm continually finding out new things about her. I like that she keeps surprising me.

It takes about two hours for her to fully make her rounds, including the bartender who hangs on her every word and offers to let her drink for free for the rest of the night. I can tell that she wasn't successful by the way her brows draw together and her smile dips as she makes her way back to me.

Maeve drops into the chair next to me and leans her head on my shoulder. She exhales a long, slow breath. "No one has seen the *Crimson Hag* in months. Most of the people here have southern routes or stick close to Drash, though, so that's not to say we won't find more information in the next place."

I nudge her beer toward her and watch as she takes a small sip. "We had our allotment of luck in finding your pelt without having to wait weeks for Bronagh to return to Khollu. It stands to reason that this part of the hunt won't be easy."

She lifts her head and smiles at me, and I'm surprised to realize I can tell the difference between her smiles now. This one isn't the expression designed to charm and disarm people. It's a little crooked, a little bittersweet, and purely Maeve. "Let's keep going, then."

But at the next bar, it's more of the same. And the next as well. Drash lays at the tip of the arch of islands that swing north from Lyari. Most ships on a north-to-south route will stop in here, whether to trade or just as a break for their crew before moving on. The fact that the *Crimson Hag* hasn't stopped in in months, not since well before Bowen was voted out as captain, seems to suggest they're still in the western part of Threshold somewhere.

That should narrow things down a bit, but this damned realm is littered with islands. Even if we pick the right direction to sail, there's every chance we could miss them entirely. Literal ships passing in the night and all that.

The thought should fill me with deep frustration, but it doesn't. I press my fingers against my chest, but I don't have a chance to examine that lack of sensation before the small hairs on the back of my neck stand on end.

Someone is watching me. Watching *us*.

I look up without lifting my head, surveying the room. I've already forgotten the name of this tavern, but it's situated much like the others we've been to. Groupings of smaller tables orbiting one larger long table with bench seats on either side, all filled to the brim. There are stools at the bar itself, each occupied by people well past their prime. With Maeve in the mix, no one seems to be paying much attention to me.

But my instincts are never wrong.

I'm about to call for Maeve when she moves back to our table. Her shoulders have dropped to a dejected degree, and she doesn't pick up the beer that I nudge in her direction. "It's more of the same. Some of these people came from the Three Sisters to the west, and they haven't seen them, either. I don't understand. Historically, that ship likes to stick to this particular route in between hunts. The fact that it's not is strange. I don't like it."

"Must be the new leadership. Maybe they have an entirely new route. We just have to find it." But I'm still scanning the room, still trying to find the source of the raised hairs at the nape of my neck. I cover Maeve's hand and bring it up to my face, urging her to lean close enough that I can speak directly into her ear. "One more bar and then we're done for the night. I think we've garnered some attention, so be careful. I'll handle it if they attack."

She stiffens but then seems to make a conscious effort to relax. "I hadn't realized anyone was paying that close of attention."

"I don't think they're in this room. Whoever they are, they're good at avoiding detection."

We pay our tab from our dwindling expenses and head for the door. I keep close to Maeve, ready to whisk her out of danger at the first sign that something's gone wrong. But no one jumps out at us as we move through the increasingly empty streets of Drash. The next tavern is up one level, but it's late enough that the lift is shut down for the night. We pass it and head for the stairs.

That's when I hear it. The soft scuff of foot against stone. I don't turn and look, instead sending my power out in a wave of sensing. No matter how good someone's magic is, if they have blood in their body, they can't hide from me.

There. They aren't too far behind us, and there's only one of them, which seems to suggest a spy rather than an intent to ambush. Or perhaps they're an assassin.

I guess we'll find out.

"Stay in front of me," I say under my breath.

Maeve gives a jerky nod and shifts to walk directly in front of me. I love her a little more for trusting me and not arguing on principle. We pass building after building as we head for the stairs. I scan the space in front of us, trying to figure out where the person intends to strike. If it were me, I would—

Our stalker chooses that moment to pick up their pace. I push Maeve forward and spin around, grabbing them by their throat and shoving them against the wall. They're taller than me, but that doesn't stop me from lifting them until their feet don't touch the ground. "Who the fuck are you?"

Instead of pissing themself in fear, they let out a strangled laugh. "Nice reflexes." Their voice drops. "But not quite good enough."

Something pricks my upper stomach, just below my ribs. I look down to see their fingers embedded in my skin, each digit ending in a claw. Shifter. A strong one at that, since most of their people can't do a partial shift like this. They could have attempted to take my heart in my moment of hesitation, but they just wait to see what I'll do.

"Answer my question."

"Call me an interested party." Their voice is low but lyrical. Their cloak hood is so deep that I can't pick out their features in the shadows. Not even with my superior vision. They turn their head to Maeve. "I know you, selkie. You've been passing secrets for years."

This person doesn't feel like one of the Cŵn Annwn, but what do I know? They're as varied as grains of sand on the beach, each unique to themselves. And what kind of ruling group would the Council be if they didn't have a few pet assassins on the books?

But Maeve doesn't seem to be terrified. She shifts closer and peers up into the hood. "Do I know you?"

"We've met once or twice." They finally shift their fingers from my skin and hold up their hands. "Peace, vampire. I have information you might find useful. You won't get it if you snap my neck."

"I *really* want to snap your neck." But I can already feel Maeve's caution warning me not to. At this point, we can't afford to ignore the possibility of answers. And so I carefully set them on their feet and release them.

They lift a hand to their throat and laugh again. "I appreciate the care. Let's go somewhere we can talk more privately."

This is absolutely a trap. I can't decide if I want Maeve in front of me or behind me, and my indecision makes me furious. "One wrong move and you won't have a throat to worry about."

"Noted." They don't sound like they're particularly worried. In fact, the gravel in their voice has already smoothed out as their magic heals the damage I did. Fucking shifters. They heal even faster than vampires, and that's saying something. Even more inconvenient, they don't need blood to do so. A bad injury might require a shift into their animal form to handle it, but I barely bruised them.

They lead us down the stairs into a small house that appears to be privately owned. I'm so tense that I'm practically vibrating, ready to spring into violence at the first sign of trouble. But there's no one in the room, or even in the house. No one except us. The stranger shuts the door between us and the rest of the village.

"I believe some introductions are in order." They push back their hood, revealing a person with tanned skin, a square jaw, and long straight brown hair. They grin, revealing straight white teeth. "I'm Siobhan."

I glance at Maeve, willing to take my lead from her. Recognition rolls over her face and all her tension bleeds away. "Siobhan! What are you doing here?" She turns to me, holding out a hand in a way that cautions me to peace. "She's a trader, though she's usually not sailing with a crew. She's come through Viedna a few times over the last few years. Tells some great stories. She's okay."

I have my doubts about that. The woman shrugs out of her cloak and drapes it over the chair, revealing a body that's tall and muscular and looks like she can run through brick walls without slowing down. Trader, my ass. She's obviously a warrior. Not to mention her instincts are stellar, because even as I was crushing her throat, she was poised to take my heart. That kind of reaction requires training. A lot of it.

"Please. Sit. Like I said, I have information that you might find helpful."

"In exchange for what?" I ignore Maeve flapping her hands in a bid to keep me quiet. "We both know that nothing comes for free, and if you simply wanted to give us some information, you could've done it at any point tonight. Instead, you skulked around and stalked us. Explain yourself."

Siobhan laughs, flashing teeth that suddenly seem a little bit sharper than they were a few moments ago. "I like you, vampire. Let's just say that I'm not unaware of your plight and your aims. The *Crimson Hag* has become a thorn in my side, and I would like it removed. Permanently."

Maeve's jaw drops. "Why do you care what the *Crimson Hag* is up to?"

"I'm afraid I haven't been perfectly honest with you in our previous meetings. Your work toward the rebellion has been invaluable. Which means that you've earned the right to know exactly who's behind said rebellion." Siobhan holds out a hand. "Me."

CHAPTER 29

Maeve

SIOBHAN IS THE LEADER OF THE REBELLION? BUT THAT doesn't make any kind of sense. The few times I've met her, she's looked more like a penniless trader than the kind of person who would inspire loyalty from someone like Nox and the rest of the rebellion. She's always alone. I've never even been quite sure how she gets from island to island, because she doesn't have a crew herself or a ship. She seems to travel with the wind, though that's a fanciful thing to think.

But this is Threshold, so perhaps not.

Even so, no one in their right mind is going to claim to be the leader of the rebellion. Not when occupying that role is an automatic death sentence once the Cŵn Annwn crews and the Council become aware the rebellion exists and has been working under their noses for years. And they will become aware eventually. We can only operate in the shadows for so long.

Even with all that in play, there's one thing I don't understand. "But why are you *here*? Why are you revealing yourself to us?"

"Like I said, I have business with the *Crimson Hag*. They're currently sailing east to Drash. There was a confrontation at one of the shifting islands a few days ago and they need to restock their supplies before they head south to Lyari."

I frown. "How could you possibly know any of that?"

Siobhan gives a grim smile that doesn't reach her hazel eyes. "I wouldn't be a very good leader of the rebellion if I didn't have a network of spies passing along information, now would I? A network that *you* have historically been part of."

Maybe I was part of that network, but I only ever got rumors from people passing through. What she's suggesting, being able to anticipate the movements of Cŵn Annwn ships, would be worth its weight in gold if the rest of the network was able to do it. I open my mouth to press for more information but stop short as what she said finally penetrates.

If she's right, the *Crimson Hag* is coming here. To Drash.

I glance at Lizzie, expecting to see elation that she's so close to her goal. She doesn't seem particularly impressed. She drops into one of the rickety old chairs around the faded dining room table and crosses her long legs in front of her. "What you're carefully not saying is that you need us to do something to that ship for you."

"You were already planning on sneaking aboard the *Crimson Hag* and stealing back what was taken from you." Siobhan moves into the dingy kitchen and pulls a dusty bottle of wine from an open-faced cabinet. "They have something in their hold that belongs to me. I want it back. Two birds, one stone."

Lizzie narrows her eyes. "That's a saying from my realm."

"Is it?" Siobhan opens the bottle of wine and rifles through the cabinets until she comes up with three tin cups. "It's an effective metaphor, don't you think? Why make more work for us individually when we're stronger together?"

There is something off here. I've spent my entire life studying people. In the few times I've met Siobhan previously, her body language was loose and relaxed. There's a new tightness to her shoulders, an edge to her words. I don't think she's lying to us, exactly, but she's very clearly not telling us everything she knows—or everything we need to know.

Lizzie examines her cup of wine, her upper lip curling. "If your information is that accurate, when will the *Crimson Hag* make port?"

"Tomorrow night if they keep their current pace and don't have any trouble along the way."

So soon. Regardless of how formidable the *Hag*'s crew is, Lizzie will prevail. She's too damn good not to. Which means that within a couple of days, she'll have reclaimed her family heirlooms and be on the hunt for a portal home. Her actual portal home was destroyed in a fight between her and Evelyn and Bowen, but that doesn't mean the way is closed to her. Threshold contains thousands of portals on its thousands of islands, and even more beneath the waves. It may take some trial and error and trust, but I've no doubt that Lizzie is savvy enough to find her way home.

My time with her is coming to a close.

I feel the weight of her gaze on me, but I don't look her way. I'm not certain I can control my expression if I meet her eyes. Not when I'm feeling so suddenly vulnerable and raw.

Instead, I focus on Siobhan. "I'm willing to hear you out, but that's *all* I'll agree to without more information. I support what the rebellion is trying to accomplish, but we both know my role to date has only been gathering information. Asking this of me, even with Lizzie involved, is asking too much on faith alone. So let's start easy. What did they take from you?"

Siobhan hesitates, and for a moment I think she won't answer honestly. But she finally throws back her wine and grabs the bottle to refill her glass. "They took someone very important to me—to the rebellion. They intend to bring him to Lyari to stand trial."

A . . . trial? There hasn't been a trial in living memory, at least not for a victim of the Cŵn Annwn. They tend to be of the mind that murdering first and asking questions never is the best policy. All they have to do is categorize their victim as a monster, and it's well within their rights, at least according to the Council. Trials are reserved for nobles.

Nobles.

I narrow my eyes. What is Siobhan doing associating with a *noble,* let alone doing it in such close proximity that she feels obligated to save him? Or is it a matter of him having information that she doesn't want to fall into the Council's hands? Impossible to say, and I don't think she'd be honest if I asked her.

I take a different route. "What's his crime?"

Again, that moment of hesitation where it's clear that she's considering lying to me. Again, she shows every evidence of telling the truth. "Glamour. Using his powers to charm the Cŵn Annwn."

Lizzie snorts. "Glamour magic is a dime a dozen. With all the magical people the Cŵn Annwn keep on their ships, they must have the shields to combat that sort of thing. I don't see why this requires a trial, no matter who this man is."

I shake my head slowly. "We don't have glamour magic,

Lizzie. Not here. Not in Threshold." It probably wasn't always like that, but when the Council took over a very, very long time ago, they couldn't risk that anyone in the realm might influence or overpower them. According to the whispers that have been passed along for generations, they wanted anyone with a drop of glamour magic removed. Permanently.

That flavor of magic is primarily held by humans, though. They had a hard time convincing the general population these people were monsters who deserved being hunted in order to promote safety for everyone. There was pushback. These days, the regular citizens wouldn't dare, but back then, the Council was so new that they bowed to popular sentiment.

They didn't hunt publicly, but when they were through, not a single bloodline that carried glamour magic remained. Or at least that's how the story goes. I believe it, though. With all the travelers who've come through Viedna, I've never met someone who could use glamour magic.

"Is he a local?" I finally ask. What am I saying? He must be if he's being carted back to Lyari to stand trial. More, he *must* be a noble. But if a noble held the power to glamour, we should've heard about it long before now. "Never mind. He obviously is. But I don't understand. How has he kept it secret long enough to reach adulthood?"

"Glamour is Bastian's secondary power. It's not one that he's ever been public about, but he's invaluable to the rebellion because of it. I can't let the Cŵn Annwn take him to Lyari to stand before the Council. More than his life is at stake."

If he's close enough to Siobhan for the rebellion to utilize his glamour magic, he's probably been privy to secrets that could get a large number of people killed. The thought makes me shiver. "If that's the case, then we need to rally your allies. Nox has an entire ship. Surely they can—"

"No." Siobhan shakes her head. "The *Audacity* is easily a week away, and while they *are* southwest of Drash, enlisting their help means Bastian will be a week closer to Lyari. We won't have another opportunity to catch the *Crimson Hag* unawares. You're here, and you have your murderous vampire with you, so it's our best chance. His best chance."

Lizzie motions with the hand holding her tin cup full of wine. "The murderous vampire in question is sitting right here. And all of this sounds like a whole lot of bullshit. If he's really that powerful, how did he get taken in the first place? Or, more importantly, if *he's* so vital, why didn't you stop the kidnapping?"

"I wasn't there." Siobhan sounds downright agonized. "We were supposed to meet up at a particular location and time, but he never showed. When I finally realized what had happened, the *Crimson Hag* had reached open water."

That doesn't quite explain how she got to Drash before the *Crimson Hag*, but I suppose it doesn't matter. "That ship is sailing with a pretty intense crew. It was one thing to potentially sneak in and steal back some jewels, but to steal an entire person who's under guard? It will be a fight, and possibly one we can't win. You're asking a lot."

"I don't have another choice. Bastian *cannot* reach Lyari."

Lizzie examines her fingernails. She's put on an air of disinterest, but I can see her mind working behind the bored look in her deep brown eyes. There are a dozen ways we could attempt to do this, but no matter which angle I look at it from, the risk is astronomical. Three of us against an entire crew? There's no way we'll all survive.

"We have to sink the ship," my vampire finally says.

I spin to face Lizzie. "We can't sink the ship."

"Sure we can. Between your power underwater and this one's strength." She motions at Siobhan. "It wouldn't take much to rip a hole in the hull. The trick is to keep it open so they don't have a chance to repair it. If they're close enough to shore, they'll abandon ship. That's when we strike."

"Or, more likely, they'll realize we attacked them and just flat out murder us," I snap.

She grins, flashing her sharp teeth at me. "That's definitely a possibility."

"The vampire has a point." Siobhan toys with the string holding her cloak together. "If the crew is in the water, it will be easier to separate the guards holding Bastian and take him back. They won't leave him to drown. He's too important a captive."

They're jumping right over a very vital portion of this plan. "I'm strong, but I'm not strong enough to break a hole in the bottom of a ship. It's far more likely that I'll charge it, knock myself out, and drown."

"I'll soften it up for you." That expression on Siobhan's face makes me shiver. She's contemplating death, and the longer I spend in her presence, the stranger I find it that I never questioned her coming and going in the past. How did I overlook the fact that she's obviously a warrior—and a dangerous one at that?

I feel very naive right now. I clear my throat. "How are you going to 'soften up' a ship's hull?"

She wiggles her fingers at me. Bones crack as they shift, forming into long, vicious claws before morphing back into mundane fingers. "I heal even faster than the vampire, and I can do a lot of damage in a very short time. I'll tear the hole open, and then you charge it to make it bigger. Between the two of us, we can get it done."

There's a *small* possibility this may work. But I've listened to Bowen and Nox discuss the *Crimson Hag*. I know all about the various crew members and many of their powers. There's plenty to worry about there, but the biggest threat is Lucky, a crew member who's half mermaid. "If they send Lucky in the water, we're both in trouble."

"I'll take care of Lucky." Lizzie appears to relish the idea. It's everything I can do not to remind her that she almost drowned less than a week ago. That the fight with the water horse scared her so badly, she ended up hurting me by accident. Saying as much now, let alone in front of Siobhan, would be unforgivable.

I keep my silence, but worry gnaws at my insides. The longer Siobhan and Lizzie talk, hammering out the details of the plan, the more I suspect the steps are deceptively simple and will fall apart the moment we put them into action. I don't have a better idea. The only thing I can do is vow to myself to keep these two alive.

Even if it means I have to sacrifice Bastian in the process.

CHAPTER 30

Lizzie

WE DON'T FORM A MORE CONCRETE PLAN BEFORE Maeve and I take our leave and head back to the room we rented for the night. The farther away from Siobhan's captivating presence I get, the more I start to question what the fuck we're doing.

Sure, Nox and I took out an entire ship's worth of Cŵn Annwn, but Nox is a force of nature beyond understanding. Between my powers and their elemental magic, we were able to subdue a large number of people in a very short period of time. Siobhan is a shifter; she'll be fierce as fuck in a battle, but it will be an out-and-out brawl instead of a mass disabling event.

Maeve could be hurt.

I'm so close to the jewels I've spent months hunting, and all I can think of is Maeve lying in that bed for two days as pale as death, her chest barely moving. I've spent my entire life being trained to think of my life as something both disposable and infinite. A dichotomy I've never questioned but one that made me fearless in fights.

It's different now. I have something to lose. Some*one* to lose. If Maeve is hurt in this fight . . .

I barely wait until the door is closed between us and the rest of the building before I turn on her. Maeve's eyes are bright, and her mind is obviously moving a mile a minute as she thinks about tomorrow. I will do *anything* to ensure those eyes aren't closed forever while chasing the ambition of some mysterious woman and the damned rebellion. "This is a mistake. Let's get our shit and get out of here."

Maeve stares at me as if I've grown a second head. "What are you talking about?"

"We'll figure out another way. One that doesn't involve you slamming your body repeatedly against a ridiculously hard surface and injuring yourself. Or battling a half fucking mermaid. I've heard the same stories you have. Lucky isn't the same thing as a water horse, Maeve. If it was a matter of stealing back my jewels alone, then I could go in by myself and retrieve them before anyone knew I was there." Probably. It would be simple enough to send the sentries into unconsciousness and slip past them. If there was a fight, it wouldn't be with the entire fucking crew.

It's an entirely different prospect to take Bastian back by stealth. They will have their strongest people watching the prisoner, especially if he's as dangerous as Siobhan says. He must be. When she originally said he had glamour power, I thought of the humans I've met who can say the same. They are able to change their appearance, but not their physical form, and sometimes they can even charm their words a bit to soften someone to seeing things their way. But that's it.

On the other hand, there's an entire bloodline of vampires whose power is glamour. A single word from them is enough to stop even the most powerful predator in their tracks and make them helpless as a babe. *That* is dangerous. There's a reason we don't fuck with them unless we absolutely have to—and when we have to, we attack from long range. That bloodline is the reason I'm proficient in sniper rifles.

Impossible to glamour me into doing their will if they're missing their head.

If Bastian's power is anywhere in *that* vicinity, then he's exactly as dangerous as the Cŵn Annwn believe. If his glamour works the same way that Wolf's paramour's does, then his guards will have him gagged. If they're smart, they'll have him gagged, blindfolded, and bound.

If the ship goes down, he'll die.

"Lizzie." Maeve steps to me and grasps my shoulders. "This might be our only chance to get your heirlooms back. It could be months or longer to track them down again, and if they go to Lyari, then they're beyond our reach for as long as they're there. No matter how powerful and formidable you are, the capital is filled with the Cŵn Annwn. It's too dangerous to risk."

I don't give a fuck about my family heirlooms.

The thought shocks me. Ever since I realized Evelyn had them with her when she disappeared, retrieving those jewels had been the thing motivating every single one of my actions. Maeve is right. I should be frothing at the mouth to follow Siobhan's orders just to get them back. I shouldn't care if anyone's hurt in the process. My mother would whip me for experiencing even a sliver of doubt, of hesitation.

But I *do* care. A whole fucking lot. More than I know how to put into words.

It's on the tip of my tongue to ask Maeve what happens if we just . . . let them go. If we stopped hunting them. If we took a different route. I have no desire to settle down in some tiny selkie town, but Threshold is vast and filled with wonder. We could spend the rest of our lives traveling it.

Except that's just another problem. I have the potential to live several of Maeve's lifetimes. She will grow old and frail and eventually slip beyond my reach, while I will still be hale and hearty. The thought makes me sick to my stomach.

What if I bit her? Not the bite of feeding but the bite of turning. Bloodline vampires don't make a habit of turning humanoid paranormals into vampires. A turned vampire is a different creature all together. They gain the life span and superhuman strength and speed, but none of the powers that come with being part of the bloodline. And their bite hurts rather than giving pleasure.

Still, it would mean she was alive.

"Lizzie," Maeve says again. She squeezes my shoulders and gives me a tiny shake. "Even without your heirlooms in play, we *cannot* let the Council get their hands on Bastian. If he's close enough to Siobhan for her to care if he lives or dies, then he's privy to secrets that will cost a massive loss of life. More than that, they'll become aware of the rebellion before we're ready for them to know. It will be an all-out war. I don't see how the rebellion can possibly win unless we have the element of surprise on our hands. We have to save him."

"Or kill him." That's the simplest solution. It means the rebellion loses their glamour mage, but it prevents the Cŵn Annwn from getting access to his secrets.

She narrows her eyes. "I realize that murder is your default, but even without the risk of him falling into the Council's hands, it cannot be overstated what a powerful tool he is. We need him."

I knew she'd say that, but it's not going to stop me from arguing. "How can you need someone who you didn't know existed a few hours go?"

She sets her jaw in a stubborn angle I'm beginning to recognize. Maeve may bend when it comes to certain things, but the moment she digs in her heels, my chances of convincing her to see things my way diminish rapidly. Sure enough, when she speaks, her voice is clipped and angry. "I understand this isn't a priority to you, but his existence can alter the course of the rebellion. Once you collect your family heirlooms, you're leaving Threshold. You don't have to continue to live in a world where we suffer every time a Cŵn Annwn crew feels like causing problems. If this man is vital to Siobhan's plan, then we need him. It doesn't matter if you think we do or not, because *she* thinks we do and therefore we *will* save him."

That's the problem with a cause. It makes martyrs of far too many people. It's clear in every line of her body and the boldness in her tone that Maeve believes in the rebellion wholeheartedly. She doesn't want to die, but she's willing to if it comes to that.

I don't understand what it's like to believe in a cause so much that you're willing to lay down your life for it. Survival is paramount. It's the only rule of my existence, aside from serving my family. But those two things dovetail together, because for the family to survive, its members must survive. I don't understand the urge to be a hero, and yet I keep finding myself in close proximity to people who possess it.

At the start of this conversation, I knew it was a long shot. For once, I wish I was wrong. "Even if I draw my line, you're going with Siobhan to attack that ship, aren't you?"

Maeve hesitates, and I can tell she doesn't want to fight any more than I do, but she finally gives a short nod. "Yes. It's too important not to. I understand that you don't understand it—"

"I understand it. I just don't agree." I scrub my hands over my face. This is a fucking mess. If I was back home, I could at least call on an ally or two to weigh the scales in our favor. But here, my only allies exist on the *Audacity*, and according to Siobhan, that ship is too far away to be of assistance.

"You don't have to do this," Maeve says softly. "I know this isn't your fight."

If she keeps saying things like that, I might scream. It's *not* my fight, but that doesn't change the fact that I'm invested despite myself. Not because I believe in the rebellion, though even I can see that the Cŵn Annwn are a detriment to this realm. If I was stuck in Threshold without Maeve at my side, I would content myself with hunting them quietly in ways that can't be traced back to me. I wouldn't start a fucking rebellion.

But Maeve's already in this up to her neck—which means I am, too. The thought makes me dizzy. The realization of just how much I care for her washes over me. Not care. This sickness inside me, this feeling that's both giddiness and dread, can only be one thing: *love*. What a fucking disaster.

"Fine. We're doing this. We'll meet up with Siobhan tomorrow and go over the details one last time, and then we'll attack as they make anchor in the bay. Satisfied?"

Maeve looks anything but. She stares at me with confusion in her inky eyes. "I don't understand you sometimes. Why put yourself at risk for something you don't believe in?"

I could lie and tell her the only reason I'm agreeing to a plan that's just this side of suicidal is because I want my family heirlooms back. It's not the truth. It hasn't been the truth for some time now. And it feels wrong to lie to her.

It's like I don't even know myself anymore.

I drag in a breath. "I'm not going to let you get yourself killed in service of some cause. Rebellions tend to value the benefit of the many over the survival of the individual. They love a fucking martyr." Even saying the words makes my chest go tight. "It's incredibly incentivizing. A name to scream as they charge into battle, wasting their lives just like the martyrs do. Well, fuck that. You aren't going to be a martyr. I won't allow it. You're going to live a long, happy life, godsdamn it. If I have to kill every single threat that comes into your sphere, then so be it. But I *will* see it happen."

Maeve's lips part, her rosebud mouth forming a perfect O. She blinks rapidly. I'm horrified to see her eyes go damp with unshed tears. "I care about you too, Lizzie. A lot," she whispers. She gives herself a little shake and eases back. "I don't want to become a martyr. I promise I won't take any unnecessary risks during this process."

I don't believe her for a moment. This is the woman who battled a water horse to save me. A creature that, by all rights, should have ripped her to pieces. But she didn't care. All she was thinking about was keeping me alive—not of the risk to herself.

That's exactly what she'll do when the ship comes. She'll dive into the fight without worrying about watching her back. She'll rip herself to pieces as long as the *Crimson Hag* goes down.

"I'll be there to ensure you don't." I close the new distance between us and cup her face with my hands. "No one will touch you, Maeve. I swear it."

"Lizzie." She gives a laugh that almost sounds like a sob. "You're terrified of the water. I can't ask you to be in the depths with me."

Her speaking my deepest shame almost unravels me. It's something I've tried very hard to cover up, to shield, to pretend doesn't exist. But it's the truth. I am afraid of the depths. It's impossible to be an apex predator when at such a disadvantage. "It doesn't matter. A promise is a promise, and I promise to keep you alive."

Her bottom lip quivers the tiniest bit before she makes a visible effort to still it. "I don't think I want to talk about this anymore." She sets her hands on my hips, her fingers pulsing. "I just want you. The risk and danger and everything will be waiting for us in the morning, but tonight, all I want is you."

She's all I want, too. Not for a single night. Not for a series of hours that will have no chance of sustaining me. I want her forever. But now isn't the time to say as much. It feels too much like confessing your love before riding off to die in battle. It's not my style.

So instead, I start backing her toward the bed. "You have me, Maeve. I'm right here. Take me."

CHAPTER 31

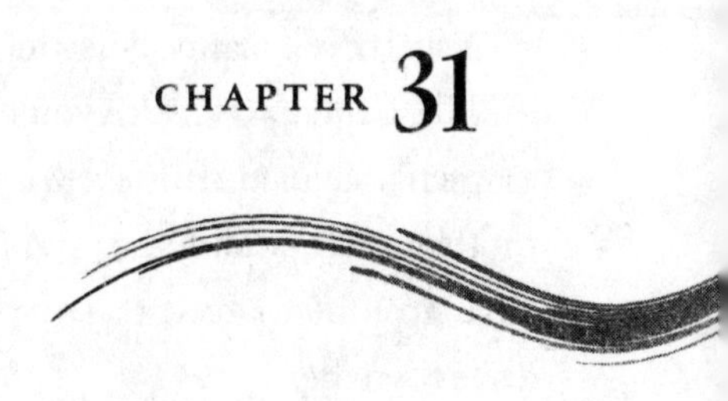

Maeve

SOMEDAY, SOMEHOW, I DESPERATELY WANT LIZZIE IN A bed that's *ours*. Not a couch or mattress or bathtub belonging to someone else. It's a fool's desire. No matter what her words seem to indicate, she's still leaving. She's always been leaving.

But not tonight.

I press her down to the bed, thankful that it's actually a decent size. It's soft and fluffy, and Lizzie bounces a little on the mattress. Her expression is as open as I've ever seen it, and the naked longing written over her features makes my heart beat faster. I care about her so much. I love her, though admitting as much aloud would make me a fool in the worst way.

So I don't.

I kiss her, filling each touch, each taste, with all the things I don't dare put into words. The thought of attacking a Cŵn Annwn ship openly fills me with the kind of fear I don't know how to combat. There will be no going back. If someone on the crew sees me, recognizes me, then my life as I know it is over. I can't go home. To do so would put my family in danger.

It might not matter. Being related to me is enough to condemn them, though if the Cŵn Annwn try to take them, they'll have the entire island up in arms. If I don't go home, if they investigate my mother and grandmother and find out—truthfully—that they have nothing to do with any rebellion, it might be enough to leave them be.

As long as I never go home again.

"Maeve." Lizzie cups my face, her eyes worried. "Are you okay?"

"I don't know." Perhaps I should lie, should keep this moment of unspoken feelings going. "So much is changing. The risks are so intense, the consequences for failure even more so. I believe in what the rebellion is doing, and I'm willing to sacrifice it all for the cause, but . . ."

Understanding dawns. "Your family."

"Yes." I shudder out a breath, glad that I don't have to explain. If there's one thing Lizzie and I have in common, it's that sense of familial obligation. We just . . . go about it in different ways. "Doing this means not going home. Not for a long time, maybe not ever." Saying it aloud does exactly what I fear—it makes it real. I might never be able to go home. As much as the shores of Viedna felt like they were smothering me at times, losing them is losing a vital part of myself.

Lizzie strokes her thumbs over my cheeks, lightly tracing her touch from freckle to freckle. "As a general rule, I don't like noble causes."

"Because martyrs," I say faintly. I have her in bed, and we're talking about death and loss. What a sad little excuse for a seduction.

"Because martyrs," she confirms. "And because for so many people, being noble means their common sense and ruthlessness go out the window. Successful rebellions need that ruthlessness, they need leaders and people willing to do horrible, unforgivable things. I don't want that for you. You're so damn *good*." She says it like it's a revelation. "It would hurt you for that goodness to die, and I'm viciously opposed to you being hurt."

From Lizzie, that's practically a declaration of love. Or it would be if I were romantic and foolish enough to believe her feeling anything for me would be enough to keep her from leaving.

My eyes burn. "Things can't go on the way they are, Lizzie. I understand that this isn't your fight, but it *is* mine."

"I know." She sighs. "I suppose, in addition to keeping you alive, I'll have to protect your goodness as well." She brushes a light kiss against my lips. "It will mean you'll have to ease your rules about murder, though. Do you think you can do that?"

I sit up, still straddling her, so I can see her face clearly. Surely she isn't suggesting what her words seem to? "Lizzie," I say carefully. "You're leaving. It might take a little time to find the appropriate portal to get you close enough to find your way home, but it won't be more than a few weeks. This conflict with the Cŵn Annwn, once it truly begins, could last for years." That's the best-case scenario, the one where the Cŵn Annwn don't crush us within a few weeks. I want to believe we have enough resources to win, but my knowledge of the full extent of the rebellion has been intentionally limited.

Easier to protect the rebellion if I were taken in and tortured.

Her hands fall to my thighs, but she's still painfully serious. "If the time difference remains as pronounced as it was between

Evelyn going through the portal and me going through one, it's been years since I left home. My mother likely thinks I'm dead."

I study her expression, trying to divine her emotions. "But you're not. You could still go home."

"I know." She lifts her hands a little and lets them drop back to my thighs. "I know," she repeats. She seems to be working through something, so I stay silent, waiting. Finally, she takes a deep breath and speaks softly, almost tentatively. "But . . . what if I didn't? What if I stayed?"

My heart soars. It's everything I can do to keep from shouting with joy. Surely she's not saying she wants to stay for *me*. By all accounts, her mother is a monster, and escaping that environment is reason enough to never go home.

"You could stay." My words are just as tentative, but they don't sit right with me. The temptation to protect myself, to retreat from vulnerability, is nearly overwhelming. She's baring a part of herself to me right now, something she's never done before, and I refuse to do anything but match her energy. "I want you to stay. Not just in Threshold. With me. I want you to stay with me."

Her hands tighten on my thighs. "We're setting ourselves up for tragedy. My life span is significantly longer than yours."

I frown. "What are you talking about?"

"I've already lived two hundred years. I probably have another few centuries in me, if my mother is anything to go by. I'm not exactly certain how long bloodline vampires live, but it's long enough for this to be tragic." She shifts up to cup my hips. "I won't age. One day I'll just . . . be gone. But that will be far too long after you've grown old and passed painlessly in your sleep."

She says it with such fierceness, as if she can will me to such a peaceful end. Happiness flickers in my chest, hope feeding it until it's a roaring fire that makes me smile. Better yet, I finally have good news to share with her. "Selkies live a few hundred years, Lizzie. I know I don't look it, but I'm fifty."

She blinks. "What?" Her brows draw together. "You're saying you've lived for *fifty years,* and I'm the first person who's eaten your pussy?"

My skin heats and I shift, which only serves to remind me that we're both naked and pressed together. "I don't know what it's like with vampires, but selkies take longer than humans to mature. I was only considered a proper adult ten years ago."

"That's still too long."

Despite everything, that startles a laugh out of me. "You're getting distracted."

"I suppose I am." She drags her thumbs over my skin. "I love you, Maeve. I might not care about the rebellion for my own sake, but I care about it for yours."

She loves me. I want her to want it for her sake, too, but I realize that's a tall ask for Lizzie. She's only been in Threshold for a few months, and she doesn't seem overly inclined to care about this sort of thing in general. Or at least she didn't use to. I study her face. "I think you might care about it more than you think. Otherwise, you'd just kidnap me and haul me off somewhere until the coming conflict had ended."

"Don't give me ideas." She smirks, but the expression melts into something softer. "And don't start getting the wrong idea about me. The Cŵn Annwn piss me off. I'd be happy killing them even if there wasn't a rebellion involved."

"If you say so."

She pulls me back down onto her. "Don't say it like that. Like you don't believe me."

I *don't* believe her. But Lizzie has taken a huge leap of faith in even having this conversation, so I'm not going to push her. I kiss her. There's every possibility that we won't survive the coming attack. I don't like thinking it, and I know better than to say as much, but it's the three of us against one of the most dangerous ships the Cŵn Annwn have to offer. If Siobhan wasn't desperate, she never would have tasked us with bringing it down on such short notice and with so few people.

But that's a fear for tomorrow. Right now, I have Lizzie in a bed that's not ours but will suit us just fine. More, she's confessed to loving me. Something I hardly dared dream would happen. "I love you, too," I whisper against her lips.

There's no more time for talking, for anything but pleasure, sealing our words in a way as old as time itself. Or that's what it feels like when Lizzie rolls us so she's on top and pulls me so close, I'm not sure where she ends and I begin. I don't need to know. Not right now. Maybe not ever.

There's no rush. We're all gently questing hands and ragged gasps. We taste and touch and weave pleasure that's only more intense for the steady build. By the time I make my way back to her mouth, our kiss tastes of both of us, a combination I never want to lose. My body shakes, sweat glistening on my skin. For her part, Lizzie is no less affected. She stares down at me, her eyes swallowed by crimson.

Her fangs peek out, just a little. "Maeve." There's a wealth of meaning in my name on her lips. An agony of wanting. "I'll kill anything that hurts you. And that includes me."

That's about enough of *that*. I dig my fingers into her hair. "I trust you."

"You shouldn't."

I tilt my head to the side, baring my neck. "Lizzie . . . I trust you."

She licks her lips. "It's a bad idea."

"I want you to." But I don't pull her head to me. I wait, giving her time to work through what she wants versus what she fears.

Finally, a small eternity later, Lizzie meets my gaze. "Are you sure?"

"Yes." There's no question. I realize it's not realistic to have her only feed from me, but being deprived of her bite is agony. I hate that she's been holding part of herself back from me. I want all of her.

She doesn't ask again. She eases down slowly and kisses my neck. When she does bite me, it's so soft at first that I hardly realize it's happened. Only the pleasure gathering in response to the nick of her teeth conveys that she's broken skin. A single swallow of blood is all she allows herself. A single pull that echoes through my entire body, sending me sweeping into an orgasm that curls my toes and bows my spine.

I cling to her as she licks the small wounds, healing them with her blood. She lifts herself enough to stare into my face, obviously searching for signs of fear or regret. There's only love.

I smile, feeling a bit goofy. "Told you."

"You've very cute when you're smug." She smiles as she says it. "I like it."

I drag my thumb over her bottom lip. "It's greed. I want to keep going."

"Mmm. Yes." She settles down on top of me. "But I like you greedy just as much as I like you smug." Her hand delves back between my thighs. "Morning will come soon enough, Maeve. I mean to have my fill of you until then."

CHAPTER 32

Lizzie

After spending the night wrapped up in each other, Maeve and I sleep well past noon. I manage to keep my hands off her long enough to drag her to a nearby restaurant and ensure she gets fed, but by the time we're done with that, the sun is sinking low in the sky.

Siobhan arrives soon after. The cloak she wore yesterday to shield her features is nowhere in evidence. She's so fucking athletic and that jaw is so strong, I have the sneaking suspicion that I could break my knuckles on it.

I belatedly realize she's holding a harness. It takes me all of three seconds to realize what she intends. To use it on Maeve. I open my mouth to protest, but Maeve anticipates me. She squeezes my hand and steps forward. "It's the fastest way to ensure we make it through the water without anyone noticing."

I don't like it. I don't like any of this. And not just because it requires me to swim through dark water where anything could be below me. I haven't gone under since the fight with the water horse, and I'm not looking forward to this experience. But the alternative is to let Maeve and Siobhan go without me, and that's no alternative at all.

For Siobhan to be the leader of this rebellion, it means that she's willing to accept losses. Not this Bastian, apparently, but Maeve is hardly a linchpin in the rebellion. If something happens tonight, then she's just another martyr along the way. A name to call as the people who care about her charge into a battle that will see most of them dead.

I'm not going to let that happen. Maeve is not replaceable to *me*. She's not some faceless martyr. She's mine. I'll do whatever it takes to protect her, even if it means striking down Siobhan herself.

Siobhan leads us down to the lowest level, where the docks are, but turns away from them and heads toward the edge of town. It's not particularly late, but the farther we get from the docks, the more deserted the gently curving street is. I catch a glimpse of light behind closed shutters, but apparently we're in a residential neighborhood and there's no nightlife to speak of.

It certainly makes it easier to sneak around without being seen.

Within a few minutes, we leave the town behind entirely. The carefully curated road turns into little more than a goat track—or whatever the goat equivalent they have on Drash is—that curves around the bay in a deceptively gentle incline. We pick our way along single file: Siobhan in front, followed by Maeve, with me picking up the rear. It takes all my preternatural skill to stay on my feet. The rock reminds me of shale, ready to crumble without a moment's notice. One wrong step, and we'll end up falling into the water crashing against the rocks below.

I've never been such a pessimist, bordering on fatalistic. Again and again, I consider knocking Siobhan over the head, tossing Maeve over my shoulder, and getting the fuck away from here. Only the knowledge that Maeve would never forgive me stays my hand.

This is fucked.

The trail ends in a neatly hidden cave mouth. Judging by the crates stacked up well past where the waterline is, this is a location used by the rebellion. Siobhan moves to one of the crates and pries open the lid. "We'll want to change out of the clothing we're in. Here." She tosses something at me and then at Maeve. I hold it up to find a garment very similar to a wetsuit. It will cover me from ankles to wrists to throat, and the fabric is thick in a spongy kind of way. It's not a proper scuba suit, as such things go, but as I strip out of my clothes and pull it on, it instantly insulates me from the chill in the air.

Next to me, Maeve has also donned her suit. She rubs her hands down her hips and makes an appreciative sound. "This is very cleverly made."

"They come in handy in a pinch." Siobhan braids her hair back in quick, efficient movements. With her suit hugging every inch of her, I reluctantly admire how powerfully she's built. Even more so than I initially realized. She looks like she could bench-press a car—not just because she's a shifter—and has inherently more strength packed into that strong frame than even a human of her same size and shape would.

"Lizzie, I need you to watch Maeve's back. I'm going to climb up into the ship through the hole as soon as we break it and retrieve Bastian. The two of you will be in the water alone for a short time."

She wants me to watch Maeve's back. I look out over the dark water. Rationally, I knew what I was agreeing to, but somehow I've been able to avoid thinking about the specifics. That's not an option any longer.

I'm more than capable of protecting Maeve on land, but in the water? With all that space in every direction, the darkness shielding anything that may be approaching? My throat spasms and I have to fight to breathe normally, to not gasp. I don't know if I can do this. I *have* to do this. Maeve is hardly helpless in the water, but she's a *seal*. Anyone with the smallest drop of offensive magic will have her outgunned.

Maeve tenses beside me. "What about Lizzie's family heirlooms? If she's protecting me and you're getting Bastian, then who is retrieving the jewels?"

Siobhan flashes a smile, too sharp. "Those jewels will go down with the ship. They'll be easy to retrieve once the dust has settled."

As plans go, it's not the worst I've heard. I open my mouth to say as much, but Maeve gets there first.

She frowns. "There's no guarantee they'll still be in the ship within a couple hours of it sinking, let alone a couple days. The bay is closed off from the greater open sea, but if it's anything like Viedna, the currents move strangely the deeper you go. It's entirely possible they'll rip the ship to shreds and scatter it. It could be months, or longer, before we're able to find all of the cargo."

Siobhan doesn't look happy with the persistent questions. She turns to me. "Well? Does the selkie speak for you?"

"The selkie has a name," I snap. It doesn't matter that I refused to say her name initially upon meeting her. We are putting our necks out for Siobhan and the godsdamn rebellion. The least she can do is show Maeve a little respect. "Is there a reason you don't want to answer her?"

Siobhan drags in a breath and seems to fight for control of herself. "I understand your priorities may not be my priorities, but I hope *you* can understand why I don't really give a shit about some jewels. They have Bastian, and if we don't retrieve him—"

"We've heard it before. Doom, gloom, the end of Threshold as we know it." I wave that away. "Give us a moment." I take Maeve's arm and tug her deeper into the cave. The space isn't large enough to have true privacy, not when a shifter's senses are superior even to my own, but it gives the illusion and that's good enough. "It's fine, Maeve. I'm more worried about you than I am about the jewels."

"It's *not* fine." Maeve jerks her arm from my grasp. "This whole time, you've had one aim, one task. I understand that we need to save Bastian, but surely we can do both. If you go into the breach behind Siobhan, then you can retrieve the jewels while she retrieves Bastian."

Which would leave Maeve unprotected in the water. "No. Absolutely not."

"Lizzie." She's so serious it makes my heart ache. "Don't you think you've sacrificed enough for other people? Ever since you've come to Threshold—and even before that, honestly—you've been on a mission to retrieve what was stolen from you. We're closer than we've ever been, and I'm not comfortable with you compromising yet again in the name of a cause that you don't believe in."

I almost laugh out loud at how she's misunderstanding things. She's right that I don't give a shit about the rebellion. I'm never going to give a shit about the rebellion. But *she* does. She cares about it, so by virtue of loving her, I care about it, too. But even then, I'd let both Siobhan and Bastian burn if it meant Maeve would be safe. She's not going to be content to sit on the sidelines.

So we're going into the water and sinking the damn ship.

"We talked about this. I'm staying in Threshold. I don't need the jewels." I take her shoulders, holding her steady when she snarls at me. I *love* that she snarls at me. "I'm not leaving you in the water alone."

"What do you think you're going to do?" She tries to pull back and swats at my hands. "I saved *you* from the kelpie. I can take care of myself. I need you to trust me to do that, because I'm not going to be an oath breaker because you don't believe I'm capable enough."

Oh for gods' sake, she almost sounds like Bowen right now. I strive for patience and mostly fail. "We took no oaths."

"You're being intentionally difficult and I don't appreciate it." She blows a hard exhale through her nose. "I know what we said, but it changes nothing. Deciding to stay is a big decision, and it's also reversible. If we lose your family heirlooms to the depths? That *isn't* reversible. I want you to have the option, Lizzie. If you stay, I want you to do it because you choose to, not because you failed and can't go home."

Fuck, I love this woman. I drop my hands. "If you want me to trust you in the water, then you need to trust me to know my own mind when it comes to those damned jewels."

Maeve makes another of those cute little growls. "If you're that worried about me, then use that vampire speed to quickly retrieve your heirlooms." She holds up a hand before I have a chance to keep arguing. "I understand your concern for me, and I respect it. Which is why, after the breach in the hull is big enough, I'll put some distance between me and the ship until you and Siobhan and Bastian are ready to escape." And then she'll drag us to safety.

"I'm not leaving you. Tonight or ever." The words have weight beyond this conversation, this coming conflict. I understand what she says about having a choice, but I already made mine. I'm not going back. I'm staying in Threshold. I'm staying with *Maeve*.

She sets her shoulders in a way I'm becoming increasingly familiar with. "Then it won't matter one way or another if you have the jewels, so there's no reason *not* to get them. Promise me, Lizzie."

I fucking hate this plan, but Siobhan isn't going to give us time to come up with a better one. And Maeve clearly won't listen to reason even if I offer her an alternative. "Damn you."

"Promise me."

I'm helpless in the face of her intensity. I would give this woman the world on a platter if she asked it of me. Instead, the thing she wants is for me to allow her to be in danger, to trust her to handle herself in the coming conflict. When did she become such a stubborn little thing? Maybe she always has been, but we've been aligned in the same direction up until this point.

I finally give a jerky nod. "Stay alive. That's an order."

She catches the back of my neck and pulls me down into a quick and desperate kiss. "The same goes for you."

We rejoin an impatient Siobhan. She wastes no time holding up the harness. "It will be simpler if you shift now."

Maeve unfurls her pelt and swirls it around her shoulders.

There's that strange shimmer of consciousness, and then a giant-ass leopard seal flops before us. Seeing her in the water was one thing. Witnessing her size on land is completely different. She's *huge*, a sleek, strangely adorable killing machine. Distantly, I wonder if I'll ever stop being amazed by her.

Somehow, I don't think so.

She moves in the awkward hopping motion that seals do to the edge of the cave and waits for Siobhan to slide the harness—a simple round leather creation with three leads hanging from it—over her head. Siobhan shoves one of the leads into my hand. "Hook your arm through the loop at the end. The tension when she tows us will keep it tight."

The better to drag us through the cold, dark sea.

I slip my hand into the loop and grip the lead. There's no more time for questions or arguing or trying to find another way. I'll do whatever it takes to ensure Maeve makes it out alive. I'll break my promise to her in a heartbeat if it means she's alive to yell at me about it.

Siobhan can go down with the ship for all I care.

Maeve slides into the water in a movement that's almost liquid. After a beat, we follow her. I'm not particularly sensitive to cold, but the suit removes what little discomfort I may have experienced. I've never engaged in water sports before, and as Maeve drags us along the surface of the bay, I vow that I never will. This is *awful*.

Maybe it's the jerking motions of her dips and dives, constantly pulling us under and then back to the surface. Maybe it's being nothing more than a buoy dragged along, completely helpless. Or maybe it's the creeping fear that we're acting the part of particularly juicy bait on a moving hook.

For future attempts to sneak aboard a ship and murder everyone, I'm going to insist on a boat.

The *Crimson Hag* crouches nearly in the center of the bay. With each glimpse I get of it as we approach, I begin to understand why Alix insisted on not fighting them. The *Serpent's Cry* felt large enough when we were on board, but compared with the *Crimson Hag*, it's the size of a child's toy. The *Crimson Hag* dwarfs even the *Audacity*. This thing is a fucking warship.

How the hell is Maeve going to sink it?

Even without the sheer size of it, surely there are magical defenses below the surface. This ship battles sea monsters on a regular basis. If a monster could simply drive up from below and shatter the ship into a thousand pieces, it would be a very short hunt. But if there are magical barriers, surely Siobhan would have said something. She might be desperate to reclaim Bastian, but she doesn't have a death wish. At least I don't think she does.

Maeve pulls us even with the ship, slowing down enough that we're basically treading water. Siobhan looks at me. "It's time. Hold your breath." She reaches out and pats Maeve. "Let's go."

As Maeve dives deep down below the hull, it strikes me that I should have asked more questions. I just hope we live long enough to regret it.

CHAPTER 33

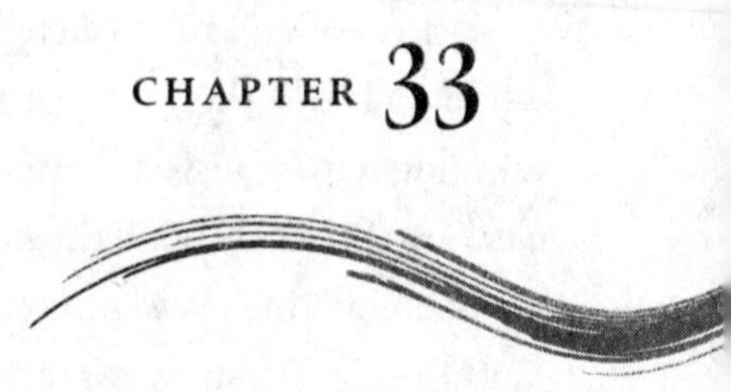

Maeve

I'M AS AT HOME BELOW THE SURFACE AS I AM ON LAND, BUT it feels different tonight. Aside from rowing out to take control of the *Serpent's Cry*, I hardly have a history of sneaking out to attack ships. The *Crimson Hag* being a Cŵn Annwn ship is almost enough to undermine my bravado. This is what the Cŵn Annwn *do*—fight and attack and kill. I've only ever killed for food . . . technically. Maybe the deaths Lizzie has committed while on this journey with me are as much my fault as hers. Maybe . . .

At this point I've been surviving off pure momentum, and it'll have to get me through to the end. That and the knowledge that if I falter, Lizzie will be focused on me instead of on what she needs to be focused on—getting her heirlooms back.

That, more than anything, gives me the strength to muscle down my fear and keep going.

I slow my pace roughly ten feet below the surface just at the curve of the hull. Siobhan pushes off me and latches herself onto the ship. It's dark enough that I can't see much, but I can hear perfectly as she rips her claws into the wood.

Even though I refused to show doubt to Lizzie, I definitely wondered how this plan would work. By all rights, it should take hours for a person to use their claws—or their bulk, in my case—to break through the hull of a ship.

But Siobhan's claws punch through the wood as if it's paper. Within seconds, she has a section weakened and a hole started. Later, I'll wonder how she could possibly manage that. Right now, I have a job to do.

I brush against Lizzie, trying to reassure her, before I dive deeper as Siobhan and Lizzie swim to the surface to catch their breath. Even now, even with the danger barreling down upon us and worry about Lizzie's fear and stubbornness, I have a moment of pure appreciation for the fact that I'm able to do this. Swim and fight and be *whole*. Then I spin around and charge back toward the ship.

Closer and closer and closer. At the last second, I twist to hit the hole with my shoulder instead of my head. It hurts. It hurts so incredibly bad. But the wood cracks further and breaks away. Another hit, maybe two, and the hole will be big enough for Siobhan and Lizzie to slip through.

There's no time to waste. I dive deep again, pushing my body faster and faster through the cold water. Distantly, there's a faint sound of a body hitting the water, but I can't focus on that right now. I have to trust Siobhan and Lizzie to keep whomever has come to investigate off me.

I barrel toward the surface and the ship and again twist at the last moment to hit it a second time. It truly gives way, my body wedging into the newly created hole hard enough that I have to fight to get free. The broken wood scratches at my skin, but I'm made of sterner stuff than that. I wiggle free and twist out into the water to find Siobhan in the middle of a fight with a shadowy figure.

I swim up underneath Lizzie and urge her to the surface again. It's only been a couple of minutes, but she can't hold her breath like I can. She fights me a little, but ultimately she's only humanoid and I'm a creature of the waves. We breach the surface and she takes a gasping breath. "We need to help her."

Siobhan's more than capable of taking care of herself. I have no voice in this form, but surely Lizzie can smell the blood saturating the water around us. It makes me a little nervous, because while there aren't likely to be a large number of predators in this bay, blood can make even the most cautious hunter forget themselves.

Lizzie curses and wraps her fingers around my harness. "Okay. I'm ready. Let's go."

I inhale deeply and dive below the surface, cutting through the water to where Siobhan is prying the hole open even further. In the distance, a body sinks into the depths, boneless in the way that only the dead are. There's no room for guilt inside me. While I have pity for those who have been forcibly conscripted by the Cŵn Annwn, the reality is that we have no way of knowing who is a potential ally and who is an enemy intent on our deaths.

If they come at us, we have to kill them.

The thought makes me sick, but I'll have the luxury to feel guilt later. If we survive this. Right now, I have to focus on getting Lizzie to that hole and inside. She's resisting me, her body tight and tense as I tow her toward it. Because she doesn't trust me to be able to take care of myself without her looking over my shoulder.

Pride is a wicked thing, and even at this point, I'm victim to it. I am so damned tired of being considered a victim. A selkie who lost their skin, a cliché that hurts me right down to my heart. Reclaiming that part of myself has gone a long way to heal that, but the wound still aches inside me. I won't let her experience even a sliver of the same regret by passing up this chance to reclaim what she lost.

Lizzie makes a sound and her fingers dig in tighter to my harness, but I'm having none of it. I twist my body back on itself and shove her into the hole, pushing her with my tail until she's all the way through. And then I dive again, taking refuge in the darkness below. If someone comes to investigate or attempt to patch the hole, I will deal with them. But my job now is to wait until Lizzie and Siobhan have returned and then get them to safety.

Even so, part of me expects to see Lizzie back through the hole, diving down to give me a piece of her mind. It's not disappointment I feel when she doesn't return. It's worry. Foolish. Lizzie is the most efficient killer I've ever met, and she won't hesitate to remove anyone standing between her and her goal. She'll live through the night. I'm certain of it. I have to be.

A body hits the water, diving deep before it turns and shoots its way toward the hole. Even in the darkness, this person is moving too efficiently to be a kind of paranormal more comfortable on land. This must be the half mermaid, Lucky.

I wait until they have their back to me, their hands frantically touching along the hole, until they shoot back to the surface to give their report. Attempting to patch it from the inside is a fool's errand. Even now, water will be rushing into the hull. The only way to patch it is from the outside. Which means that the mermaid will be returning.

Mermaid. I shudder at the thought. I have only seen mermaids once in my life, and once was more than enough. They frenzy, killing each other and their victims at the same time. They're damn near unstoppable, not needing to surface to breathe, not needing to slow down. It defies belief that someone associated with one of them long enough to breed a half-human child. I desperately don't want the details of that union.

But that's the least of my problems. Lucky is back, and this time they have a webbed bag full of tools to patch the hole. *Not on my watch.*

I wait until they turn to their task before I shoot up out of the darkness. I move fast as lightning, intent on surprising them. They're part mermaid, they can't drown, which means I'll have to find another way. A broken neck, like the water horse. Or blunt force.

But the moment before I strike, Lucky spins. Ready for me. Hands outstretched and a wicked grin on their face. *A trap.*

And I swam right into it.

I'm going too fast to divert my charge. That's the only thing that saves my life. I catch sight of the glint of a knife in their hand as we collide. If I had turned, they would have attempted to gut me.

I knock them into the side of the ship hard enough to rattle my brain in my skull, and pain pricks my side as they drive the knife into me. But I won't go down that easy. In this form, I have a thick shield of blubber to keep me warm in even the coldest temperatures, and it protects me now. Being stabbed hurts, and

I won't be able to fight indefinitely, but I'm not going to slow down yet.

I thrash, battering them against the side of the ship with everything I have. If I can make them drop the knife or knock them unconscious, the fight will be over. They cling to the weapon, stronger than they have any right to be. Over and over again they stab me as I slam them against the ship repeatedly, desperate to end this.

I break away, but I'm moving far less smoothly than I was previously. I shouldn't have taken my protection for granted. My blood joins Siobhan's victim's, coating the water around us. I dive deep, desperate to put some distance between us, to assess how bad the injuries actually are, but the mermaid follows me, intending to attack my exposed back.

I twist at the last moment, slapping them with my tail and sending them spinning away from me. They catch themselves almost immediately. I can't see how they're moving so well, not when they're mostly humanoid. They aren't quite as fast as I am, but they're agile enough to be a threat.

They charge me, and it's everything I can do to spin away before they make contact. I might be able to hold my breath for a very long time, but that doesn't change the fact that I *do* have to breathe eventually, and the fight is taking more energy than I expected. If I make it out of this alive, I'm going to train in underwater combat so that I'm never this helpless again.

Lucky keeps coming. I dodge again and again, but far too late I realize that they're driving me deeper into the depths. Farther away from the air I need to survive. In desperation, I swat at them and bolt past, heading for the surface.

I can feel them behind me, and if they're not gaining, they

are close enough that I'm not certain I'll make it. Even as the thought crosses my mind, their hand closes around my tail and jerks me back. Bubbles escape my nose, precious oxygen.

We're close enough to the surface that I can see the light of the moon glinting off the waves above. To my right is the lurking darkness of the *Crimson Hag*. So close, and yet with this mermaid crawling all over me, slashing and stabbing, it might as well be on another realm entirely.

I was so confident when I told Lizzie I didn't need her to watch my back. What a fool. My thoughts go muddy and strange, but I keep fighting even as my movements weaken, becoming sluggish and slow. The mermaid's bleeding me out, a thousand small cuts to do their dirty work more effectively than one big attack.

I catch movement out of the corner of my eye, and my despair gains wings. I could barely hold my own against a single combatant. How can I possibly do it against two? It's over. I'm dead. I don't stand a chance.

I'm sorry, Lizzie. I love you. I'm sorry.

But when the third person collides with us, it's not me they go after. They wrap their hands around the throat of the mermaid, and even as blurry as my thoughts are, I can hear the snap as they break Lucky's neck and then rip their head from their body. Blood is so thick in the water that I can't see, can't think.

Instinct guides me to the surface, to take the breath that I desperately need. It's as if that influx of oxygen conveys to my brain just how desperate my condition is. It's bad. Really, really bad.

My savior surfaces next to me, her dark hair plastered to her face. "Maeve! Maeve, talk to me."

Lizzie.

I might laugh if I had the mouth for it. Talk to her? I'm a leopard seal. But as she runs her hands over me, my thoughts slow further. Is she . . . stopping my bleeding? If I had my human voice, I would tell her that I think it's already too late, that I've lost too much blood—for real this time. That it's not her fault.

But maybe it's a blessing in disguise that I can't speak the truth, can't take away her hope. I've brought Lizzie so much suffering. I've broken through her cold exterior only to hurt her again and again. I just wish I could be sure I'd live long enough to say I'm sorry.

CHAPTER 34

Lizzie

THE *CRIMSON HAG* LISTS DRUNKENLY IN THE WATER, BUT it doesn't seem to be going down in a hurry. I could give a fuck. Not with Maeve listlessly treading water beside me. Hurt. She's so fucking hurt. There's as much of her blood in the water around us as there is the mermaid's. *Too much.*

Her body ripples, and I barely have a chance to get my arm around her as her skin falls away and leaves the human woman behind. I make a mad grab for the pelt. There's no fucking way I'm letting that sink to the bottom of this damned bay. When Maeve wakes up—because she *will* wake up—it won't be to learn that she's once again missing a vital part of herself.

The pelt is heavy, the fur large and waterlogged, dragging at me. I may be significantly stronger than a human, but I've never been the strongest swimmer. It doesn't matter. It *can't* matter. If I go under, then Maeve dies, and Maeve cannot die tonight. The thought shakes me to my very core. "No dying," I pant. "You don't get to . . . declare your love and then pass . . . tragically." I do another pass over her with my magic, pressing it into her wounds to keep her from bleeding out. I've never tried to do something like this before. I'm so much better versed in killing than in healing. Except this isn't healing at all. I'm only commanding the blood in her body to *stay* in her body. Or trying. It feels more slippery than normal, whether that's because my concentration is split or Maeve's blood is resisting my magic . . .

I don't know if I'm doing enough. I'm terrified that I'm not.

She lolls in my arms, unconscious. If not for the faint pulse of her heartbeat, I might believe she'd already slipped beyond my reach. "*No.*" I fight my way through the waves, foot by agonizing foot. "Live, Maeve. You have to *live*."

I drag Maeve and her pelt through the water. If she was conscious, she would tell me to stay, to make sure Siobhan gets out safely, but she's not and so I'm getting her away from Siobhan and the *Crimson Hag*. The whole damned rebellion can burn for all I care. Maeve is *not* dying tonight. "Stay alive, baby. Keep breathing. You have to keep breathing." With every stroke of my free arm, I curse myself for leaving her unprotected. And for what? Some fucking jewels. As if those lifeless gems could ever compare to the woman in my arms.

I should have ignored her insistence that I go for them. Should have fought my way back into the water faster after she shoved me through the hole. Should have . . .

A ripple of water is my only warning before a dark head pops up above the surface. I start to lash out, but they easily catch my foot. "Don't be a fucking fool, vampire. I don't want her dead, either."

Siobhan.

I don't allow myself to feel relief. We're still hundreds of yards from the shore, and I may have stopped more of Maeve's blood from leaving her body, but that doesn't mean she's going to be okay. My power pings over and over again with the sheer number of wounds she carries. She must've fought for so long. She should have run, should have protected herself instead of trying to ensure the ship kept sinking. I pull Maeve closer. "This is your fucking fault, shifter."

"Let me *help* you."

This is what Maeve's life will be like if she's left to her own devices. Fodder in a war fought by people more powerful than her. A martyr. Maybe not even that; maybe she'll just be a body that's fallen by the wayside as others pursue their ambitious goals. She deserves better. She deserves to have someone watching her back, ensuring that she reaches that ripe old age.

I don't deserve her. I have no illusions about that. She's too good, too honorable. But *she* deserves *me*. I'll make the calls she's too decent to make, and I won't hesitate to bloody my hands to keep her safe. I'll do anything to keep her safe.

I've already fucking failed.

"I'm going to rip out your throat," I gasp.

"Noted." Siobhan dips beneath the waves again, and then she's at our side, easily pushing me away from Maeve and wrapping her arm under Maeve's chest. "I've got her."

I'm having a hard enough time carrying the pelt, weighted down with the water the way it is. And Siobhan is taking obvious care with Maeve, which is all I could ask for. As much as I want to keep her in my arms, to measure the beat of her heart with my arm over her chest, Siobhan is obviously the stronger swimmer. She won't let Maeve drown. She better fucking not. I clutch the pelt to my chest. "If she dies, you die."

Siobhan ignores my threat. We swim toward the shore in strained silence as Maeve's color gets paler and paler. She's not actively bleeding, but obviously she's not anywhere close to waking up. To being okay.

I might lose her.

The thought is incomprehensible. Last night we exchanged words of love, and now her heartbeat is slowing to the point that, without my powers, I would think it's not beating at all. I barely came to terms with the fact that I don't want to leave, and now *she's* leaving *me*.

It takes far too long to reach the rocky beach near the cave we started the night in. Siobhan touches down first, sweeping Maeve into her arms and whisking her up onto dry land. I follow a few steps behind. My muscles quiver and shake, and the pelt feels approximately five thousand pounds. I don't think I've ever been this tired in my pathetically long life, but I keep putting one foot in front of the other. Maeve needs me. I won't falter. I can't lose her. I fucking *refuse*.

I reach the cave in time to see Siobhan lay Maeve down carefully on the floor. "Second crate down," she says without looking up. "There are medical supplies."

I don't take the time to argue. I shove the top crate away and rip open the second one. Some of the medical supplies look vaguely familiar, but most of them are completely foreign to me. Whether that means they're magical or simply a different technology is anyone's guess. I've hardly spent my time worrying about how to heal people when my blood—

My blood.

I grab bandages and rush back to them. "My blood can heal her." I wasn't willing to take the chance on the *Serpent's Cry*. I had been out of my mind with worry, but it was clear she was recovering. That's not the case now. I don't know what happens if a selkie imbibes vampire blood, but if she doesn't, it's increasingly looking like she might slip away permanently.

I won't let her die. No matter what it takes.

Siobhan has been busy in the seconds that I was away, using her claws to cut the suit from Maeve's body. The wounds revealed make my stomach twist. I'm hardly queasy when it comes to evidence of violence, but this is *Maeve*. Stab wounds cover her entire body. I have no idea how she fought as long as she did. The bandages in my hands won't cover half of them. I drop them, my chest so tight, I'm having a hard time drawing breath. "You said no martyrs, Maeve," I whisper. She should have run. Why didn't she fucking run?

"If we—"

"Shut up. You've done enough." Any doubt I had about giving her my blood disappears. It's the only choice we have. "Get out of the way."

"You don't know what that blood will do to her. Neither of us do."

Even with my powers artificially sealing her wounds, they gently ooze blood. She's going to die if we don't do something, and out of all the outcomes that I've played through my head, different scenarios with varying degrees of heartbreak, her dying is unacceptable. I won't allow it.

"It's our only option." It shouldn't be enough to change her, but no matter the outcome, at least she'll be alive to hate me if it comes to that. I drag my nail along the inside of my arm. "Hold her head."

Siobhan hesitates for the faintest heartbeat, and then she's moving, shifting behind Maeve to lift her head and shoulders as I press my bleeding arm to her lips. Too cold. She's too damn cold. I barely even registered how deliciously warm she is all the time until that heat is nowhere in evidence. My blood dribbles into her mouth, but she doesn't swallow.

"Come on, baby. You have to live." I gently massage her throat, artificially urging her to swallow. It's tempting to give her more blood, but a few mouthfuls should heal even the most mortal of wounds. It just takes time.

Siobhan rises and walks deeper into the cave only to return with a stack of blankets. She props a folded one under Maeve's head and covers her with the other two. "So . . . Now we wait?"

"Now we wait," I confirm. I've healed people with my blood in the past, but I've never cared about the results as deeply as I do right now. I measure every slow beat of Maeve's heart, searching for some indication that the blood is working. It will heal her. It has to.

"He wasn't there."

I'm so busy focusing on Maeve, it takes me a few moments to realize that Siobhan has spoken at all. And a few moments more for her meaning to penetrate. "Bastian?" Obviously I registered that we hadn't acquired a fourth person in our retreat, but I honestly don't give a fuck about Siobhan or her goals. If the glamour mage drowned, then he drowned.

"Yes. He had definitely been on the *Crimson Hag*, and recently. His scent was all over the cell in the brig, but it's at least a few days old. They must have passed him off almost as soon as they captured him."

She's obviously upset, and she *did* help me get Maeve to shore, so I don't make a derogatory comment about shifters and their noses. I think that's called growth. Maeve will be proud of me if she wakes up. *When* she wakes up. I swallow hard and search for the appropriate response, the words Maeve would instinctively know. "I'm sorry."

Siobhan scrubs her hands over her face. For the first time since I met her, she looks startlingly young and almost vulnerable. It strikes me that she can't be more than thirty, maybe thirty-five. Practically a baby, and yet she's carrying around a burden that I can barely comprehend. Whether she picked it up willingly or it was thrust upon her is anyone's guess, and frankly I don't give a fuck.

But Maeve cares and so I try. "I'm sure you'll find him. You just have to retrace the route the *Crimson Hag* took and find out where they dropped him off."

"That will take too much time. He's headed for Lyari, and whether or not I know which ship he's on . . . fuck." She turns and punches the wall, and I'm startled to watch cracks form. Shifters are strong, but this is on another level entirely. "We'd have to search every ship sailing in that direction, and there's no way to guarantee that would be enough. Even if I wanted to try that, we don't have that many ships or that many people. It's impossible."

Again, I wonder who this man is to her, and if it's as personal as it seems. Obviously he's helping with the rebellion, but there are plenty of powerful people helping with the rebellion. This is something more—and not just because he has the ability to glamour people into doing his will. "Who is he to you?"

"No one now. But he was once." She holds up her hand and watches her knuckles heal, the skin knitting back together where it had been broken by her punch. "No matter what you believe, this *isn't* personal. His powers can change the course of the rebellion. If he dies, I don't see a way forward."

I snort. "That's a whole load of bullshit. You have Nox, who can take out an entire crew in a series of heartbeats. And Bowen, who can probably level an entire fucking island with that damn telekinetic power. They are just two people who believe in your cause. There are others, and I imagine they must have a range of powers. Pull yourself together."

"Nox . . ." She gets a strange look on her face. "You're right. I'm letting frustration get the best of me. I really thought we'd save Bastian tonight and everything would be back on track." She crouches down next to Maeve. "Her breathing has evened out."

I scan Maeve again with my powers. The wounds have started to close, though it's slower than I'd like it to be, but more importantly, her blood is once again flowing in a regular rhythm. Relief makes my knees weak. "Her heartbeat, too."

"Look, I know this is shitty, but time is of the essence. I have to go. No one will look for you here, but I would stay out of the village. When she's up for it, follow the trail past the path where it branches back toward the village. It will take you to the top of the cliffs, and you can skirt around to the east side of the island. There's a sea cave there with a small sailboat. It's not much, but it's stocked with food and water and supplies. It can get you to the nearest island. You should be able to catch a ride on a trading ship from there."

Obviously the sailboat in question is hers and how she's been traveling without a crew. But that begs the question: "Where are you going?"

"A local captain owes me a favor. The *Audacity* will be sailing south of here in a day or two. If I can flag them down, then Nox will be honor bound to help me retrieve Bastian."

I'm not so sure about that. I want nothing more than to see the back of Siobhan, but as I look down at Maeve, I can't help hearing her voice in my head. *Help her.* I don't want to. Putting the rebellion behind us would be my preference, anything to keep Maeve out of danger. And yet I find myself speaking: "No reason to split up."

"Excuse me?"

"It will be quicker if you wait for Maeve to wake up and we take your ship . . . together." I'm feeling my way, Maeve's palm warming against mine where I hold her hand. "This one won't be content to sit by and watch others take risks going forward, and I won't let anything happen to her. We're headed back to Nox as well. We might as well travel together."

Siobhan studies me, her body tense as if she wants to spring into motion. "Very well. I'm going into town to make a resupply run and see if I can find any information about what might have happened to Bastian. I'm sure the *Crimson Hag*'s crew will have made landing by now." She stalks to the crates and digs through them until she comes up with a cloak that looks identical to the one she wore when we met her. "Meet me at my ship by dusk tomorrow."

"We'll be there."

"Maeve will be fine." She flips the hood of the cloak up around her face and hesitates. "Sorry about your jewels, though."

I'd all but forgotten them. Again, I wonder what the fuck I've been doing. Chasing down some godsdamned inanimate objects, putting Maeve at risk to do so, and for what? To go back to a life where I was just going through the motions. I've lived so fucking long, and this last couple of weeks is the most alive I've ever felt.

I don't want to go home. I don't give a fuck about the jewels. I just want Maeve to be okay.

As Siobhan slips out of the cave, I settle down next to Maeve and take her hand. I can carry her to Siobhan's ship if I need to, but I'm going to give her as much time as possible to sleep and let my blood continue to heal her.

There's nothing to do but wait.

CHAPTER 35

Maeve

Everything hurts. It's a strange sort of pain, weighing me down and making it hard to open my eyes. But it's not sharp like I expected to experience when I woke up . . . if I woke up at all. If not for Lizzie—

Lizzie.

My eyes fly open and I try to sit up. Or at least my brain gives the command. All I'm capable of is a jerky movement that barely raises my body off the hard surface I'm lying on. Hands press to my chest, easing me back down. Then Lizzie's face appears over me, concern etching lines that bracket her mouth and spider from the corners of her eyes. "Steady, Maeve." She sounds exhausted, too, more tired than I've ever heard her. She takes my hand and guides it to a damp fur folded neatly next to me. My pelt.

"What happened?" I croak.

"You're alive." She gives a faint smile and brushes my hair

back, her touch gentle and filled with so much emotion that my throat tries to close. "Take things slowly. My blood healed you, but accelerated healing is hard on the body in its own way when you're not used to it."

She's calm. Too calm. Last time I woke up in what amounts to a sickbed, she was beside herself with worry. "Are you okay?"

Her smile warms. "I am now." She studies me. "I'll tell you what happened if you agree not to try to sit up again until I'm done."

Considering I was about to do exactly that, I flush. I force myself to relax and survey our surroundings as much as I can without moving. Judging from the dark arch of rock overhead, we're back in the sea cave. I have no idea how we got here. The last thing I remember is being underwater, pain lashing my entire body as Lucky stabbed me, and then . . . nothing at all.

I swallow hard. "Your jewels?"

Lizzie curses softly under her breath. "You have a one-track mind even when on death's doorstep."

"That's not an answer."

"No, it's not. I'll tell you everything if you promise to lie there quietly for the duration."

I huff out a breath. I wish I could say she's overreacting, but even that deep breath causes something deep in my chest to ache. There's no way I'll admit as much, though. She's worried enough about me. "Yes. Fine. I promise."

"Good." She quickly details what happened. Bastian missing, the swim back to the cave, the plan to meet up with Siobhan at the sailboat waiting for us on the other side of the island. Through it all, she keeps up those little touches as if reassuring herself that I'm alive and well enough to talk. She finally sits back on her heels. "Say the word and we'll find another way off the island. We can go back to Viedna and live there."

I search her expression, finding only sincerity. She really means it. I lift my hand and she immediately takes it. "Why did you agree to sail with Siobhan? You don't even like her. You don't believe in the rebellion."

"Maeve." She squeezes my hand. "You just asked a question you already know the answer to."

My flush deepens. She did it for *me*. "I guess I do. Are you sure?"

"As sure as I am about anything." Lizzie gives a wan smile. "Besides, there will be plenty of murder in my future. Keeping you safe as you charge off into danger is a full-time job."

The way she's talking . . . I grab her hand. "Lizzie, what about your family heirlooms? Did the *Crimson Hag* sink?"

"No." She glares at the cave opening. "It's still listing like a drunk asshole, but they managed to get the hole patched after we fled. I suspect they'll make asses of themselves searching the town, but we'll be long gone by then."

I desperately want to believe she's saying what I think she's saying. That she's coming with me. That she's staying. I know what we spoke of before, but that was in the heat of the moment. I might be naive about some things, but even I know that words exchanged when sex is involved don't necessarily hold the same way in the cold light of dawn. Even as I want to ask her if that's what she means, I recognize it for the selfish desire it is. I love her and I want her with me. But it goes against every single thing she's done since coming to Threshold. "But the jewels."

"Maeve, I am going to say something, and I need you to actually listen to me." She shifts closer until her knees bump my arm and her face hovers over mine, almost kissably close. "Are you listening?"

"Yes," I whisper.

"Fuck. Those. Jewels." She bites out each word. "I've existed two hundred years, but I didn't actually start *living* until I met you. I'm not going to retrieve those heirlooms and fuck off to my realm when you're here—and not just because you're liable to get yourself killed if I'm not here to watch over you. I *love* you, Maeve. I'm not leaving you. I'm staying in Threshold. If I have to kill every single fucking Cŵn Annwn to make sure the rebellion succeeds, then I will. Because it means you'll be safe." She takes a ragged breath. "Because it means you'll be happy. And happy is all I want for you."

The burning in my throat gets worse and I fight to swallow past it. "I love you, too. I want you happy, too." Even if that means leaving me.

"*You* make me happy." She cups my face. "I just want you, Maeve . . . and perhaps a little murder from time to time to keep things interesting."

"Lizzie!"

"Don't worry. Rebellions tends to be soaked in blood. I'll have plenty to keep me busy." She strokes her fingers over my skin. I suspect she's tracing my freckles. "We'll survive it, baby. And go on to live nice, long lives filled with plenty of joy and fucking."

I don't know if a person can die from blushing, but I might melt into a puddle right here and now. "But you hate sailing."

"I like sailing. I hate the water." She shrugs and eases back.

"If you don't want this, just say so. I'll respect it, though I will haunt your steps through the coming conflict to ensure you stay alive."

It's almost impossible to wrap my mind around. The entire time I've known her, I've had to come to terms with the fact that someday she'd leave and I'd never see her again. Even as I fell in love with her, I knew it would end in heartbreak. To suddenly have the possibility of what I so desperately wanted . . .

"I want you. I want everything you've said and more." I clasp her hand and bring it back to my face. "I want everything."

"Then you shall have it." She grins suddenly and swoops down to press a quick kiss to my lips. "Let's try to sit you up and see how that goes."

Relatively well, as it turns out. I have a brief dizzy spell, but it passes quickly. It doesn't take long to convince Lizzie to get moving, likely because she's concerned Siobhan will sail off without us if we don't meet the dusk deadline. Without that easy exit from Drash, we could potentially run into problems securing a ship while the crew of the *Crimson Hag* turns the town upside down.

The less said about the hike to the other side of the island, the better. It's brutal and exhausting and highlights just how unwell I am after the attack. We find Siobhan's sailboat exactly where she promised. The ship is larger than I expected, but it's got a clever design that means only one person can successfully sail it.

Siobhan appears through a hatch and smiles tightly when she sees us. "Good. I was worried you wouldn't make it in time."

Lizzie holds my hand as she helps me step onto the gently swaying ship. "Did you have any trouble in town?"

"Nothing I couldn't handle." She nods at me. "Glad to see you back on your feet."

"Glad to be here," I say faintly. What I don't say is that I'm minutes away from collapsing.

Lizzie, of course, knows. She wraps an arm around my waist. "Tell me there are decent cabins in here."

"There are." Siobhan nods at the hatch. "There's only one extra room, but I assume that's not a problem. Bath and a small kitchen are below. We'll share both. I don't need you to help get us moving, so you might as well head down and make yourselves at home."

A bath. Gods, I would commit atrocities to get clean. My body aches with each move I make, and while I adore salt water, I *don't* adore what it does to my hair. Plus, the journey to this part of Drash has left me shaky and covered in sweat. "Thank you."

It's only when we've settled in the cabin below, the ship swaying gently as we head for open water, that I broach the topic that really needs to be dealt with. "How am I alive?"

Lizzie pauses in the middle of filling the tub. "I gave you my blood. Not a lot. But it was the only way to heal you." She glances at me over her shoulder. "It will still take time for your body to replenish the blood you lost, so you're going to take it easy for the next couple days and let me and Siobhan do all the work."

I worry my bottom lip and try to decide how I feel about that revelation. It seems like it should bother me, but it just . . . doesn't. Except for one thing. "Will I turn?" If I do, surely that means losing my ability to transform.

"No." She turns off the faucet and twists to face me. "Turning someone into a vampire—if it's even possible with a selkie—takes a massive exchange of blood and, according to my mother, a ritual. I don't know if the latter is true, but I only took a mouthful from you the night before last, and I only gave you the bare minimum required to heal your wounds and keep you alive." She's so incredibly serious when she says, "I won't pretend I wouldn't make that decision for you if the alternative was your death. There was some concern my blood might affect you negatively, but"—she shudders out a breath—"you were dying. I had to try."

"I'm glad you did." I don't feel any different, aside from the exhaustion weighing me down. "Come here."

She walks over to sit on the bed next to me. I lean my head against her shoulder. "You know, when the rebellion is successful, there won't be many enemies to murder your way through. What will you do then?" I *have* to believe the rebellion will be successful. The alternative doesn't bear thinking about.

"There are always enemies, baby."

"Lizzie."

She carefully wraps her arm around me, tugging me into her lap. She props her chin on the top of my head, but I swear I can feel her smile. "I'll love you, Maeve. Beyond that, Threshold is massive, and I think I'd like to explore it. If we get bored with that, we could always take jaunts into different realms in between visiting your family. It sounds like a good life, don't you think?"

I smile against her throat. "Yeah. I think it sounds like a really good life. A perfect one, even."

CHAPTER 36

Lizzie

THE JOURNEY SOUTH IS PEACEFUL. SIOBHAN ISN'T MUCH of a talker, which suits me just fine. I try to keep Maeve confined to bed, but after three days, she's out and about. Sometimes she helps Siobhan sail. Sometimes, she swims beside the boat, her pale gray body cutting through the waves even more efficiently than our ship.

There may come a day when seeing her swim in the open sea doesn't make my chest tight. It won't be anytime soon. I worry. Fuck, I worry about her so much. If she's healing as well as she seems to be, how will I keep my virtuous selkie from throwing herself headfirst into the first conflict we come across? What will it take to make sure she survives the rebellion?

The nights are my favorite, though. I finally get to properly map the freckles on her body, though it takes me hours, and we're both shaking by the end of it. The sex is outstanding, of course, but some of my favorite moments are when we lie next to each other as our bodies start to cool, listening to the steady rhythm of her heart. Again and again, it hits me that she almost died. That if I don't do something drastic, she *will* die. Not of old age, safe and peaceful, but in the coming battle.

That fear drives me from our bed and out onto the deck while the stars are still bright in the night sky. Siobhan sits near the helm, her hands moving steadily as she mends some piece of cloth. I settle down next to her. "If you take Bastian back from the Cŵn Annwn, there will be no more hiding in the shadows. It will be a full-out conflict between them and the rebellion."

"I know."

I can appreciate how frank she is. It makes it easier to be blunt right back. "I'm not going to let Maeve die for you."

Her lips curve in a grim smile. "You're formidable, but I don't think even you can sway the course of what will become a war."

War.

Once, I relished the very idea. It was a chance to shuck off my thin veneer of respectability and bathe in the blood of my enemies. I suppose . . . I still *do* relish the idea. Just not the potential cost. I inhale the salty sea air. "In a battle of attrition, you're going to lose, no matter how extensive your network is."

Siobhan snorts. "You have something to say, vampire. Stop dancing around it and *say* it."

She's right. My days of not caring are in the past. I *do* care about Maeve, and by extension, that means caring about what *she* cares about. The rebellion. Stopping the Cŵn Annwn from abusing their power. Taking down the Council. It means surrounding myself with rebels who have stars in their eyes. "I'll stand at your side through whatever comes, and I'll make your enemies my enemies. At least until the Council is no more and you've set up some kind of new ruling system here."

Siobhan sets down her mending and turns to face me fully. "You don't believe in our cause."

"I wouldn't go so far as to say that. The Council is aggravating in the extreme, and I like being able to move freely."

"Lizzie."

I sigh. Fine. The truth, then. "I would kill the whole fucking world if it means keeping her safe. She won't approve of all the methods required, but I'd do it anyways. Maeve will join you in the coming confrontation. That means I will, too."

"I won't lie. You're an asset, and I'm glad to have you, no matter how reluctant." She tilts her head back and inhales deeply. "We'll reach the *Audacity* in two days. Rest until then. Enjoy your selkie. There won't be much time for either once things get started."

I rise and head back down belowdecks. Maeve is awake and sitting up, her eyes a little too wide. I pause inside the doorway. "You heard."

"I heard. I know what you said before, but . . ." She smiles a little. "I really shouldn't find it romantic that you'd kill the world for me. That's terrible."

"Maybe you shouldn't find it romantic. But you do." I cross to the bed and lean down to press a kiss to her temple. "I think I'm rubbing off on you."

Maeve laughs and pulls me down on top of her. "I can feel the bloodlust rising in me as we speak."

"More like just lust." I kiss her and ease down so we're lying on our sides facing each other. I brush her hair back from her face. "You *will* survive the revolution—or whatever it ends up being called."

"So will you. Promise me."

It's not a promise I have any business making. If I've learned anything since arriving in Threshold, it's that life holds no guarantees. "I promise." I pull her close. "When this is all done and our enemies are all in pieces, what will we do?"

She smiles against my throat. "Skipping right to the good part, I see."

"Just call me an optimist."

She trails her fingers down my spine. "I'd like to see all of Threshold. There are so many islands I've only heard of in stories. We could spend several lifetimes getting familiar with them." She hesitates. "But I would like you to meet my family. If you're okay with that."

It warms my heart for her to take such care with me. I don't deserve this woman, but that's not going to stop me from loving her with every bit of my corrupted heart. I kiss her temple again. "I'd like that. I promise to be on my best behavior."

Maeve shoves me onto my back and moves to straddle me, her expression going wicked. "That's two promises tonight. *And* you voluntarily signed on for a noble cause." She presses the back of her hand to my forehead. "Are you sure you're feeling well?"

I playfully bat her hand away. "I suppose you bring out the best in me."

"It was there all along." She leans down and kisses me hard. "I love you, Lizzie. Thick and thin, no matter what the future brings, I'll be at your side. I promise."

The words have the sensation of a vow. I hold them close,

letting them settle inside me. Letting myself hope. It's a strange sensation, almost as if a pair of wings unfurl in my chest. I think I like it.

I dig my fingers into her hair and tug her down. I speak against her lips, whispering the vow right back, binding us together. "I love you too, Maeve. Thick and thin, no matter what the future brings, I'll be at your side. I promise."

LOOK OUT FOR

Rebel in the Deep

THE NEXT BOOK IN THE CRIMSON SAILS SERIES

Author photo by Bethany Chamberlin

KATEE ROBERT (she/they) is a *New York Times* and *USA Today* bestselling author of spicy romance. *Entertainment Weekly* calls their writing "unspeakably hot." Their books have sold over two million copies. They live in the Pacific Northwest with their husband, children, a cat who thinks he's a dog, and two Great Danes who think they're lapdogs.

VISIT KATEE ROBERT ONLINE

KateeRobert.com
Katee_Robert
AuthorKateeRobert
Katee_Robert